"AND YOU WILL ATTEMPT TO CURB YOUR— YOUR NATURAL TENDENCIES?"

Whitshire thought for a moment. At least, he thought he was thinking, but his mind did seem to be all of a muddle. And when the words slipped out, he was most amazed. "No," he heard himself drawl rather lazily, "I do not think that I will be able to do that, Miss Virtue—to curb my natural tendencies. Not this time."

"You will not?" Honor's eyes fairly blazed.

"No, Miss Virtue, I believe I will not," repeated Whitshire. "In fact, I am becoming quite certain that I would not be able to curb them even if I did wish to do so," he mumbled, standing and taking the wineglass from her hand and setting it aside.

"But, my lord, you must! It is for your own good."

"Is it?" he asked, standing over her.

"Indeed. You do not wish to be ruined completely. Oh, I know you are blinded by your need and do not think such a dire thing could possibly happen to you, but—"

Whitshire found himself most inexplicably leaning down toward her, toward that most enchanting face. . . .

A SEASON
OF VIRTUES

Judith A. Lansdowne

Zebra Books
Kensington Publishing Corp.

http://www.zebrabooks.com

To Rosemary Stevens:
ThankyouThankyouThankyou for
helping me to believe in myself!

ZEBRA BOOKS are published by

Kensington Publishing Corp.
850 Third Avenue
New York, NY 10022

First Printing: January, 1999
10 9 8 7 6 5 4 3 2 1

Printed in the United States of America

Chapter 1

Garrett Forester, earl of Whitshire, content in the belief that he had disposed safely of his charge, Mr. Justice Virtue, by sending him off in the company of Mr. Alex Donnering to Astley's Amphitheater—a place where neither of those cubs was likely to fall into any sort of scrape whatsoever—climbed neatly over the first floor balcony rail at the rear of Longbourne House in Russell Square, then stopped just outside the French doors to listen for any sound from within. Hearing nothing, the earl plucked from his waistcoat pocket a hairpin he had long ago purloined from his mother's little pin box and kneeling, applied the pin to the lock.

It was a very chancey thing this business of breaking into houses. He had done it any number of times, but it was chancey nonetheless. A gentleman could quite easily get himself shot to death before he could say one word in his own defense if he were not extremely careful. Strolling into someone else's establishment in the middle of the night, especially strolling in through a previously locked set of French doors, did tend to place one in a most vulnerable position and a virtually indefensible one to boot.

Whitshire grinned as the lock clicked open beneath his educated fingers. He waited for a very long moment before pushing the doors inward and entering Longbourne's Grand Saloon. Then, standing solid and still in the silence and the shadows, he listened closely to the groanings and creakings and cracklings of the house.

At the front of that very same establishment, Mr. Andrew Millard, dressed to the nines and looking the perfect dandy, leaned as nonchalantly as he could manage against a lamppost and fiddled with his cane. Then he tilted his high-topped beaver down low over his brow and sighed. Then he fiddled with his cane again, tapping it upon the flagstones. Devil it, he thought, how do I let Whit talk me into these things? I ain't generally such a beetle-brain. But there is something about him when the light of a new theory dawns in his eyes. I am a veritable fool not to hastily depart whenever I see that particular light, and a fool not to take cover instantly when he begins to rub at his chin and mumble to himself, too. And why I cannot shut my ears to every single word that Whit utters following "Do you know, Andrew, I have just now had the most interesting idea," I cannot think for a moment. I know what will follow. Some harebrained scheme will follow. If only I could do that—just refuse to listen once he begins upon that tack—I might have some hope of becoming an old man and dying of natural causes in my own bed.

Any number of times in the course of his twenty-nine years Mr. Andrew Millard had pondered the sagacity of remaining the Earl of Whitshire's best friend. But for all of his doubts and qualms upon the subject he was not likely to change his mind at this late date. Whit is a great gun, he told himself for at least the fifteenth time since he had taken up his post. He has stood by me and supported me since we were boys, no matter how deep into the briars I have fallen. Yes, and he thinks nothing of leaping into the briars after me if there is no other way to get me out. How can I not do likewise for him? It is merely that this business of breaking into houses in the middle of the night makes me jittery. "Oh, botheration," Millard muttered under his breath as he caught sight of the watchman making his way leisurely up the street.

The Watch was not particularly difficult to spot. He came at a goodly pace with lantern in hand, whistling a particularly catchy tune. Millard took up the melody himself, whistling loudly and tapping his cane noisily upon the cobbles to the rhythm of the song, hoping against hope that Whitshire would hear him and not come climbing out some window or other right this very moment.

"I say, sir," called the watchman as he approached to within hailing distance. "Lost, are ye?"

"No, not lost," replied Millard, straightening and pushing his beaver farther back upon his head. "Standing about waiting upon a friend is all. All's quiet at this end of town, eh?"

"Quiet as kin be," nodded the watchman. "Not but that it weren't a reg'lar hubble-bubble here a bit back."

"What? In Russell Square?"

"Aye. Did ye not be reading about it in all the papers? A gentleman were murdered. Right there in that very house," the watchman declared, pointing to the establishment directly behind them. "A baronet, he were. Sir Nathan Longbourne. Attacked an' killed right in his own bed. Robbers it was. Stabbed the gentleman to death and run off with all his val'ables. Ter'ble tragedy. Ter'ble. And no one having an idea who it was done the deed nor how they got inside with never a one of the servants hearing 'em. Wickedness and greed," nodded the watchman knowingly.

"Appalling thing," Mr. Millard responded.

"Indeed, sir. I have been akeeping of an eye out ever since. Had the Runners ever'where about the square for weeks, we did, but never seed a sight of them villains what done it. Still as all, it ain't safe to be standing about by yerself, sir. Not anywhere in London. Not even in such a peaceable place as Russell Square. Them as done the deed might come back. Do sometimes, the Runners say."

"Indeed," nodded Millard. "I shall give my friend another five minutes and then be off."

"A excellent idea," agreed the watchman. "But two is all I would be agivin' him. Never know but some of them villains could be watching us even now." And with a knowing nod of his head and a swing of his lantern, he bid Millard farewell and continued up the street, his whistling once again echoing through the night.

Inside the establishment Whitshire smiled to himself as he heard the Watch depart, the whistle fading into the distance. He stepped out from beside the armoire in the master bedchamber where he had huddled at Millard's signal, and after one last, hurried look about the now abandoned room where Longbourne had supposedly died, he floated like a fog out into the second floor corridor. His boots barely whispered across the carpeting as he made his way to the staircase at the front of the house and down it to the ground floor. He stood for a moment, a shadow among shadows, listening for the merest hint of sound. Nothing. He drifted like a cloud down the corridor to the midway point and stepped into a small chamber on the right, closing the pocket doors soundlessly behind him. Tugging a candle stub from his coat pocket, he set it upon a table top and taking his flints in hand, lit the thing. His glance darted hastily about the room. The draperies had all been drawn. The light would not be noticeable from the outside. That, at least, was a relief.

Whitshire lifted the candle stub and carried it with him to the cherrywood desk that occupied the far corner of Longbourne's library. Setting it down, he ran one gloved hand over the bare and shining top of that fashionable piece of furniture, attempting to remember if the desk had been so clear of papers the last time he had been here. No. It had been a veritable rat's nest of books and letters. Someone had been busily putting things in order.

Frowning the slightest bit he took up the candle and knelt with it in hand to examine the patterned Aubusson carpet near the desk and all about the place where Longbourne's chair stood. He fumbled for his quizzing glass and squinted through it at the carpet, then he let the quizzing glass fall and placed his rather patrician nose a good deal closer to the floor. A quiet smile suffused his countenance. "Not so excellent a scrubbing as it appears," he murmured, and he reached out to touch one tiny spot and then another and then a third.

Feeling most encouraged, the earl sat back upon his heels and studied the desk itself. It presented him with four locked drawers. These he opened easily—a talent which, much like opening French doors, he had acquired in his youth through considerable practice with his mama's hairpins. The drawers, however, contained little of interest—except for a ring which had been shoved to the very rear of the bottom drawer and buried beneath a stack of ledgers. This Whitshire slid into his jacket pocket. He thought for a long moment and then, candle stub in hand, ducked beneath the desk and peered upward. "Just so," he mumbled as the candle flame glinted off a tiny pair of hinges at the rear of the center drawer. "Enrico Caldari did fashion this piece."

He had just managed to open the hidden compartment when Millard began to whistle again. This whistle was not quite so musical and a good deal louder. Snatching the papers that lay within Longbourne's secret hiding place and thrusting them hurriedly into his coat pocket, Whitshire doused the candle stub and then ceased to move at all. Footsteps. There were footsteps coming toward him from the front of the house. Someone carrying a brace of candles or a lamp had descended the main staircase or Millard would not have taken note from his position on the street. Thank goodness the windows beside the front door were covered only by lace curtains so that the light had shone through.

Moving with the grace and silence of an apparition, Whitshire floated toward the nearest window, stepped behind the draperies and lifted the casement latch. At least, he attempted to lift the casement latch. He attempted it any number of times. His fingers encased in York tan gloves scrabbled at it. But the thing would not budge. Across the chamber, the pocket doors slid open. And from somewhere beyond the window Millard whistled compellingly.

He could not actually see the light as it entered the library, but the Earl of Whitshire knew when it did. It was as if he could feel it and taste it and hear it. And with it, he began to distinguish the slight shuffle of slippers across the carpeting. Whoever held the light, Whitshire knew, was turning toward Longbourne's desk whose center drawer he had left, in his haste to depart, open wide—the hidden compartment laid bare beneath it. With a distinct sense of panic, the earl fumbled again at the casement latch.

"By gawd, but someone has been snooping about Sir Nathan's desk!" roared an excited voice. "You were right, Diggens! Look about quickly. Perhaps the dastard has not yet escaped us."

"Where ought I to look, Mr. Curbridge?" asked what Whitshire thought to be a child's voice.

"Everywhere, Diggens. Look everywhere." Small bare feet moved across the carpeting and then a small pale face with enormous green eyes beneath sleep-tousled hair of brown poked between the draperies and stared up at Whitshire in pure amazement. The earl brought one finger to his lips, urging the child to keep still—which, he thought immediately, is a perfectly stupid thing to do.

"Not there, you fool. Why would a thief stand waiting for us to find him behind the draperies?" came the voice that had roared but a moment before. "I vow, Diggens, you have not one brain inside that misshapen skull of yours. Tomorrow I take you myself to be apprenticed to Mr. Collins. I vow it! Look up the chimney and beneath that sopha and in the window box. There ain't even a window box in that window where you be, you blasted half-wit! I am going to check the kitchen and raise the alarm."

The slippers that had shuffled into the library made a rather loud and hasty exit and could be heard pattering heavily off down the hall. The enormous green eyes continued to stare up at Whitshire, and then a skinny little body in a flannel nightshirt made its way completely behind the draperies, climbed upon the window sill, and shoving Whitshire gently aside, tugged a piece of metal from out the latch, then lifted the latch and opened the casement wide. "I ain't be no fool," murmured the scratchy little voice. "I knows 'ow ta open up a lock, I does."

"Indeed," whispered Whitshire, stepping down onto the flagstones at the side of the house. "Who is Mr. Collins?" he asked looking upward.

" 'E be the gent what buries people."

Whitshire stared at the child. He knew he ought to take off at a run, seize Millard and chase down the nearest hack. There would not be much time before the staff began pouring over the house and the grounds, but he could not quite get his feet to move. And then he was reaching out and lifting an emaciated little body into his arms. "I cannot possibly leave you behind," he murmured, shifting the feathery weight of the boy to one arm and pushing the casement closed with the opposite hand. "You have seen my face after all, have you not?"

"Yes, an' I knows ye be Quality, too," nodded the tyke. "Even if ye don't be dressed all up ta snuff."

"Exactly," agreed Whitshire. "So, I cannot allow you to remain behind and open your duffle to the Runners, can I?"

"Uh-uh," replied the child, resting his head quite comfortably upon one of the earl's broad shoulders as Whitshire turned and made his way as quietly and as hastily as possible toward Millard and the relative safety of the square.

Honor took one last, long look out at London—at least at as much of it as she could see from her bedchamber window—then pulled the casement to, padded barefoot across the elegant Persian carpet and climbed into the delicately carved sleigh bed. The very sight of that bed made her smile. That a gentleman should have picked such a remarkably dainty white piece with pink roses on the headboard and at the foot from among all others to place in his guest chamber! What an extraordinary gentleman the Earl of Whitshire must be. And to think that an exact match to this bed already cradled her sister in the adjoining bedchamber. Truly, if it had been left up to her own papa to select beds for his guest chambers, every one of his guests would sleep in huge solid mahogany monstrosities hung with purple and puce velvet draperies—and most likely they would all die from lack of air!

Of course, Lady Whitshire had told the girls over and over again on the long drive into London that the earl was a most extraordinary man, but Honor had not quite believed her. Lady Whitshire was his mother after all and did not all mothers think their sons extraordinary?

"But I am forced to reconsider," Honor whispered to herself as she climbed between the fine linen sheets. "Perhaps Lady Whitshire was not seeing him through a mother's eyes at all, but simply telling us the truth. Though, if he is so extraordinary, one would expect him to be polite enough to be present to welcome us upon our arrival in town."

That *faux pas* upon the earl's part had been most distressing. Lady Whitshire had pretended to take no umbrage at such cavalier treatment by her son, and Prudence had simply rolled her eyes toward the ceiling, but Honor had been rightfully affronted. And when she had discovered the next instant that her very own brother had not remained at the establishment to welcome them either, she had not known what to think!

As she lowered her lamp wick and lay her head upon the beautifully embroidered pillow case, Honor wondered again where Justice and the earl could be. Perhaps some dire exigency has occurred, she thought, that has drawn both gentlemen away quite unexpectedly. Yes, that is precisely what has happened. Lady Whitshire surely advised them of the day and the time of our arrival and I know that Justice would have been here had not something most urgent forced him to be elsewhere. And just as certainly, she thought as she closed her weary eyes, no gentleman who furnishes his guests' chambers with such pleasing and delightful furniture as this wonderfully comfortable little sleigh bed can be such a barbarian as to ignore his own mama's arrival upon his doorstep. Certainly not.

Mr. Millard stared at the nightshirted child who had fallen asleep in the hackney with his head nestled against Whitshire's shoulder. "I hardly think that you require a tiger badly enough to steal one, Whit," he murmured. "You do not even own a curricle."

"I did not steal him, Andrew. I abducted him. He is just about the right size for a tiger, is he not? That's the answer then. I shall go off to Hadley's and order up a curricle tomorrow. No, truly, Andrew, I could not just abandon the boy. He helped me to escape for one thing, and he saw my face."

"And," sighed Millard, "whoever the man was, he threatened to apprentice the tyke to an undertaker first thing in the morning. But you cannot just abduct him, Whit. You have not got his apprenticeship papers for one thing. What will you do if his master spies him and sets the law upon you? What else did you pilfer?"

The earl raised one eyebrow slightly.

"No, do not give me that particular look, m'dear. I have not been your chum for all these years without knowing how incredibly sticky are your fingers."

Whitshire chuckled. "Yes, well, but I do not pilfer things, Millard. I merely appropriate them for further study."

"Indeed. And what exactly, besides a raggedy little boy, have you appropriated from Longbourne House?"

"Merely some papers and a ring and a hairbrush I discovered lying behind Sir Nathan's armoire. Sir Nathan's bedchamber has been cleared of almost everything. Even his clothing is gone. And his library desk has been gone through quite thoroughly."

"The Runners most likely."

"Perhaps. But it was a Caldari, Millard, and they missed the hidden chamber beneath the center drawer. That is where I discovered the papers, but I had no time to read them. The carpet beneath the desk has been thoroughly scrubbed," he added, "though not thoroughly enough that a few blood spots did not remain."

Millard whistled lowly.

"Just so," nodded Whitshire. "I do believe my theory is correct, Andrew. At least a part of it."

"Are you going to confide in Sir John, Whit?"

"No."

"But, Whit—"

"No, Millard, I am not. Sir John's Runners are always stepping in and ruining everything."

"Pardon me, but was it not two of Sir John's Bow Street Runners who stepped in last year and kept you from having your brains cudgeled out and spilled all over the cobbles?"

"Well, yes, but that is neither here nor there, Millard."

"It ain't?"

"No. I should have come about before my brains were spilled. I was merely taken by surprise. In a moment or two more—"

"You would have been dead."

"I would not," protested Whitshire. "I would have divested that miserable devil of his club, blacked both his daylights and trussed him up like a stuffed guinea hen."

Mr. Millard thought to protest this rather whimsical memory of what had been one of the worst days of his own and Whitshire's lives, but he merely shrugged and let the matter drop. "So, what's to do next then?"

"Study the papers I appropriated, Andrew, to see if they might hold some clue as to our murderer's identity. And we shall need to look into the ring and the hairbrush.

Other than that, I have not the faintest idea. I cannot do much of anything these days with Virtue's cub always following me about. Devil it, but I cannot for the life of me understand what came over Mama. To tell Sir Loyal Virtue that I would be pleased to sponsor his son into Society and bearlead him about, and then to send the cub off to me in London without once consulting me. There I stood in the vestibule, Andrew, my hat upon my head, my gloves in hand, stuttering and stammering at a stripling I had never seen before and not making the least bit of sense. I must have seemed to him a total lack-wit. And all because Mama did not once think to tell me a thing about any of it."

Millard chuckled quietly.

"It is not a laughing matter, Andrew," protested Whitshire, though his eyes in the light of the passing streetlamps bubbled with humor. "I was that nonplussed, let me tell you, attempting to divine what was expected of me without letting on that I had not the least idea who Virtue was or why he should be standing upon my doorstep. If he had not at last remembered to produce that note of thanks from his papa—Truly, Millard, if I were not so inordinately fond of my mama, I would ride into Warwickshire this very night and wring her lovely neck."

The fifty patent lamps of the grand chandelier blazed above the sawdust ring and turned the spangles upon Miss Desdemona Jackson's silver tights to diamonds and the braiding upon her military-style tunic to burnished gold. The Astley band's spirited rendition of "Cannonade"— bugles blaring, drums pounding, a trumpet spiraling up to high C again and again—stirred her enormous gray to a hectic pace and sent Miss Jackson's heart to soaring. As Jasper's iron-clad hooves thundered around and around the ring, Miss Jackson danced breathlessly upon air. Like a fairy in flight, she twinkled and floated and fluttered along the great beast's back, then spun heels over head to the ground and flew upward again and somersaulted down to the opposite side.

With short red curls forming a halo of fire about her head and silver-spangled slippers flashing dauntlessly, she raced through the sawdust to vault onto Jasper's back once more. And then she stood, fearless and proud, as the throng of spectators just beyond the lights applauded wildly. In that moment, a particular gentleman, in a cloak with pea green lining, bobbled into and out of her vision. Miss Jackson's blue eyes widened, her breath caught in her throat and she forgot to lean inward as Jasper came around, forgot to take advantage of the centrifugal force that kept her upon his magnificently broad back and Miss Desdemona Jackson went soaring to the west as Jasper turned south.

Mr. Justice Virtue had merely popped out of the box he shared with his friend, Mr. Donnering, to go in search of a convenience. And if he had gotten turned about and had become confused in the maze of Astley's backstage area upon attempting to return to his seat, it was certainly not his fault. Nor could it be called any shortcoming upon his part that he had taken a wrong turn and had come to a most confused halt beneath the lights at the very edge of the ring in which Miss Jackson performed. But Justice did feel particularly dull-witted as he peered upward at the sound of a plaintive squeal to discover a veritable pixie in silver spangled tights plummeting down at him.

Of course Mr. Virtue was not so very dull-witted as to ignore this situation. He immediately dropped his cane and the bag of oranges he had acquired upon his wanderings and opened his arms to catch the girl. What gentleman would not have done the same?

The sheer force of Miss Jackson's descent drove Justice to his knees as she landed with an ooph! in his arms.

"Let me go," Miss Jackson ordered breathlessly.

"Just so," Justice responded, rising from his knees and setting her firmly upon the arena floor. To his amazement, the sprite took his hand in her own and led him several steps forward. "Bow with me," she whispered, tugging at his hand. "Everyone will think this a part of the act if you bow as well."

It did occur to Justice that at least one member of the audience certainly knew that he was *not* part of the act, and any number of others might well suspect it, but the very sight of a little tear silently making its way down one of the young woman's cheeks decided him. He clasped her hand tightly and bowed grandly at her side. A great wave of applause pulsed through the audience. And then the twinkling, bespangled sprite turned, abandoning the bag of oranges where it lay, and tugged him from beneath the lights into the dimmer backstage area where together they dodged amongst horses and clowns and shuffling scenery.

I ought to say something, Justice thought, running a hand through his hair and staring down at the girl who led him in and out amongst the throng of backstage workers. At the very least I ought to introduce myself. But for some reason he could not quite bring himself to utter one syllable.

It was Miss Jackson, in the end, who turned toward him and, staring upward as tears dribbled down both her cheeks, introduced herself and thanked him sincerely for coming so expediently to her aid. And then the petite young woman stood upon the verimost tips of her silver-spangled slippers and kissed Mr. Virtue's chin, which was as high as she could reach.

Justice's heart lurched and his ears reddened considerably.

And then Miss Jackson became a quivering mass of sobs and sniffles, grabbed at Mr. Virtue's lapels and attempted to bury her face in Justice's new and very natty red and gold waistcoat.

What could Virtue do but put his arms around her and hold her and pat her back as if she were one of his sisters?

"Hush," he whispered, rocking her gently. "You are safe now, my gel."

"No, I am not," sobbed Miss Jackson, burrowing deeper into his waistcoat. "It was he. I am certain it was. Whatever will I do?"

Chapter 2

"You will sleep here tonight, Miss Jackson, and tomorrow we shall discuss what is to be done," Mr. Virtue stated confidently as he set his candle upon the top of a dresser and crossed the room to deposit Miss Jackson's portmanteau upon the bed. Except—there appeared to be feet beneath the coverlet! Justice stared at the bumps beneath the quilt in some confusion.

"What is it?" asked a bewildered voice from the head of the bed, and a young lady with blond hair in a long braid beneath a charmingly ruffled nightcap popped up, clutching the bedclothes to her with one hand and rubbing at sleepy green eyes with the other. "What is it? What has happened?"

"Prudence?" Mr. Virtue stared in wonder. "Prudence, is that you? What the deuce are you doing here?"

"Justice?" Miss Prudence Virtue blinked and blinked again. It *was* her brother and he *was* standing at the foot of her bed with a portmanteau in his hand. And then she noticed the young lady behind him. "Oh, my goodness!" she gasped. "Justice, are you planning upon—upon—And you forgot that we were to arrive—Oh! Oh! I shall get up and leave at once, shall I? You must only hand me my robe. Except—I expect all is spoiled already is it not? Or does it not matter?''

"Does what not matter?'' asked Mr. Virtue.

"Well, I mean—*Can* a gentleman make love to a lady when he is aware that both his sisters are in the next bedchamber over?''

"Honor is here too?'' asked Virtue, astounded.

"M-make love to?'' whispered Miss Jackson in a hushed voice.

"Of course Honor is here, you ninny,'' continued Prudence. "Would I come to London for the Season without Honor? I should think not!''

"M-make l-love to?'' whispered Miss Jackson again, and then, putting her hands to her adorable Cupid's bow lips and giving the tiniest of squeaks, she fainted dead away.

"You truly did not expect us?'' asked Honor, pushing Justice before her out of her bedchamber, through the connecting sitting room and into Prudence's bedchamber. "His lordship did not say one word to you about our coming for the Season?''

"Not one word,'' murmured Justice. "I expect he intended it for a surprise. And I was surprised to discover Prudence in that bed, let me tell you.''

Honor was not quite certain whether to laugh at her brother or give him a proper scold for bringing a young lady home to spend the night, no matter what the reason. But as she settled upon Prudence's bed beside the slowly awakening Miss Jackson, she did neither. "Are you feeling more the thing, Miss Jackson?'' she asked instead, giving the girl's hand a bracing pat. "I assure you, Justice was not about to take advantage of you.''

"I never had the least intention to do any such thing,'' declared Justice self-righteously.

"No, of course you had not,'' smiled Honor. "That was all Prudence's imagination. You must forgive my sister,

Miss Jackson. She is forever imagining things about people upon the most insignificant of grounds.''

"She is?"

"Yes," nodded Prudence repentantly from where she sat at the foot of the bed. "It is my greatest failing."

"Oh." Miss Jackson's big blue eyes looked up into Justice's warm brown ones and a smile wavered across her face. "I knew you would not think to—to—It was only that I did never once so much as imagine—and then she said—and I—"

"The mere thought was a shock to your sensibilities," provided Honor neatly with a reproving glance at Prudence.

"Yes," agreed Miss Jackson. "And then I thought what I must seem, you know, allowing myself to be sneaked into a gentleman's establishment through the rear door and up the back staircase."

Honor stared at her brother in disbelief. "Justice, of all things! How could you?"

"Well, but we could hardly walk straight in past the butler, Honor. Mr. Donnelly would not have countenanced my bringing Miss Jackson into the house for one moment, much less my taking her upstairs to a bedchamber."

"No, most certainly not." Honor managed a stern look for her brother's sake, but she discovered that she could not maintain it in the face of Miss Jackson's quivering lower lip. "Do not cry, dearest," she said softly, giving the little hand in her grasp a quick squeeze. "It is none of it your fault I am certain."

"It is *all* my fault," murmured Miss Jackson haltingly. "I wish I had never been born." And with a tiny sniff, the young lady sat up straighter upon the bed and began to relate a tale of the most hideous and unbelievable depravity. All three Virtues were quite taken aback by it. "And so I ran away," continued Miss Jackson with a sniff. "I thought to find myself a position as a governess, but no one would have me."

Honor nodded wisely at that. No married woman in her

right mind would hire such an alluring young lady. Why every man upon the staff would be captivated by her, possibly even the master of the house or an elder son. No, to hire any young lady with such an adorable face and figure as Miss Jackson's as a permanent member of one's household staff would seem most ill advised.

"Well, I had to do something," continued Miss Jackson, noting that three pairs of eyes were fastened upon her, enthralled, and quite satisfied with that reaction. "I had no more money to pay Mrs. Dingley at the boarding house, you see, and I had had nothing to eat for a week at least. And so—I cut my hair and changed my name and took the position at Astley's. My true name is Miss Patterson. Miss Julia Patterson," she added in a whisper, "from Nottingham. And this was my very first actual performance, and I—I—Oh, I cannot bear it! How he knew to look for me there, I cannot think! Now I cannot possibly return to Astley's."

"Of course you cannot," responded Prudence with some vehemence. "Why that villain will be upon you the moment you appear. You must stay right here with us. You will be perfectly safe here. Honor and Justice and I will see to that."

"Yes," nodded Honor, tucking a stray curl tenderly behind Miss Patterson's ear, "though how we are to see to it, I cannot think."

"I shall tell Whit the whole of it," declared Justice, his eyes squinting in anger. "It is the outside of enough, let me tell you! The nerve of your uncle! And that—that—piggy-eyed villain! Set out to take untoward advantage of young ladies, will he? We shall see about that! You must not worry any longer, Miss Patterson. It is my duty as a gentleman to protect you from such perversion and Whit will see it as his duty as well."

"You call his lordship Whit? Justice, how can you?" asked Honor aghast. "He is an earl."

"Everyone calls him Whit, Honor, even some of the ladies. He is a great gun and will be certain not only to offer Miss Patterson sanctuary, but to take this piggy-eyed villain to task should he so much as show his evil face around her again. Yes, and he will seek out this Uncle Monty and give him what for as well."

"Perhaps," agreed Honor tentatively, for she had not as yet set eyes upon the Earl of Whitshire and so could not purport to know the least thing about his propensities. "We will not worry about it now, however. It is enough that Miss Patterson is safe for this night. Now we must all retire and allow her to rest. Prudence, you will not mind to share my bed for one evening, will you? No, I did not think that you would." And with that, Honor sent her brother off to his own quarters, her sister to the chamber she, herself, had been given, and murmuring words of support, she unpacked little Miss Patterson's portmanteau, helped that young lady into her nightrail and tucked her safely into bed.

Whitshire's eyes widened considerably. "No," he said. "Two more of them, Tyrel? What the devil is going on around here?"

"I cannot say, my lord," replied the valet as he helped the earl doff his coat. "Her ladyship and the young misses arrived shortly after you departed this evening. I assured Mr. Donnelly that I would remain awake tonight to give you warning."

"For which I am immensely grateful, Tyrel. They are Mr. Virtue's sisters, you say?"

"Yes, my lord. That is my understanding."

"My mama has retired, I expect."

"Yes, my lord."

"Are they pretty, Tyrel, Justice's sisters?"

"I do believe so, my lord. It was Martha helped them to unpack and she did mention that she thought them both most handsome. The misses and her ladyship were speaking, my lord, of plans for the Season," Tyrel added, unlacing his lordship's inexpressibles.

"Well, I'll be deviled!"

"Just so, your lordship. We did think, Mr. Donnelly and I, that you would prefer to know of their existence before you made their acquaintances at breakfast."

"And do you know the names of my newest house guests, Tyrel?"

"Miss Virtue and Miss Prudence Virtue, my lord."

Whitshire slipped into the nightshirt that Tyrel held for him and then sent the valet off to bed. With a sigh, he poured himself a brandy and sat down in the wing chair before the hearth in his bedchamber. It was the outside of enough! In one night he had gained a tiger who was tucked up asleep in the grooms' quarters above the stables and two young ladies who were tucked up in the floral bedchambers and obviously expected to spend the Season there. He had made the decision to take the tiger into his charge, of course, but the Misses Virtue—Why the devil had his mama not so much as asked whether he wished to accept the responsibility for the Misses Virtue? And then he chuckled. It would not have made a bit of difference if she had asked. He would have taken them in. He could not disoblige his mama in anything.

After all she has done for me, I would be a brute to oppose her or to criticize her in any way, he thought. *If Mama were not precisely the woman she is, I would be completely destitute and attempting to sell my title upon the marriage mart in exchange for some fortune that smells of the shop.*

It did occur to him, however, that he ought to request to know, at the very least, why his mama was so concerned with Sir Loyal Virtue's children. That was a puzzlement. She had offered his services on behalf of Virtue's heir and now, apparently, she had offered his services on behalf of the gentleman's daughters as well. Great heavens, he had never heard Sir Loyal's name spoken before but once in his life and now his life was overflowing with Virtues. "I am becoming a most virtuous gentleman," he chuckled. "Virtually drowning in Virtues."

* * *

The Dowager Lady Whitshire, whose chambers were merely two doors down from her son's, had heard him arrive home. But the ormolu clock upon her mantel put the hour at two o'clock and she could not think that Garrett would be at all pleased to have her pop in upon him at such an hour. Not that he would frown upon her and stick his nose into the air and request that she refrain from any conversation until a more reasonable hour. His cousin, Freddy, might well do such a thing, but Garrett would never think to react in such a manner. Still, he was likely as exhausted as she was herself, and he would not find sleep hard to come by as she had been doing of late.

He has likely fallen directly into bed and is snoring away at this very moment, she thought. With a tiny sigh, she wiggled her toes as she stretched out in a most unladylike fashion upon the sopha in her sitting room and leaned back into a plethora of pillows. Really, she was quite exhausted. The trip to London had taken a much greater toll upon her than it had once used to do. "I am old," she murmured to herself as she opened a beautifully carved and painted jewelry box and lifted a sparkling diamond and sapphire necklace into the light of the candelabra that burned just beyond her left shoulder. "I am so much older than I ever thought to be."

She played the necklace through long, slender fingers, her eyes alight with pleasure at the blue and white fire that danced before her eyes. "This is the very necklace you gave to me upon our engagement, Anthony," she whispered to her long-departed husband. "Do you remember? It was always my favorite. I wore it everywhere the first year of our marriage. It was perfectly dastardly of you to turn it into paste before you died—and without telling me a thing about it! And it was dastardly of you to leave me all alone and overwhelmed with debts and with a babe in arms as well. But Garrett has grown into an exceedingly fine gentleman, the debts have all been settled long since and I have turned my necklace back into its true self again, dear heart, so I forgive you."

The tiniest line appeared between the dowager's perfectly drawn eyebrows as she set the piece back into the box and lifted out a brooch of rubies and emeralds upon beaten gold shaped into the semblance of a rose. "But how you come to be here, I cannot imagine," she murmured to the piece. "You must have come at Christmas because that is the very last time that I saw Caroline, and you are most certainly Caroline's brooch. Edgar gave you to her the very year that Edgar, Jr., was born. Oh, she was so very puffed up about you at the time. She wore you everywhere. Once she even wore you pinned to that absolute nightmare of a pink muslin gown with the red velvet trim. I shall never forget that gown. It ought to have been consigned to the fire before she ever donned it. But I could not bear to tell her so. She pinned you upon it and I thought I should faint from the sheer horridness of such a combination. But I did not, thank heavens. And you," she added, setting the brooch aside and lifting a diamond bracelet into the light. "I have no idea at all to whom you belong. I must set my mind to pondering upon you until I can remember where it is you ought to be. You ought not to be in my jewelry box, I am certain."

With a tired sigh the dowager replaced the bracelet, snapped closed the lid and set the box aside. Really, it was distracting to have other people's folderols forever turning up amongst one's own beloved treasures. For a moment she wished that her Anthony were there, holding her in his strong arms, so that she might confess to him how very discomposed she was becoming about the odd collection of objects she had discovered—not only amongst her jewels—but in the various nooks and crannies of Freeman's Hill as well. Anthony would know immediately how to soothe her and set her silly fears to rest. Truly, he had never been the best of husbands when it came to his unfortunate bent for gaming and bad investments. He had all but left her and his heir paupers. But he had always known the best of ways to calm her nerves and cure her fidgets and make her feel genuinely blessed. If only he were there beside her now. But her adorable Anthony had been dead for near thirty years, and though she still found herself speaking to him and remembering his shining eyes and boyish smile, she knew very well that she could expect no aid from that quarter.

I will confide my puzzlement in Garrett, she decided at last, rising from the sopha and making her way to her bedchamber, depositing the little box upon her dresser as she passed. Yes, that is exactly what I shall do. He will discover what has made all these trinkets and folderols come wandering into my life and he will put an end to it directly. I shall confide in him the very first thing tomorrow morning. "Well, perhaps not tomorrow morning," she whispered as she slipped out of her dressing gown. "Perhaps I shall wait for a time—until the dear boy has adjusted to the Misses Virtue being about the house. He will grow accustomed to them. Of course he will. How can he not? He is already quite fond of their brother. He must be, for he has not sent the boy packing."

It did occur to Lady Whitshire that she had been quite remiss not to inform her son that Mr. Justice Virtue would arrive upon his doorstep nearly a month ago and that she had been equally remiss not to warn him of her own arrival this evening with Honor and Prudence in tow, but she merely shrugged at the thought. What could she have done after all? Confess to him that she was bringing Sir Loyal's daughters to London for the express purpose of providing him with a wife? That would never do. "And besides," she whispered with a smile as she climbed into a pretty tent bed with rose silk draperies that her son had purchased solely for her delight three years earlier, "Garrett will not complain in the least at any of it. He is kind and generous and not at all stiff-rumped when it comes to having his life disarranged on the spur of the moment."

* * *

Whitshire rested one elbow upon the breakfast table and his chin upon his fist and stared, bewildered, at Justice. "An equestrienne from Astley's?"

"Yes, but she has only performed there for one evening, Whit. She was called Miss Desdemona Jackson, but that is not her *true* name. And she is in the most dire of circumstances. I assured her that you would see it as your duty to protect her, just as I do."

"An equestrienne?" Whitshire could not quite seem to keep himself from repeating that. It was not that he had the least intention of turning the young lady out of his house without any further discussion, not when he could see quite clearly the determination to help the girl in Justice's eyes, but had the cub informed him that he was to give sanctuary to a paper and pins girl it would not have set his mind to reeling quite as much as did this most novel profession. "So, for one evening she was an equestrienne at Astley's. And before then? Perhaps it is merely too early in the day, but I do not think I have got it all straight."

"And before then she was forced to run away from home because her uncle, who is her guardian, wagered her in a card game and lost. Well, she would not be forced to marry some old rogue, Whit. And she could certainly not remain in the custody of such a man as her uncle. There was no one to whom she could turn."

"And last evening a piggy-eyed villain who is not the winner of this infamous card game but someone she knows not at all—a villain who has been chasing her all over London and from whom she has been hiding—appeared in the audience at Astley's and she recognized him at a glance, whereupon she fell from her horse directly into your arms?"

"Exactly. You have got it perfectly. Now she is at point-non-plus, Whit, let me tell you. No one will hire her as a governess—because she is young, you know, and quite pretty—and now that that piggy-eyed villain has discovered her there, she cannot possibly return to her position at Astley's."

"No, of course she cannot. Be a regular rattlebrain if she did," muttered Whitshire. "And she is staying here? In my house?"

Justice nodded enthusiastically. "M'sister Prudence gave Miss Patterson—that is her *true* name, Miss Julia Patterson—Prudence gave her the loan of her chamber last night and slept with Honor."

"Indeed," sighed Whitshire, recalling the presence of those two young ladies under his roof. "Miss Virtue's name is Honor?"

"Uh-huh, but that is neither here nor there, Whit. We are speaking about Miss Patterson. It is a gentleman's duty to rescue a lady from dire circumstances, is it not?"

"Indeed it is," agreed a voice from the doorway. Whitshire gained his feet immediately and went to greet his mama with a kiss upon the cheek as she entered the morning room. Justice followed, bowing smartly over the dowager's hand. "How nice to see you again, my lady," he declared.

"You are looking quite up to snuff, Justice," smiled Lady Whitshire, studying young Virtue from head to toe. "Garrett has not introduced you to his own tailor, I perceive."

"No, Mama. I took him to Schweitzer and Davidson instead," grinned the earl. "Justice does not aspire to such sartorial depths as I do myself."

"And thank the heavens for it," declared his mama, gazing askance at her son's peacock blue morning coat, which was most unfashionably cut and allowed the most extraordinary white- and gold-striped waistcoat to peek out from beneath it. "Dear heart, you are the worst example of a gentleman of fashion that I have ever seen," she said with a charming wink at Justice. "But I did warn Mr. Virtue of that before I sent him to you, did I not, Justice? You may be guided by Garrett in all things, I said, except dress. And that is quite the truth. In everything of honor and loyalty and friendship, there is no man in London more worthy to be emulated than you, dear heart.''

"You have met Miss Patterson," stated Whitshire with assurance as he escorted his mama to table and poured her a cup of chocolate. "You would not be praising my honor in my presence else."

The Dowager Lady Whitshire smiled benignly and waved her son away to the buffet to fetch her some nourishment.

"She was an equestrienne at Astley's, Mama," he informed her as he filled her plate. "Did you know that?"

"She said that she was," nodded Lady Whitshire. "Because she must eat and pay for her lodgings, dear heart, and it was the only position that offered. But it lasted merely for one evening and she did quite right to use a false name. Had she used her real name, we should not stand a chance, of course. She would have set herself quite beyond redemption. But I highly doubt that after such a brief foray into the public she will be at all recognized as this Desdemona person. Proper clothes, you know, and proper companions make all the difference in how a young woman is perceived."

"Proper clothes and proper companions," nodded Whitshire, knowing beyond doubt what was to come.

"Indeed. I have decided that Miss Patterson shall accompany the girls and myself into Society. She is gently bred, dear heart, and quite obviously of Quality."

"She is?" asked Justice, astounded.

"Oh, indeed. One may tell that immediately by her speech and her manner and the way in which she presents herself."

Justice envisioned the manner in which Miss Patterson had presented herself to him and choked the merest bit on his tea.

"Do not stare at me so, Garrett," continued the dowager. "It is not as though I intend to present the child at Court for goodness' sake. I simply intend to take her about with us to some of the less demanding entertainments. We will introduce her as one of the Misses Virtue's friends from the country who is at present visiting with us. What harm can there be in that?"

"None," Whitshire smiled. "Unless, of course, one or another of our acquaintances should recognize her as the dashing Miss Desdemona Jackson. I assume she was dashing, was she not, Justice?"

"Extremely."

"Pooh!" declared the dowager. "If anyone says a word about that, we will simply say that they are much mistaken."

"So, we are adopting this one as well," said Whitshire.

Lady Whitshire's left eyebrow rose the merest bit. "Adopting this one as well? What on earth can you mean by that, dear heart?"

What he meant by that was that his mama had decided to take up Miss Patterson in the same offhand manner as she had unaccountably taken up Mr. Virtue and his sisters. She was about to make him responsible for another young person about whom he knew not the least thing. But Whitshire had the good grace not to say as much while one of those young people happened to be present.

"I shall instruct Donnelly to have the striped chambers readied for her, shall I?" he asked instead. "We cannot have the Misses Virtue sharing a bed when the striped chambers require little more than a good airing out."

"Just so," nodded Lady Whitshire. "My thoughts exactly. Come in. Come in, my dears," she added, her gaze directed toward the doorway and a most welcoming smile upon her face.

Whitshire gained his feet again and Virtue with him as three remarkably pretty young ladies entered the room.

"Garrett, may I present Miss Virtue, Miss Prudence Virtue and Miss Patterson," his mama said as each of the girls curtsied quite properly. "Come, my dears. Do not stand upon ceremony. Breakfast is quite informal at Whitshire House. You must simply help yourselves at the buffet and take whichever seats you prefer."

"Indeed," Whitshire agreed. "You are members of this household now and must think of yourselves as such."

"We—we are?" asked the tiniest of the young ladies, whose bright red curls fairly blazed in the sunlight that streamed through the morning room windows. "M-myself as well?"

"Oh, most certainly, Miss Patterson," Whitshire replied gravely. "And you must set your mind to rest about that villain who plagues you. If he dares to harass you while you reside under my roof, he will regret it immensely."

"Garrett will offer the man grass for breakfast," declared his mama confidently. "That means he will call him out, my dear."

"But only if he proves to be a gentleman, Mama."

"And if he is not a gentleman, you will thrash him to within an inch of his life."

"Yes, Mama."

"Or take the buggy whip to him."

"Or break his fingers one by one until he sees the light," murmured Whitshire to himself, a most impish twinkle in his eyes.

Honor, overhearing the murmur, smothered a giggle behind her hand. That brought the earl's gaze upon her instantly, and he grinned the most infectious grin.

Chapter 3

Mr. Millard was in alt. "You are not hoaxing me, Whit? The Incomparable Melinda is truly in Town, and she intends to remain?"

"For the entire Season. Do attempt some decorum, Andrew. You are grinning like a fool."

"Well, but it is The Incomparable Melinda!"

"Indeed. And she has brought two more Virtues with her. Miss Virtue and Miss Prudence Virtue. They intend to reside in Park Lane for the Season as well."

"Incredible. Are they pretty, Whit, the girls?"

Whitshire took his gaze from the horses presently being put through their paces in one of Tattersall's rings and stared off into the distance.

"*Are* they pretty, Whit?"

"I expect. Miss Prudence has hair like Mama's and her eyes are green and she is not too tall."

Millard rolled his eyes. Whitshire had never been the person to ask about a woman's appearance. "And Miss Virtue?"

"Yes, I expect she is pretty as well. In a different sort of way. She looks much more like Justice than she does the younger sister. But not quite like Justice. And there is a third young woman, but she is not a Virtue at all. She is a Miss Patterson from—ah—I do not believe anyone mentioned where she was from."

Mr. Millard stared as the earl explained about Miss Patterson. "I do not believe a word of it," he muttered, as Whitshire concluded. "It sounds like a plot from a Minerva novel."

"Yes, well, I am almost certain it is, Andrew. If not, Miss Patterson ought to be writing Minerva novels, I think. Still, she is gently bred. Anyone can tell simply by holding conversation with her. And one can see she has had a rum go of it. Ran off from home for some cork-brained reason and is afraid to go back now that she thinks she has ruined herself, I expect. But Mama will put an end to those fears simply by taking the girl about with her from time to time. Eventually we shall be able to discover her direction and reunite the miss with her family."

"What of this man she claims has been following her about?"

"Well, I did promise Mama to call the fellow out, or beat him to within an inch of his life or some such if he should ever bother Miss Patterson again. But I doubt he exists, Andrew. I think it is all a Canterbury tale."

He had the most speaking eyes and they were quite the most beautiful she had ever seen on man or woman. Violet, they were, and large and surrounded by the darkest, longest lashes. Not at all like her own plain hazel eyes. Of course his nose was a bit long, and his shoulders were not quite as wide as they might have been and he dressed in the oddest fashion. But oh, his eyes were enchanting, and his hair was thick and black and curly and his voice—his voice was just the sort of voice she imagined for every hero in every novel she had ever read.

"Honor, the coach is stopped, the door is open and we are getting out again," whispered Prudence. "Are you not feeling just the thing? I vow my own poor feet are about to fall right off from all the walking about we have been doing.''

They had been shopping for the last three hours, the three girls trailing about in Lady Whitshire's wake like little dinghies behind a yacht. They had been to Madame Estelle's and to the Exeter Exchange; to R. Willis in Fish Street Hill for slippers and to Mayfair to browse among the boutiques; to Dalton House, Haberdashers; to a silk mercer's and a linen-draper's in Oxford Street and most unaccountably to Hunkelman's cabinet shop. With quick steps and many cries of delight, Lady Whitshire had led them in and out of London's most fashionable and expensive emporiums, filling her footman's arms with packages all the way.

''We are almost finished,'' whispered Miss Patterson. ''Lady Whitshire says this is the very last stop.''

''I do hope so,'' giggled Prudence. ''I am beginning to feel as though I have walked barefooted all the way across London. And that is no small thing.''

''Oh, it is Rundell and Bridges,'' exclaimed Honor in a hushed voice. ''Prudence, this is the very shop where Papa bought Mama's topaz necklace and earrings!''

Honor, gentle memories of her mama placing a most becoming smile upon her face, tucked her hand companionably through Miss Patterson's arm and, with Prudence doing likewise, the three strolled quietly into the store behind Lady Whitshire.

''Pearls,'' declared that lady with authority, sending the clerk behind the counter scampering. ''Pearls are the most suitable,'' she added, beaming upon her three charges. ''There will be time enough for jewels when you are older. We do not wish you to seem gauche by flashing diamonds and emeralds about, not when you are just now making your debuts.''

With a pleasant smile and a marked deference, the clerk laid out upon the counter a number of exceptionally fine pearl necklaces from which Lady Whitshire chose three quite lovely ones. "And now I wish to see some of your snuff boxes, the silver ones, and those quaint little shepherdesses as well. They are Italian, are they not? Yes, just as I thought. Terintino's."

With notable enthusiasm the clerk fetched Rundell and Bridges' entire collection of silver snuff boxes, which was considerable, and laid them upon the counter beside the line of pearl necklaces that Lady Whitshire had not chosen. Then he brought down piece by piece the most beautifully rendered statuettes that Honor had ever seen. They were remarkable in their delicacy and detail and had all three of the girls and Lady Whitshire oohing and ahing as one.

And that was when it happened. Lady Whitshire lifted one of the shepherdesses from the counter to view it more closely and taking a step back, trod upon Prudence's aching toes.

Prudence gasped and stumbled against Miss Patterson. Miss Patterson, who had been leaning forward to gain a better look, was tipped sideways into Honor with such force that Honor fell to the floor with a great and most unladylike "Ooph!"

Honor had never been more embarrassed. Her cheeks flamed and she could feel her ears begin to burn a bright red beneath her bonnet. The clerk rushed out from behind his counter to help her to her feet and every other clerk and patron in the shop came running as well. It was truly mortifying. But then Honor's sense of humor claimed her and she began to smile as she was helped to her feet. From this moment forward, she thought, her smile widening, I shall likely become a noteworthy person—known to all Society as "Miss Virtue, the young lady who was so very clumsy as to fall upon the floor in Rundell and Bridges."

Justice led the big gray through the streets of London gathering any number of stares from gentlemen who were suitably impressed by exquisite horseflesh when they saw it. He had had the devil of a time to get the gelding away from the stablemaster at Astley's. It had taken him, in fact, most of the afternoon. And in the end, he had had to leave his card with his direction inscribed upon it and had departed with his ears reddening under dire warnings that horse thieves, dressed as gentlemen or not, were still hanged in England.

"And after I gave him Miss Jackson's note, too," he muttered under his breath. "Who would it be writing him to give me her bloody horse if not Miss Jackson—I mean, Miss Patterson?"

The very thought of Miss Patterson sent a ripple of excitement through Justice's sturdy frame. Truly, she was the most adorable, impish, alluring young woman he had ever met. And she had proved to be even more enticing in the sprigged muslin dress she had donned that morning than in the silver-spangled tights of the evening before. It was no wonder that the people at Astley's had been devastated to learn that she was abandoning the circus ring in favor of a more circumspect existence. Any number of gentlemen, Justice was certain, might have taken to attending the performances at Astley's simply to get a glimpse of the daring and delicious Miss Jackson. "But I must remember to call her Miss Patterson now," he reminded himself.

Holding tightly to Jasper's reins, Justice turned his own horse and the gelding into Park Lane and wondered—not for the first time—how he had come to be so very lucky as to reside in such a first-class establishment in the company of such a capital fellow as the Earl of Whitshire. It had been all Lady Whitshire's doing, of course, but it was not as though she were his godmother. She was not even godmother to one of his sisters. In fact, until the day her coach had pulled to a stop in his father's courtyard, he had never so much as heard Lady Whitshire's name mentioned in his household. Perhaps she had been one of his mama's friends—but it was odd that he could not recall his mama ever having mentioned her. And she had not been in attendance at his mother's funeral, nor had she sent condolences that he could recall. Of course, that had been three whole years ago, and he had not read every single letter of condolence.

"I say, Virtue!" a voice called from just behind him, and in a moment Mr. Millard and the earl were urging their own mounts up beside Justice. "Where did that bit of blood come from? Is that Miss Patterson's?" asked Millard. "What a splendid animal."

"You know about Miss Patterson?" Justice asked in surprise.

"Millard knows all," nodded the earl. "No, do not look at me in such amazement, Cub. Millard can be trusted not to give the girl away, I assure you. And he may be of help in protecting her from this supposed piggy-eyed villain."

"Supposed villain? Do you not believe that a man is following her about then?"

"No," replied Whitshire. "I rather think this person a figment of Miss Patterson's obviously fertile imagination. But you must admit that Millard will be a good man to have upon our side should Miss Patterson's piggy-eyed villain actually exist. You are certain that is Miss Patterson's horse, are you?" The Earl of Whitshire studied the gelding with a most experienced eye as they turned into the mews backing Park Lane where he stabled his own hacks.

"Yes, sir," Justice nodded, as one of Whitshire's grooms came running to meet them. "Jasper, she calls him."

"Mr. Millard is staying awhile, so unsaddle Monk as well and put the gray in the rear stall, eh, Nev?" Whitshire ordered. "Name is Jasper. See he is fed and coddled a bit, won't you? How does the boy go on? Not afraid of the horses, is he?"

"No, m'lord, not one bit. Brazen as a bedbug that un when it comes to horses. Did ye order up a curricle, then?"

"I did. And went to Tat's to purchase a pair to pull it, too. They will be upon you in the morning. A pair of blacks. One with a blaze and the other a stocking."

The groom grinned and shook his head. "Ye cannot bear ta be fashionable in no way, m'lord. Never could since ye were a tyke. 'Tis matched blacks what be fashionable."

"Ha!" Whitshire's grin stretched from ear to ear for the man who had set him upon his first pony. "As if you know a thing about fashion, Nev! I would eat my boots to see you all decked out in the height of fashion. That I would."

With long strides, Whitshire led the way from the mews through the back garden and into the house. "Horse is worth a veritable fortune," he muttered, his spurs jingling as he crossed through the kitchen into the long corridor that led to his study. "If Miss Patterson had thought to sell that beast she could have lived years upon the purchase price."

"Yes, I thought so too," agreed Justice.

"Where did she come by it, do you think?" Millard asked.

"I should most heartily like to know," responded Whitshire, "because unless I miss my guess, Millard, that hack is one of Sir Nathan's. No, I do not miss my guess. It is the star gives him away. He is the image of Longbourne's Moonraker. Devil it, but Sir Nathan could never be cajoled into selling even one of Moonraker's offspring. Prinny went so far as to call upon his patriotism to get one of the colts for himself. Sir Nathan still would not sell."

"Thunderation!"

"Yes, just so, Andrew," agreed Whitshire, placing his hand upon the doorknob. "If Longbourne would not sell even to Prinny, how did our little Miss Patterson come by the beast?"

"Who is Sir Nathan Longbourne?" queried Justice. "Are you saying, Whit, that you think Miss Ja—Patterson stole that horse? But you cannot be saying that. She would never have done such a thing. How could she? She is barely big enough to steal a mouse."

"I doubt she stole him, Cub," Whitshire replied. "But she acquired him from someone. You were not in London then, but Sir Nathan Longbourne was a gentleman murdered a few months back."

Mr. Virtue stared at the earl, openmouthed. "And you think that Miss Patterson—"

"No, of course not. What reason would a dab of a girl like Miss Patterson have to wish old Longbourne dead? Man was old enough to be her grandfather. But if Miss Patterson will tell us where she got the horse, it may lead to something." The Earl of Whitshire, a hopeful smile lighting his face, turned the knob, opened the door and strolled into his study.

"Lead to something?" murmured Justice in confusion. "What—what sort of something?"

"Avast, ye scurvy bastards!" croaked a hoarse, gravelly voice from the shadows in the far corner of the room. "I'll scuttle ye where ye stand!"

Without one second's hesitation Whitshire dove to the floor and scrambled behind his heavy mahogany desk. Millard scuttled after him on all fours, followed quickly by Mr. Virtue.

"This is what comes of consorting with murderers," grumbled Millard as he came to a halt behind the earl.

"Consorting with murderers?" gasped Justice, barely avoiding a collision with Mr. Millard's back.

"I have told you over and over again that you would end up awash in your own blood in the middle of your study, Whit," Mr. Millard continued.

"Quietly, Andrew," whispered the earl. "Did you get a look at him? He is near the windows, I think."

"Get a look at him? How was I to get a look at him with the drapes drawn and the fire cold and not a single candle lit as yet? It is dark as blazes in here."

"Not so dark as that," muttered Whitshire. "Shadowy is all. Do not upset yourself, Andrew, nor you, Cub. I have a pistol in one of these drawers and it is at the ready."

"One of these drawers? Do you not know which one?" asked Millard more quietly.

"No, not actually. It is forever in my way and so gets moved about. But it is in one of them." Slowly, carefully, the earl reached toward the lowest of the drawers and, holding his breath, he eased it open and felt around the inside.

"I'll scuttle ye!" cried the most intimidating voice.

Millard clamped a sweaty hand upon Whitshire's wrist. "Hold, Whit. He sees what you are doing."

"How the devil can he see what I am doing?" hissed Whitshire. "*I* can barely see what I am doing."

"Muffle them mumblers!" ordered the voice angrily.

"Do what to what?" asked Justice, huddling more closely against Millard. "What is he talking about?"

"Yer scurvy guts," came the voice again. "Scum o' the earth. Blasted bungler! Awwk!"

Whitshire's hand came slowly out of the drawer and one eyebrow tilted in puzzlement. "Awwk?" he whispered.

"Awwk," nodded Millard, releasing his grasp upon the earl's wrist and hunkering back upon his heels.

"In all of my years I have yet to hear a murderer say awwk," murmured the earl. All three of the gentlemen rose to their knees and peered cautiously over the desk top.

"Shiver me timbers!"

"Be deviled!" exclaimed Whitshire, gaining his feet and stomping across the carpeting. "It's a deuced parrot!"

"It *is* a parrot," murmured Justice, gaining his feet and crossing the carpet as well.

"By Jove, I did not know you possessed a parrot, Whit," chuckled Millard, joining them.

"I do not possess a parrot," responded Whitshire, glaring at the red- and green-feathered fowl that strutted about upon a perch beside the study windows. The earl opened the draperies upon the lingering light of dusk to take a closer look at the bird. "I was not in possession of this parrot when I left the house this morning and I have no intention of being in possession of him now."

"Thing is ancient," observed Millard, peering down at it through his hastily raised quizzing glass. "And ugly as sin."

"Villain!" muttered the bird. "Feed Ferdy! Feed Ferdy!"

"I expect that will be its name," grinned Justice, gazing at Whitshire who stood with his back to the window, his fists planted firmly upon his hips, glaring at the parrot. "Yep. Ferdy the birdy, I expect, don't you, Millard?"

"That is not humorous, Virtue," the earl grumbled.

"Then why are your lips twitching, Whit?" asked Millard.

"They are not."

"I beg to differ with you. They are most definitely twitching. Give over, Whit. You are going to laugh at any moment. He will belong to The Incomparable Melinda, mark my words. Who but she would take such an ugly old fowl into her heart and your home?"

"Who but she?" echoed Whitshire.

"Bloody bungler. Feed Ferdy."

Millard cocked an eyebrow and tugged at an earlobe. "Speaking to you, I gather, Whit."

"Mama!" roared Whitshire, breaking into whoops of laughter as he dashed out into the corridor. "Mama! Come here at once!"

"I do not think that I shall ever forgive you for shouting for me along the corridor as though I were some fishmonger's wife," declared Lady Whitshire, settled comfortably after dinner upon a satin-covered sopha in the long drawing room and staring up at her son as he leaned against the drawing-room mantel. "Everyone must think you were brought up in the stables with the grooms."

"I do beg your pardon, Mama," the earl replied. "But there was a parrot in my study. And he is still there, madam."

"Well, I cannot help that, Garrett. We were on our way home when we passed the most interesting gentleman who had the bird upon his shoulder and wished to sell it—for merely two shillings six pence, dear heart. I did intend to keep Ferdy right here in this drawing room, as an object for discussion when we have visitors, but then he began to speak. Well, I cannot have such language spouted about in my drawing room, Garrett. It would be most unseemly. You know it would."

"Indeed," nodded the earl. "And so you thought to put the thing in my study because I would not mind such language, having been raised in the stables by the grooms and all."

"Exactly so," Lady Whitshire smiled. "I knew Ferdinand could say nothing that you had not heard before, dear heart. And he is truly remarkable. And he was such a bargain. I would have been foolish not to have bought him. Certainly you can see that, Garrett. *You* can see that, can you not, Andrew?" she asked, turning hopefully to that gentleman.

"Of course, my lady," replied Mr. Millard, his eyes twinkling. "And I promise to see all from your perspective for the remainder of the evening since you were kind enough to invite me to dinner."

"Every gentleman ought to have himself some sort of beloved pet," offered Justice with a quiet smile.

"Exactly so!" exclaimed Lady Whitshire, quickly pouncing upon this notion. "What an intelligent young man you are, Justice. And Garrett has not so much as one tiny dog or cat to his name."

"I am not fond of dogs, Mama," the earl stated as he stretched one arm along the mantel and began to play aimlessly with a statuette sitting there. "Or cats. Or squawking parrots."

Honor thought she would burst into giggles at any moment and Prudence and Julia, she noted, were likely to do the same. Really, they could all of them tell from the look in his lordship's eyes that he was going to keep that ridiculous parrot. If he only knew!

"The particular pirate who sold you that wretched bird, Mama, is not going to buy him back. I can assure you of that," drawled Whitshire. "Fellow is likely dancing a jig right this moment at being shed of the delightful Ferdinand. Did you bring this shepherdess with you from Warwickshire? I do not seem to recall its being here before. It is a Terintino, I think. Remarkable craftsmanship. And this snuff box," he added, setting the statuette aside and picking up the object next to it. "Do you know, I saw one quite like it in Rundell and Bridges only last week. Wanted a veritable fortune for the thing, too. Was this one Papa's?"

Honor stared up at the silver snuff box the earl held out toward his mother. Why, it was very like one of the boxes Lady Whitshire asked to see when we visited the jewelers, she thought. It was almost exactly like.

"No," Lady Whitshire said. "I cannot think it is one of your papa's, Garrett. Perhaps one of your friends left it behind him after a visit. You must ask around, dear heart. It appears to be a most expensive article."

"I shall look into it," nodded Whitshire.

"And you will keep Ferdinand," his mama stated hopefully.

"Yes, I expect I will keep the ridiculous bird. Though what I am going to do with him—"

"You will enjoy him, dear heart. He will keep you company and brighten your day with his nonsense. Now, since that is settled, I think we ought to do something entertaining," continued Lady Whitshire. "After all, this is quite likely to be one of the very few evenings that our little family will have all to itself once the girls have been introduced into Society. I do include you, Andrew, in our little family, as I have always done."

"Because it is so very difficult to exclude him," offered the earl, his violet eyes overflowing with laughter.

"Because he has always been the most charming of boys, and because I yet hope that he will teach you how to dress with some degree of fashion," declared Lady Whitshire, raising a most intimidating eyebrow in her son's direction. "Although why I continue to hope for what is clearly impossible, I cannot say. Honestly, dear heart, a puce coat, a lavender waistcoat, and lace at your collar and cuffs?"

Mr. Millard, who had taken the time to return home and change into the black and white evening clothes that Brummell had made fashionable, chuckled as the earl appeared to study, quite innocently, the difference in their ensembles.

"I cannot think that there is anything wrong with what I am wearing, Mama," drawled Whitshire, his incredible violet eyes opening quite wide. "At least I am not wearing scarlet and epaulets and braided cord and brass buttons like Prinny."

"Oh, thank the Good Lord!" his mama exclaimed, and the entire party burst into the most merry laughter.

Chapter 4

Honor stood before the open window of the sitting room that lay between her own and Prudence's bedchamber and stared out into the moonlight. She would close the window shortly because the breeze was somewhat chill and there was a smell of rain in the air. But just for a moment she wished to inhale the sweet breath of the night. She inhaled as well the distinct odor of a cigarillo. It must be his lordship, she thought. Justice has not taken to smoking as yet. And Mr. Millard left for home directly after tea.

The thought of his lordship brought a smile to Honor's face. His absence from home upon their arrival had set her teeth on edge, but his every word and action toward herself and Prudence since had proved most welcoming and congenial. And though he did never apologize for his *faux pas*, yet his manner toward them both, and Justice and little Miss Patterson as well, was so kind and welcoming as to be apology enough. Truly, he seemed the finest, most considerate gentleman. But, Honor reflected with a grin, he is a terrible tease. Still, if he does tease Mr. Millard and Lady Whitshire mercilessly, it is only because they tease him with equal abandon. To think that he is going to keep that parrot. And Lady Whitshire bought it merely as a prank to set him off. She said as much when she stopped the coach to inquire if the man would sell it to her. I do wonder what his lordship would say if he knew that?

Most likely he would say nothing, she thought then. Most likely he would fall into whoops of laughter and then go out tomorrow and attempt to do something equally as absurd to her ladyship. "Perhaps he would buy her one of those truly ugly turbans I have seen the other dowagers wearing and cajole her into accepting it as she did him into accepting Ferdinand."

Honor giggled. His lordship was extremely good at cajolery. This evening in the drawing room he had gone so far as to coax them all into playing charades. It was a game at which none of the Virtues excelled and one that Honor had always detested—before. But this evening the generally serene guessing game that made her most self-conscious had been converted into a wild and rousing conflict in the midst of which all her inhibitions had been blown completely away. The earl and his mama had transformed a drawing room full of generally sane and polite people into a veritable battleground of wits. Lord Whitshire, with his disarming violet gaze, along with his sapphire-eyed, exquisitely beautiful, and resolute mama had instilled in all present the determination to taste of victory for their respective teams.

Really, Honor thought, her smile broadening, such a pair they make! I should never have suspected Lady Whitshire to be so obstinate and wily or a son of hers to prove so relentless and so terribly devious. Why, they had us all battling to win as though our very lives depended upon it. Those two rascals turned us into a group of rowdy rapscallions! "And I cannot remember when I have enjoyed an evening more," Honor whispered to herself. "Nor the last time I have seen Justice and Prudence laugh so heartily. And little Miss Patterson—I am certain little Miss Patterson forgot completely every one of her troubles in the midst of the battle."

Another whiff of cigarillo smoke floated to her upon the breeze and with it the soft murmuring of the Earl of Whitshire's voice. "Ah, Virtue, we have a thing or two to discuss, eh? You have been studying me out of the corner of your eye all evening as though I were a most interesting specimen of bug."

"Yes, well, I did not intend to do that. It is merely that Mr. Millard said in the study when that parrot—Well, about your cavorting with—I did wonder, but I knew you would not wish to discuss it in the presence of the entire household."

"You are correct there, Cub. In fact, I do not generally care to discuss it at all but ..." The Earl of Whitshire's voice faded, as though he had turned and stepped back into the house. And then it returned again. ". . . referring to my hobby horse."

"Your hobby horse?" queried Justice.

"Indeed. I am a collector. That is what I call it at any rate, though Millard has been known to call it a great many other things. Well, he is right to rail against it and call it scruffy names at times, because it is not at all an acceptable hobby. But there is not ..." And once again the earl apparently wandered off.

Honor told herself that she was quite blatantly eavesdropping and moved to close the casement upon the conversation. But then the earl's incredible baritone returned and said, " . . . murderers."

Honor gave the tiniest gasp and leaned out over the window sill the slightest bit. Her brother's voice met her ears. "Does—does anyone know that—that you—?"

"Well, Mama knows. And Millard and Sir John Fielding at Bow Street. But it is something I prefer not to have bandied about. Hard to explain, you know. Any number of people would find it bad *ton* for me to be collecting murderers and studying them. They would drop me at once. Others might not go so far as to drop me, but they would find my interest in the subject most peculiar. And I do not choose to be thought any more peculiar than they think me already. At the moment I am merely considered a bit eccentric, but if word of my—hobby—should be mixed into the scandal broth . . .''

He is jesting, thought Honor, suddenly feeling quite warm and removing one of her bedroom slippers to fan at her face with it. Of course he is jesting. A Lord of the Realm does not go about collecting murderers. Of course he does not. How would he do it? Would he wander about in the night with a stick like the Runners? Great heavens, cannot Justice tell when he is being hoaxed?

"Have you ever actually captured a murderer, Whit?" asked her brother then, his voice reaching her ears quite clearly.

"Oh, a few. But none without Andrew. Millard has always been around to lend me a hand, though in general he would rather I developed a new hobby horse, I think. The thing of it is, Virtue, that was all Millard referred to in my study when he mentioned my cavorting with murderers. It is not as though I generally have a house full of them. You will not mention it to anyone, will you?"

"N-no," Honor heard her brother stutter. "I should not think to—How do you capture them?"

"Any way I can," murmured Lord Whitshire. "Any way I can."

Another puff of smoke wafted upward and Honor leaned farther out the window. She caught sight of the top of the earl's head, his curls shimmering darkly in the moonlight, and then his shoulders which looked a good deal broader than they had before, and finally his waist which appeared a good deal trimmer.

Because he is in his shirtsleeves, she thought. His coats are cut so fully that they disguise the true breadth of his shoulders and the trimness of his waist.

"It is a devil of a thing, Justice," the earl's voice intruded upon her thoughts. "I am not mistaken. The horse is Longbourne's."

Now what were they speaking of? Honor could have kicked herself for musing upon the width of the earl's shoulders and the trimness of his waist. She had obviously missed a portion of the conversation going on below and had not the faintest idea how a horse had come into it. With a perplexed frown wrinkling her brow she ceased to lean over the sill and came back inside, closing the casement quietly behind her. Great heavens, what a dreadfully uncivilized thing to do, to blatantly listen in upon a private conversation! She could not think what had come over her.

Yes, she could. At first it had been the pleasant aroma of the earl's tobacco and then the sound of that most incredible voice. And then—then—

"Murderers?" Honor whispered, trailing off into her own bedchamber. "Lord Whitshire collects murderers? He captures them and studies them?" No, she told herself as she set her candle upon the night table and climbed up into the bed. He was merely hoaxing Justice is all. He likes to tease and most likely will be laughing himself to sleep tonight over such a tale as he has spun for my brother. It cannot possibly be true. And if I cannot get to sleep because of wondering over it, I am well served for listening in upon them when I ought not have done.

Word of the Dowager Lady Whitshire's presence in London for the Season rolled through the *ton* like sand through an ocean beneath hurricane force gales. There was not a drawing room in which ladies gathered where The Incomparable Melinda's return after a three-year absence was not the main topic of conversation. While daughters of marriageable age wondered what about a dowager countess could possibly arouse their mamas to such a high degree of excitement, the elder ladies whispered together with enormous enthusiasm, suggesting one after the other that perhaps the dowager's return had less to do with presenting the Misses Virtue and a great deal more to do with a son who had reached the age of thirty-two without once advancing close enough to a parson's mousetrap to smell the cheese. Speculation ran high that Lady Whitshire had had quite enough of her son's dawdling and that the earl would find himself leg-shackled by June. Feminine eyebrows lifted and feminine lashes fluttered and feminine lips twitched in anticipation of the entertainment to come.

At White's and Watier's and The Guards, at Brooks' and Arthur's and Graham's, The Incomparable Melinda became the main topic of conversation as well. While the younger men deliberated over what could be so very intriguing about a dowager countess, and Whit's mother at that, the gentlemen of a certain age—bachelors, widowers and married men alike—sighed softly and murmured about a pair of glorious blue eyes and riotous curls the color of fresh-churned butter and a demeanor designed by God Himself to set any man's heart to pounding in his throat just to be addressed by her.

And she had brought with her to London Sir Loyal Virtue's daughters—masculine eyebrows cocked and masculine lashes lowered and masculine lips pursed in reflection and meditation and then smiled softly in anticipation of a new London theatrical performance about to begin.

The staff of Whitshire House was at sixes and sevens for two weeks running. John Coachman was constantly in demand to carry the ladies to Madame Estelle's for their fittings, to drive them about of an afternoon, to take them sight-seeing throughout London. And Mr. Donnelly would no sooner close the front door than he would be called upon to open it again to receive another calling card or another invitation or some trinket carried by one or another gentleman's footman to welcome Lady Whitshire back to town. In the kitchen Whitshire's chef, Andre, drove his assistants near to the breaking point in an effort to please m'lady to the extent that she would wander down into his domain late in the evening and bestow upon him her most wonderful smile. And as for the maids and the footmen and the fireboys and the little pot girls, well, they were kept hopping with so many people to wait upon, where before there had only been the earl—and he often absent.

The only servant quite unaffected by the presence of her ladyship, the Misses Virtue and Miss Patterson was his lordship's valet. But Tyrel's life was not nearly so calm as it was used to be. Where once he had been called upon to dress only the master of the house, now he found his expertise required by a young Mr. Virtue, who, quite unlike the earl, had a most commendable taste in fashion and actually cared about the set of his coat, the creases of his neckcloth and the number of fobs upon his waistcoat.

Honor was as swept up in the hubbub of fashions and fittings and folderols, of visiting the British Museum and Westminster Abbey and the Cadiz Memorial as were Prudence and Miss Patterson, and the conversation she had overheard between her brother and the Earl of Whitshire quite faded to the very back of her mind where it lingered in quietude, rising only once to the forefront when his lordship had asked Miss Patterson over a dinner how she had come by her Jasper and that young lady had related gravely another story of her uncle Monty and a friend of his by the name of Connors or Constairs or Conway who had staked the gelding in a card game and lost. "And then I—I—stole him from Uncle Monty," Miss Patterson had confessed, one lone tear falling from her eye. "I had come to love Jasper and could not bear to be parted from him and so I brought him to London. Which I should not have done because it is terribly expensive to keep a horse in Town, is it not?"

"Very expensive," the earl had agreed, his violet eyes squinting the tiniest bit. "If you were so in need of money, Miss Patterson, you ought to have sold him, you know. That particular beast would have brought you near fifteen hundred pounds at Tat's."

Honor had gasped and drawn the earl's remarkable violet eyes full upon her. "But young ladies, I expect, have little idea of the prices for which cattle sell. I can see that by the awed expression upon Miss Virtue's face."

"Fifteen hundred *pounds?*" Honor had managed to stutter at last. "It cannot be."

"Indeed it can. She might have supported herself quite nicely for a long while had she thought to sell the horse."

"Oh, but I could never sell Jasper," Miss Patterson had proclaimed. "He is very dear to me."

"And how did you get him to London, Miss Patterson," the earl had asked. "You did not ride him?"

The sweet young face had crinkled into a most impish grin. "Yes, I did. I dressed in one of the groom's clothes and strapped my portmanteau to the saddle, and not once was I accosted by anyone. Everyone thought me a lad in the service of a gentleman."

And then the earl had asked if Miss Patterson's uncle Monty were acquainted with a gentleman by the name of Sir Nathan Longbourne, and Honor, who was seated beside her, noticed how Miss Patterson's face had gone quite pale for the briefest of moments, though she had instantly denied ever having heard that gentleman's name. After that the swirl of preparing for the Season had taken over Honor's life once again, and once again the memory of the conversation she had overheard from her window waned.

Lady Whitshire chose, as the first introduction of her chicks into Society, an invitation from her old friend, Lady Eldridge, to a rout. "It will prove the perfect thing," she smiled, glancing from one young lady to the other over evening tea. "And Garrett and Justice will escort us, will you not?"

Mr. Virtue, hovering possessively behind Miss Patterson's chair, nodded and grinned the most besotted grin, which made Prudence smile and Honor's eyes glow with good humor. Surely, Honor thought, Justice is smitten with Julia. It is so obvious. He will escort her anywhere. But then the earl groaned and all eyes in the room turned to where he stood with his back to them, staring out through the window into the shadows of Park Lane.

"Lady Eldridge is your godmama, Garrett. You will be pleased to attend her rout," declared his mama.

The earl turned from the window, teacup in hand, and cocked an eyebrow at his mother in the most expressive fashion.

"Most certainly her Aunt Sophy has been sent off to Bath by now!" Lady Whitshire exclaimed at sight of that brow.

The eyebrow cocked to an even greater degree.

"Do you mean to tell me that Adeline has not—Oh, my goodness. She has the patience of a saint."

"Just so," murmured the earl.

"Well, but you will accompany us regardless, dear heart. I know you will. And perhaps Andrew—"

"Millard has already made the infamous Aunt Sophy's acquaintance, Mama. Several times. I doubt even you can convince him to enter the portals of Eldridge House again."

"That is complete nonsense," replied Lady Whitshire. "Adeline's Aunt Sophy is merely a bit eccentric."

"Completely mad," corrected the earl with a glance at Honor.

"What, completely?" responded Honor, noticing a most disconcerting glint of humor in those incredible eyes of his.

"Oh, yes," nodded Whitshire. "Every bit of her brain dribbled out her ears years ago."

Justice choked upon a guffaw; Prudence put a hand politely to her lips and giggled behind it; Julia grinned impishly and Honor's own eyes fairly bubbled with laughter.

"No!" she exclaimed. "How terrible!"

"Indeed," agreed Whitshire soberly, though his lips twitched and his eyes sparkled. "Only two years ago she attached herself to Millard's arm in the midst of one of

Lady Eldridge's routs and carried him off to the kitchen to help her bake strawberry tarts.''

"Well, but that is not so very bad," smiled Honor.

"Andrew was to be one of the strawberries," finished the earl with a flourish, and then he could keep a straight face no longer and a merry round of chuckles escaped him.

But Mr. Millard could be convinced to face the dreaded Aunt Sophy again if it meant that he would have Miss Prudence upon his arm. And he bowed very solemnly before the pudgy little lady in red satin who sported a heart-shaped patch just below her right eye as the Whitshire party entered the Eldridge establishment. Aunt Sophy on her side behaved quite properly as well and welcomed Mr. Millard and the others of the Whitshire party with great decorum. Apparently she had forgotten all about her strawberry tarts. She did, however, pat Miss Patterson upon the top of her head and wish her a happy Christmas.

It was a sad crush, Lady Eldridge's rout. Every public room of the house seethed with people. Why, there is barely enough room to turn around, thought Honor, clinging tightly to Lord Whitshire's arm. For a moment she stood upon her toes in search of Prudence and Julia but she could not locate either one of them.

"Are you afraid to be alone with me?" asked the earl, laughing down at her.

"Of course not. I merely thought—Well, the others were right beside us when we entered this saloon."

"And now they are gone. And so it always is with Lady Eldridge's routs. People appear and disappear like magic. Which is why I did not make much of Millard's absence the year Aunt Sophy wished him to be a strawberry. I am expected to introduce you to any number of people, you know."

"You are?"

"Indeed. And Millard is to do the like for your sister and Justice for Miss Patterson. Those were my mother's instructions. She ought to be the one doing it, but she will be detained by any number of gentlemen. Every gentleman here, I believe, who is beyond the age of fifty will attempt to detain her."

"Truly?" asked Honor.

"Truly, Miss Virtue. They think I do not know, but at one time or another they have all of them been in love with Mama. She was The Incomparable for four years running and declined a prodigious number of proposals before she accepted my father. Do you know anything at all about my mother, Miss Virtue? I mean, did your mother or father ever speak of her when you were growing up?"

"No, my lord, they never did."

"Did you not think it odd, then, that she arrived upon your doorstep and arranged to bring yourself and your sister to London?"

"I thought it most odd, but my papa welcomed her heartily and assured me that the two of them were the best of friends. Is there something wrong, my lord? Do you wish she had not brought us?"

Whitshire's eyes met Honor's directly. "Never, Miss Virtue. I have only been wondering—Ah, Mrs. Carstairs, Miss Carstairs," he interrupted himself, bowing over two proffered hands. "May I present to you Miss Virtue?"

From that moment on Honor found herself so occupied in making new acquaintances that she had not one free moment to ponder what it was the earl had been about to say or even to wonder where the rest of their party had gone.

It was precisely three o'clock in the morning when it came on to rain. There had been no particular warning, not even the rumble of thunder or a flash of lightning. It simply began to pour down over the city in a steady torrent, drenching everyone from opera dancer to duke alike who happened to be, for some unaccountable reason, out of doors at such an hour. The Earl of Whitshire found himself soaked through to the skin in a matter of moments, and swore under his breath as a particularly heavy gust of wind swept his high-topped beaver from his head and sent it swirling into the gutter where the water had collected so rapidly that the hat was carried away into the night, bobbing and twirling like a ship on a storm-tossed sea. Whitshire could feel his hair plastering itself to his head as a virtual cannonade of water droplets exploded into his collar and across the bridge of his nose at one and the same time. "Be deviled!" he grumbled, looking about him for the nearest doorway, all the while knowing that it was much too late to even think of taking shelter. He was as wet as he was ever likely to be. With a shrug, he abandoned his search for shelter, tugged the collar of his coat as high as he could get it, shoved his hands deep into his pockets and turned his steps toward home.

He had been everywhere since seeing his mama and her charges home from Lady Eldridge's rout—to Watier's and White's and The Guards, to Arthur's and Graham's and Boodle's, even to The Pigeon Hole and The Two Sevens and every other gaming hell that he could remember existed. His purse was heavier by half than it had been when he had left home, but his heart had grown heavy as well, and the sogginess of his clothes only matched the sogginess of his spirits. The light of hope that had flickered in his mind at his first sight of Miss Patterson's Jasper, that had begun to blaze when she had attempted to name the man who had accompanied her uncle from London and lost the horse in a card game, had sizzled out. "It was just another of her Canterbury tales, I collect," he muttered to himself. "I should have guessed as much at the time if I had not been depending upon her to steer me straight upon the trail of Longbourne's murderer."

Whitshire had gotten not so much as a sniff of the gambler named Connors or Constairs or Conway. Nor had anyone so much as nodded in recognition of a regular Captain Sharpe of medium build with unruly brown hair and blue eyes and a birthmark the size of a crown upon his left cheek, which description he had pried from Miss

Patterson that very afternoon in the midst of the rout. And that is that, he thought with a frown and a sigh as he turned his steps toward home. What blasted luck!

He waved down a hackney whose driver looked as sullen and soggy as he felt himself and gave the man his direction. Then he stepped inside the thing and leaned back against the oddly smelling squabs. He reminded himself that his efforts of late had not all been for naught. He did have the papers from Longbourne's hidden drawer and they were interesting to say the least. And he had the ring, which Millard had discovered had been fashioned ten years earlier by a Mr. Harding who worked for Rundell and Bridges. That gentleman had recognized it at once. He had created it from a design given him, he'd said, by a man named Paxton.

All of which ought to cheer me considerably, Whitshire told himself. They are all pieces of the same puzzle. Pieces I did not have a month ago. But I was depending upon Miss Patterson's fictitious gambler to provide the key for fitting them together.

Whitshire sighed and stretched his legs out as far as he was able. He could well understand why Miss Patterson would think to tell everyone a bouncer about why she had run away, but why should she lie about the horse? Unless, of course, *she* had stolen the beast from Longbourne's stables. But that could not be. How would she even begin to steal one of Longbourne's horses, virtual infant that she was? It was beyond imagining.

Well, but it did not matter. He would begin again with something else. The hairbrush perhaps. There had been red hair in the bristles, and Sir Nathan's hair had been whiter than a pond duck's belly. It did occur to Whitshire that little Miss Patterson had red hair, but he was very tired of thinking about little Miss Patterson. Yes, and he was tired of pondering over Longbourne's murder, too. He rested his wet head against the back of the seat and let his thoughts drift off in a different direction entirely.

Whitshire smiled wistfully at the vision of Miss Virtue in

an afternoon dress of thin white muslin as it twirled into his mind. He had actually dreaded attending Lady Eldridge's rout—always considered a prime event of the Season—because he became inordinately edgy when great crowds attempted to inhabit tiny spaces and he found himself penned within them. With Miss Virtue upon his arm, however, he had not felt himself the least bit trapped and breathless amongst the crush. Truly, he had not thought about the number of people surrounding him at all. He had thought only about Miss Virtue and her sleek brown hair with golden lights sparkling through it, and her changeable hazel eyes that flashed and danced and laughed and her laughter itself that from time to time he could induce to tumble out into the room for his own personal enjoyment. Her sister Prudence was a good deal prettier than she—Millard had informed him of that—but Prudence was not the one whose smile Whitshire found enchanting and whose laughter chimed most enticingly in his ears even now.

Chapter 5

Honor could not believe it. She came to a halt and stared disconcertedly about. The sunlight and the fields and the glorious spring day through which she wandered had vanished and in their place had arisen a forest of tortured trees and prickling hedges and a night lit only by bits of cloud-swept moon. Now, the birdsong of the afternoon had faded and somewhere close behind her she heard instead the ominous howling of wolves. Only the most meager of paths dwindled off into the distance before her, a path she did not at all recognize. And all about her a wind blew, chill and sinister. Honor's heart began to pound with fear. They were hunting her, the wolves. She knew it to be so. They were coming closer and closer, circling about, approaching from three sides, their cries splitting the silence of the deepening night like the shrieking of specters. Honor stared panic-stricken at the path. It must lead to somewhere, to some shelter. What matter if she did not know what sort of shelter? Anything was preferable to the prospect of becoming supper for a pack of hungry animals. With a tiny squeak of fear, Honor began to run. And as she ran, the rain began to fall, hard and steady, though not one flash of lightning lit the sky nor one roll of thunder reached her ears. It fell with a vengeance, churning up the earth and pounding down into it until the path became a sea of mud that sucked at the soles of her evening slippers and made each frightened step a battle.

Why was she wearing evening slippers and in such a place as this? The thought stopped Honor in her tracks for a moment. I am dreaming, she told herself then. Oh, most certainly, this is nothing but a dream. But the wolves howled again, sounding fierce and feral and very, very hungry, and once again Honor was racing away from them. Her legs ached; her lungs burned; the mud clung, slowing her, slowing her, until she thought she might not take another step without falling to the ground from the weight of it. But she dare not fall. The wolves were already close upon her heels and they would have her if she fell.

And then she *was* falling. Drifting through air like a bird in flight, but circling downward, ever downward. Toward what? She could not see. She could not guess.

And then she heard the most tremendous crash followed by a pain-filled "Confound it!"

Honor sprang straight up in the bed and then sprang out of it. It had been a dream, all but that final crash and curse. She was certain of it. That crash and curse had been real. She heard the cursing still. Hurriedly she donned her dressing gown, seized the lamp from her bedside table and, turning up the wick, rushed out into the corridor.

A series of muttered oaths led her in the direction of the staircase and she peered down over the rail. "Oh, great heavens," she gasped, discovering below her a scene quite as frightening as the dream from which she had just awakened.

In the vestibule, the long table had been overturned and lay with its beautifully carved legs upward like a dying animal, while beside it the Earl of Whitshire was attempting to rise to his knees all the while slapping frenziedly at something that burned fiercely around him in the darkness.

"Stop!" Honor called, hurrying down the narrow stairs as best she could while balancing the lamp in one hand and keeping her nightrail free of her bare feet with the other. "You must find something to throw over it. You must smother the thing. Do not slap at it. You are only making more breeze to fan the flames!"

"Blasted lamps," came the angry reply. "Death traps in the making is what they are. Do be careful, Miss Virtue, or you will slip and kill yourself and likely drop your lamp in the process. Between us the entire house will burn to the ground," the earl added under his breath as he stood, struggled out of his soggy coat, and tossed it over the burning pile of cloth upon the parquet.

"Whatever happened?" asked Honor as she reached the bottom step and spun toward him. "You are not on fire, my lord?"

"Me? No. My great-great-grandmother's tapestry, yes. Burning like a regular Yuletide log," growled the earl, stomping upon his now smouldering coat with first one foot and then the other. "I simply came inside, closed the door, turned to pick up the lamp and tripped over something," he mumbled, looking about him as the fire died. "Began to fall. Grabbed for the dratted table. Overturned it. Lamp hit the floor and I went tumbling. Grabbed for the tapestry to keep my feet. It came down in the burning oil with myself beside it."

"Oh, my heavens," gasped Honor, staring at the man in shirtsleeves and waistcoat as he frowned down at her in the lamplight. "You are certain you are not burned yourself?"

"No, no. My shirt cuffs are a bit singed is all. My coat will never be the same again, and I smell like a moldy old hackney soaked in lamp oil. Still, I expect I have been most fortunate. Be careful, my dear," he added, noticing her bare feet for the first time. "There is glass everywhere. Do not take another step. I should hate to have to explain to my mother how you came to bleed to death in my vestibule in the middle of the night.''

Honor grinned.

''Yes, and well you may grin, Miss Virtue. You would not be the one called upon to explain the thing after all. Really, I cannot believe how ungainly I have become. What is that?''

''What, my lord?''

''There.'' With remarkable grace for one who had just barely avoided setting fire to his own house, Whitshire moved toward her and bent down to kneel at her feet. ''Devil it, how did this get here? Pardon me, Miss Virtue, I did not mean to say devil it in your presence.''

''And so you have now managed to say it twice,'' Honor pointed out in good humor as he regained his feet.

''Yes, well, I am the least bit flustered. This must be what tripped me, but dev—ah—drat if I can think what it is doing here. Has my mother been rearranging the furniture?''

Honor stared at the little footstool he held in his hand.

''I do never remember a footstool being anywhere in the hall before,'' murmured the earl, perplexed. ''Come to think of it, I do not remember this particular footstool being anywhere in my house before. By Jove, this is not my footstool. I have never seen this particular footstool before in my life.''

''You have not?'' Honor attempted with all her might to keep from grinning, but it was useless. The extraordinary shadow of bewilderment that traveled across his lordship's proud face as he stared down at the offending footstool absolutely forced the grin to her own face. ''Perhaps you have merely never taken such close notice of that particular footstool before, my lord.''

''Well, that could be, but—there is nothing at all familiar about it. You do not suppose it crawled down here from my attic and put itself in my way just so that I would notice it, do you?'' Whitshire shifted his gaze from the offending footstool to Honor and, for a moment, she felt as if she

might gasp aloud at the startling brilliance of his eyes.
Though a bewildered frown still played in tiny lines across
his brow, his incredible violet eyes sparkled with laughter.

"I can see it now," he said, his lips twitching upward.
"Dastardly footstool sitting off somewhere in a corner of
the attic muttering to itself of my neglect and plotting how
to reach the vestibule before I arrived home this evening."
He chuckled and gave the neat needlepoint top of the
stool a pat, then set it in the corner beside the front door.
"Great heavens, Miss Virtue," he said once he had disposed of the offending piece of furniture, "are you the
only one who heard and came to my rescue? I should have
thought my bit of pandemonium would have awakened
the entire household."

"Is it very late? Perhaps everyone else is fast asleep."

"It is well after three, Miss Virtue, and *you* ought to be
fast asleep. I am sorry I woke you."

"I am not," smiled Honor. "You might have had us all
burned in our beds the way you were flailing about at those
flames."

"Yes, well, I expect I would have thought to doff my
coat and smother the thing sooner or later, but I am not
particularly well known, Miss Virtue, for my immediate
response in a crisis."

"You are not?" Honor grinned. "What are you known
for then?"

"Oh, a rather long nose, enormous ears, an odd manner
of dressing and muddling through mainly. And having the
most remarkable mother in all of England. Would you
care for a glass of wine and some cakes, Miss Virtue? It is
the least I can do after jolting you from your sleep. Donnelly will have left some for me—and a fire burning—in
my study." Without so much as a by-your-leave, the earl
set her lamp upon the newel post, swept Honor up into
his arms and carried her, crunching across shards of broken glass, down the corridor and into his own private
sanctuary.

"But you are drenched from head to toe," protested

Honor as the earl set her down in one of the matching wing chairs before his study hearth. "You will catch your death."

"Devil it, I forgot about that. I beg your pardon. I did not intend to say devil it again, but I did forget I was wet clear through. Are you completely sodden as well now, Miss Virtue? I ought not to have carried you, I expect, but I did not want you to cut your feet upon all that glass."

"I am merely damp in a few spots," responded Honor. "And I shall dry nicely before this fire, but you, my lord, will not."

"Well, I will not linger long, Miss Virtue, but I do need a brandy after the night I have had. And something to eat as well. I am on the very edge of starvation. May I pour you a glass of wine?"

"Danged rumpot," mumbled Ferdy, taking his head from beneath his wing and blinking groggily at Whitshire.

"And if you will, Miss Virtue," the earl added, lifting a cut-glass decanter from a long buffet against the far wall, "please remind me to shoot that bird in the morning and send it to Andre for a parrot pie, will you not?"

"You never would," laughed Honor. "You would never do anything to hurt your mama's sensibilities."

"Only because she would have my guts for garters if I did, Miss Virtue. Wretchedly violent about her sensibilities is my mama." He grinned, handed Honor a glass of wine and then set a little dish which held five seed cakes and three lemon tarts on the table between the chairs. "Eat up, my girl. There is nothing better for you when you have been awakened by an awkward earl busily setting the hall ablaze than a bite to eat and a glass of wine to soothe the nerves. Are you warm enough? There is a quilt lying about here somewhere. Perhaps I ought to—" The wet curls bounced most enticingly upon that handsome head as Whitshire turned one way and then another, seeking the quilt that he had once brought down from his bedchamber for some long forgotten reason. "Devil it, but I thought—" He ceased to look about and stared directly at Honor, his ears reddening. "I do beg your pardon again, Miss Virtue. Apparently I cannot speak a word this evening without referring to Old Nick."

"Blathering half-wit," grumbled the parrot.

"Ferdy, be quiet or be stew," returned Whitshire, his offhand tone as well as his words setting Honor to giggling.

"You are hopeless," she offered merrily.

"Oh, yes, completely," nodded the earl, recollecting that he had tucked the quilt away inside the window seat below the bay window. "Has no one yet mentioned that to you? I should think Mama or Millard would have informed you of that by this time," he tossed over his shoulder as he lifted the hinged seat and began to dig about in the window seat's innards. "Ah ha! I knew it was here!" he exclaimed quietly. "Here you are, Miss Virtue. Now you will be more comfortable." And without the least pause, he strolled up before Honor and tucked the brightly striped quilt cosily about her. "And it covers your feet as well," he observed happily. "You will be warm as toast in no time." Then he crossed back to the buffet, poured himself a brandy and came to sit beside Honor in the matching wing chair. His long-fingered hand lifted a seed cake from the plate. It disappeared in two bites. He took another, consuming that one with equal rapidity.

"Have you not eaten anything at all today?" Honor asked, her own lemon tart lingering in her hand with only one tiny bite gone from it.

"Well, I did eat breakfast and I did manage to procure a bit of meat and bread at the rout—remember, I got you some as well—but I have not had a thing since."

"You had no dinner? But I thought you were going to White's?"

"Yes, I did—go to White's I mean. But not to eat. I was playing whist. And then I went to Watier's for macao and Brooks' for faro and—"

"Great heavens!" exclaimed Honor, her eyes widening. "You are an inveterate gamester! I never would have guessed! Oh, my lord, I beg you to exert some self-control.

Innumerable gentlemen have been completely ruined by—'' Honor brought herself up short as she noticed the earl's jaw drop. His great violet eyes stared at her. "Oh, I should not have—'' she began again hesitantly. "You must forgive me, my lord. It is certainly not my place—'' And then her eyes lit with golden fire. "Well, but I find I do not care if it is my place or not. I happen to think you are a very nice person, and I am become quite fond of your mama. I cannot remain silent and see you ruin both of your lives. You must overcome this need to gamble and you must do so at once, my lord! To think that you should choose whist and macao and faro over dinner. It is too—''

"Depraved?" asked Whitshire quietly, taking another sip of his brandy and reaching for another cake. "Corrupt? Unnatural?"

"Unconscionable!" declared Honor.

"Um-hmmm," nodded the earl around a bite of lemon tart.

"Um-hmmm? Is that all you have to say."

The earl, chewing, shook his head in the negative and swallowed. "No, Miss Virtue," he said then. "I mean to say that I quite agree with you. My papa gambled away everything before he died. You are right to warn me against the same folly."

"Oh! I never knew. It is a weakness in the blood then? But—but—you must perceive after such an experience that what I say is true and you must heed my warning. Truly you must! It is even more important for one with your background to separate yourself from the games than for one without such a—a—''

"Weakness of the blood?"

"Yes. Precisely."

Whitshire would have laughed outright. He knew he would have done so if this dire warning had come from Millard or another of his friends or even from Justice Virtue, but he discovered that he could not laugh in the face of those changeable hazel eyes which had at present turned a most beautiful topaz aflame with zeal. Nor could

he think to laugh at the sight of that lovely, intense face
which scowled at him from out the depths of the chair
beside his own. He took another sip of brandy and rolled
it about on his tongue thoughtfully. No, laughter was not
at all what came to mind. What came to mind was something far from it, something that warmed him despite the
chill of wet clothing, warmed him more quickly and much
more effectively than the brandy.

"Have you nothing more to say upon the subject, my
lord?"

Whitshire swallowed. "No, Miss Virtue. I feel you have
covered it all quite competently."

"And you will attempt to curb your—your natural tendencies?"

Whitshire thought for a moment. At least, he thought
he was thinking, but his mind did seem to be all of a
muddle. And when the words slipped out, he was most
amazed. "No," he heard himself drawl rather lazily, "I do
not think that I will be able to do that, Miss Virtue—to
curb my natural tendencies. Not this time."

"You will not?" Honor's eyes fairly blazed.

"No, Miss Virtue, I believe I will not," repeated Whitshire feeling somewhat dazed as he finished off his lemon
tart and set his brandy aside. "In fact, I am becoming quite
certain that I would not be able to curb them even if I did
wish to do so," he mumbled, standing and taking the
wineglass from her hand and setting it and the remainder
of her tart aside as well.

"But, my lord, you must! It is for you own good."

"Is it?" he asked, standing over her.

"Indeed. You do not wish to be ruined completely. Oh,
I know you are blinded by your need and do not think
that such a dire thing could possibly happen to you,
but—"

Whitshire found himself most inexplicably leaning down
toward her, toward that most enchanting face, placing a
hand on each arm of her chair.

What in heaven's name was he doing? Honor's voice

caught in her throat as she stared up into those mesmerizing eyes. The dewy violet of them came nearer and nearer as the earl leaned closer and closer. Quite without intending to do so, Honor gasped the tiniest gasp as a wave of heat, sudden and fierce and unexpected, engulfed her entire body. His absolutely perfect lips, which had parted the merest bit, closed on the instant. He blinked, and quite of a sudden, he released the arms of her chair, stood erect and walked off across the carpeting to the bay window.

Honor, her heart beating wildly in her breast, stared wide-eyed at his back.

"I was wrong, Miss Virtue," the earl said quietly as he turned to face her. "Apparently I *am* going to be able to curb my natural tendencies. I do apologize for having let them get so very far out of hand. I cannot think what came over me. You are a guest in my house and a gently-bred young lady and I ought never have—"

"Oh!" Honor exclaimed. "Oh! You were going to—"

"—kiss you, Miss Virtue," the earl sighed. "Damnation, but I am sorry. I am generally most circumspect when it comes to young ladies. It is just that—I have come to think your laughter the most wonderful sound, and I have come to find you charming when you catch my meaning from across a table or from across a room and then attempt not to giggle and I have grown accustomed to both. But I have never before seen your eyes so aflame with passion, Miss Virtue. You have the most marvelous eyes, do you know? And your lips—your lips when you were scolding me turned so very tempting. And I knew as you continued to ring a peal over me that I would give my good right arm to be allowed to see your hair fall free and to be allowed to—And there you sat, so innocent and so intent upon saving me from the horrors of gaming and—No, it is no excuse. I ought not to have bid you join me for a snack. I should have told you to leave me the moment the fire was out in the hall. I would have told any other young lady to do so. I know what ought to be done. I have kept myself a bachelor for years just by knowing exactly what is permissible and what is not. But my brain turned all fuzzy of a sudden and I chose to follow my inclinations, and now I have gone and compromised you."

"You have what?"

"Compromised you, Miss Virtue."

"Great goodness! Do you truly think so?"

"Yes."

"Even though you did not kiss me?"

"Yes. Because I have caused us to be alone together and you are in your nightrail, Miss Virtue, and I in my shirtsleeves."

"I am veritably smothered, my lord, in a flannel gown, a flannel wrapper and your striped quilt. I am more fully covered tonight than I was at Lady Eldridge's rout this afternoon. And shirtsleeves or not, you look like nothing more than a drowned rat, sir. No one could imagine you at all bent upon seduction."

"Nevertheless, in the eyes of Polite Society I have compromised you and I am honor-bound to offer for you."

"Well, offer then," Honor said.

"Just like that?"

"Yes."

"Very well," declared Whitshire, throwing back his shoulders and lifting his chin. "Miss Virtue, will you marry me?"

"No."

"No?"

"Certainly not. Of all the beetle-brained things I have ever heard!"

"It is not beetle-brained," mumbled Whitshire, returning to the wing chair beside her and taking up his brandy and another seed cake. "It is the right and proper thing to do. There are any number of young ladies who would love for me to compromise them, and they would have said yes to my offer, too."

"You are hoaxing me," declared Honor, attempting to keep a smile from her face. Truly, he sounded like a petulant little schoolboy. Yes, and at the moment he looked like one as well. "Any number of young ladies?"

"Yes."

"And they would truly wish to be married to an inveterate gamester who would quite readily gamble away his entire fortune without even thinking to stop for dinner?"

"Oh, that. Well, I am not actually a gamester—not to such a degree as you think. It is simply that I have been out seeking this person who lost Jasper to Miss Patterson's uncle. And the best way to locate a Captain Sharpe in London is to go about and join the games and ask if anyone has seen him."

"And has anyone seen him?" asked Honor.

"No. At least, I have not found anyone who will admit to knowing him. I think the whole tale was a bouncer, myself."

"Do you? But I cannot think why Julia would lie about such a minor matter as a horse."

"It is not a minor matter."

"It is not?"

"No. It is possible—I think—Well, I cannot tell you what I think, but it is not a minor matter. Would you have said yes to my proposal if you had known beforehand that I was not a confirmed gambler, Miss Virtue?" he asked quietly, staring at his brandy glass as he spun it slowly in his fingers.

Honor studied him for the longest time even though he would not meet her gaze. The more she thought, the more she became certain that his brag about any number of young ladies being willing to accept his proposal was not so, because anyone could see he did not fit into one of the generally accepted molds and most young ladies preferred gentlemen who did. And Mr. Millard had confided in Prudence that she and Honor were the very first young ladies the earl had escorted anywhere in more than a year. It occurred to her at that very moment that perhaps Lord Whitshire was not the confident gentleman he appeared to be. Perhaps his self-confidence was merely a facade behind which lay a most vulnerable man. Perhaps he believed what he had said of himself in the vestibule—that he was known only for his long nose, enormous ears, his odd manner of dress and the ability to muddle through. What a frightful way to think of oneself! And it is even more frightful, Honor thought, if he has come to believe that the entire opposite sex thinks of him in just that way too.

With a determined tilt of her chin, Honor reached out across the little table between them and lay one finger upon his fingers as they held the glass. "You have the most beautiful eyes," she said then. "Your nose is long, but not offensively so. And your ears are not enormous at all. You may not dress in the height of fashion, but you look quite handsome despite that. Your curls, my lord, are most seductive even when they are sopping wet. And you have a title and a considerable fortune, all of which must be seen in your favor, you know."

"Does that mean you would have said yes to my proposal had you known?" asked Whitshire, his gaze rising to meet her own, and a most contagious twinkle sparkling in his eyes.

"No."

"Why not?"

"Because it is the most beetle-brained thing I ever heard—for us to marry one another because you tipped over a lamp in the vestibule in the middle of the night and I came running down to help you put out the fire and quite without thinking we found ourselves to be alone together. Who, I ask you, is to know we were together at all?"

"Ferdy," squawked the parrot, and such an appropriate response brought laughter to hazel eyes and violet alike.

Chapter 6

Donnelly stared at the footstool, blinked, and stared again. "It is not ours," he stated flatly.

"No, I did not think it was either, but it must be ours, Donnelly. How else would it come to be in this establishment? All I wish to know is who left it in the middle of the vestibule. Someone did. And there must have been a reason for it."

"No one of my staff left this particular footstool in the vestibule, my lord," Donnelly enunciated with all the preciseness of a butler bent upon protecting his footmen and his own good credit. "It is not our footstool."

"Perhaps it came from the attic."

"It did not come from the attic, not from our attic, my lord. We have never possessed such a footstool in all of our lives."

Whitshire ran his fingers through his hair, untaming all the curls it had taken Tyrel a good fifteen minutes to tame that morning. "Then I do not understand," he murmured. "It is not that I doubt you, Donnelly, but I did trip over the thing last night. And how would a footstool that is not ours come to be in the vestibule after everyone but myself had sought their beds?''

"Burglars, my lord," declared Donnelly.

"Burglars?" A swift smile played across Whitshire's face followed by a most serious and thoughtful frown. "Let me see if I follow your line of thought. Burglars broke into this house last evening, took nothing, left us a footstool and then departed through the front door, locking it quite properly behind them?"

"It does sound rather odd," murmured Donnelly.

"It does," nodded Whitshire.

"But it has happened before, my lord."

"What?"

"Burglars have broken in before this and left things here," declared Donnelly in a rather faint voice. "I did not mention it until now because—because . . ."

" . . . it sounded absurd," finished the earl for him.

"Exactly so. How is one to say, I ask you, that someone has broken into our house and placed a shepherdess upon the drawing room mantel? And a snuff box as well. And deposited two new china plates in one's pantry, too. And a silver bell on the cherrywood table in the second-floor corridor."

"Burglars," mumbled Whitshire, stuffing his hands into the pockets of his buff inexpressibles. "Perhaps I ought to call in Bow Street then."

"And tell them what, your lordship?" asked Mr. Donnelly over his high white collar.

"Yes, I do take your point. They will think me quite as balmy as I think you, will they not?"

"Precisely."

"Do you mean to tell me, Donnelly, that the Terintino and the snuff box in the long drawing room are truly not ours?"

"Not," replied the butler succinctly.

"So," drawled the earl, a most bewildered look appearing upon his face. "Why did you not say something earlier?"

"I could not quite find the words, my lord. And with the ladies and Mr. Virtue added to the household, I thought perhaps that one of them—But of course, they had not."

"Had not?"

"Brought the things with them, my lord, and just left them lying about. I knew that was so because of the dishes. Who would bring two dishes? And neither one matching the other? But I did not discover the dishes until last evening."

"And I was out."

"Yes, my lord."

"You will tell me if something else appears, will you not?"

"Indeed."

"Good. That's the ticket. We will discover for ourselves where these things are coming from and then do whatever must be done."

"Burglars," nodded Donnelly. He handed the earl his hat and gloves and opened the front door where Spider, a veritable vision in livery made especially for him, waited at the curb holding his lordship's new team of blacks in check. A beam of sunlight glinted off the bright yellow spokes of one of the new curricle's wheels and a fresh breeze blew after the heavy rain of the night before. Despite the mystery of the footstool and the other folderols, Whitshire discovered that he could not help but smile in the face of the thoroughly pleased-looking little tiger, the new curricle, this likely-looking day and especially the phrases which Miss Virtue had uttered last night in the study which seemed to roll about in his mind continuously. No, he could not help but smile any more than he could keep a rather jaunty spring from his step as he strolled to his vehicle and climbed to the box.

"I dare say she did not mean a word of it," he murmured as he pulled out into Park Lane, "about my eyes being beautiful and my curls seductive, and my nose not being too long or my ears too enormous. But it was most kind of her to think to say it."

"Pardon, lor'ship?" asked Spider who had hopped up onto his little perch behind the box.

"What? Oh, nothing. Merely thinking aloud, Spider. Are you certain you truly wish to be called Spider? You are not going to fall, are you? Would you not rather sit here beside me? It is your first time as a tiger after all."

"Yes, lor'ship, but I have been apracticin'," announced the boy proudly. "Mr. Nev has bin adrivin' of this here charmin' vehicle about the park in the mornin' when there be no one about an' I have been apracticin' settin' right here on me little perch with me arms crossed across me chest. An' I am a sight!" the boy exclaimed joyfully.

"You certainly are," agreed Whitshire, glancing behind him. "A most spectacular sight. I only hope that no one from Longbourne House recognizes you."

"Niver 'appen, lor'ship," declared Spider. "I does not look a bit like what I was used ta do. I looks el'gant now, I does. Bein' 'ducted were the best idear I ever did 'ave."

That very afternoon had been designated for the girls' first drive through Hyde Park as part of the daily Promenade. In afternoon dresses precisely matched in design but one of blue, one of pink and one of jonquil muslin along with matching bonnets and stockings and exquisite jean half-boots, the young ladies found it hard to contain their excitement. But it was not an easy task to be put in charge of displaying such a plethora of treasures as had come to live in Whitshire House, and Lady Whitshire, herself looking cool and elegant in a sapphire silk, could not be satisfied with the arrangement of her charges.

"I cannot think what we are to do," sighed Lady Whitshire, tying the bow of Miss Patterson's bonnet sweetly below her right ear and adjusting just the tiniest bit the lace trim upon Prudence's blue silk parasol and patting one of Honor's long curls into just the right position. "Andrew has brought his curricle and Justice, dear boy, has offered to drive Garrett's stanhope, all of which are most proper vehicles for promenading, but I cannot like the thought of dividing you amongst them. It would be so much more effective to have you all in the same vehicle."

"Effective?" asked Honor.

"Yes, dear. One charming young lady is indeed a pleasure to look upon, but three charming young ladies together, matched as you are in those wonderful frocks—well, the gentlemen of the *ton* would be bowled over by such a sight. It is rather like the difference between a bouquet of flowers all daintily arranged for one's enjoyment and a single blossom. Not that a single blossom is unappealing, but a perfect bouquet is breathtaking."

"Breathtaking," echoed the earl, appearing in the doorway to the summer parlor. "Mama, you have outdone yourself. We are like to be ridden down upon by hordes of gentlemen and Millard, Virtue and myself forced to take up arms to keep the beaux at a respectable distance from these belles of ours. I have sent them around to the stables, by the way, to dispose of their vehicles. Nev will see them mounted upon the best of my lot."

"To dispose of their vehicles?" Lady Whitshire eyed her son suspiciously. "And how are we to drive in the Promenade without the gentlemen's vehicles, dear heart? Garrett, you are not thinking to drive the girls and myself in your town coach? It is all closed up. No one will gain any but the briefest sight of them."

"No, I am not thinking to drive them in the town coach. I am thinking to drive them and yourself, ma'am, in my new landau. I have been all morning seeing the finishing touches put upon it. And if you will grant me a mere fifteen minutes, I shall put a number of finishing touches upon myself and then we will be off."

Lady Whitshire's blue eyes fairly beamed with glory as the landau turned in through the entrance and joined the long line of promenading carriages. With both sides of the top lowered and two ladies upon each of the banquettes,

their parasols twirling merrily in the sunlight; with Lord
Whitshire at the reins, splendid in a high-topped beaver
and russet morning coat; and with Mr. Millard and Mr.
Virtue riding Whitshire's high-stepping bays regally beside
them, they were the most splendid sight to be seen in
all of Hyde Park. Even the most jaded of promenaders
abandoned their acquired masks of ennui and with obvious
delight slowed their progress more than usual to address
the occupants of the landau, to welcome Lady Whitshire
back to London, to joke with Whitshire and Millard and
Virtue, and most of all to gain introduction to the three
lovely flowers of Lady Whitshire's little bouquet.

The earl gave thanks that he had thought to order up
the landau at the same time as the curricle. It had seemed
at first an extravagance, but he, himself, had wondered
how best to present three such lovely young women while
keeping his mama as chaperon beside them and the landau
had been the only answer. Obviously the correct answer,
for it seemed to Whitshire as if every gentleman in the
park had approached him or Millard or Virtue wishing to
be presented to the Virtue sisters and Miss Patterson—yes,
and wishing to be reintroduced to his mama as well.

The house will be overrun with beaux by tomorrow, he
thought, turning his team for the last time back down the
path toward the gate that would lead them into Park Lane.
He could not help but laugh as he heard his mama declare
behind him, "We are a triumph! A triumph!" And because
her words sent the young ladies in the landau, the earl,
and the gentlemen riding beside them into laughter, not
a one of them noticed the medium-sized man in a dull
brown coat and buff breeches who trod the foot path across
the way, his eyes pinned upon Miss Patterson and a look
of triumph upon his plain face that quite matched the
look of triumph upon Lady Whitshire's own.

Dusk gathered over London and deepened into an
extremely warm and humid night. A thick, white fog rose

lazily from the Serpentine and sent blind tentacles streaming through Hyde Park to grasp at the shrubs and trees
and entwine themselves about the lamp posts as far as Park
Lane and farther. Behind the brightly lighted windows of
Whitshire House, however, only one person appeared to
notice. The impromptu celebration that had arisen following the Promenade and had continued right on into a
most informal dinner and then into a blithely musical
evening in the grand saloon, appeared likely to go on
forever and his lordship's valet, Tyrel, could wait no longer.
With measured steps he approached the earl across the
brightly carpeted room. His lordship's fine baritone faltered and then fell silent as Tyrel whispered in his ear.
The wonderful violet eyes swept the room, and then turned
full upon the servant. "Are you certain, Tyrel?"

"Indeed, my lord. Since you returned home this afternoon."

Honor watched, puzzled, as the servant departed the
chamber, leaving behind him a master whose face swiftly
abandoned the humor that had abided there throughout
the day and donned instead a most worried scowl. In
another moment, Lord Whitshire was whispering in Mr.
Millard's ear and the lean fingers, that had long since
joined Prudence's own in coaxing spritely melodies from
out the pianoforte, ceased their jaunty dancing upon the
keys. Prudence then faltered in her own playing, and on
an instant all the enthusiastic singers in the saloon stuttered into silence.

"I very much fear I must be off," Mr. Millard announced
quietly. "Whitshire reminds me of an early appointment.
I do thank you, Lady Whitshire, and ladies, for a most
enjoyable day." With that and a bow, Mr. Millard was out
the door and disappearing down the corridor.

"Well, of all things!" Lady Whitshire exclaimed. "Garrett, what did you say to him?"

"Nothing, Mama. Only that we are both promised to
meet with a certain gentleman at White's soon after eleven
tomorrow morning. And you know Andrew. He is barely

awake by ten after a late evening. And it takes him forever to dress. If he stays any longer tonight, he will not arrive at our meeting tomorrow until well after noon. Speaking of which, I do believe I am for my bed as well." With a bow to the room in general, and what Honor could only consider a most serious frown, Whitshire exited the chamber.

"Something," declared Lady Whitshire quietly as her son's footsteps faded, "is clearly afoot."

"Do you truly think so?" asked Honor, who was seated beside the dowager on the long, flowered sopha.

"Indeed. And it all began with Tyrel. I do wish Garrett had never employed that man. It is most unnerving to have a murderer about the house."

"A—a murderer?"

"Oh! I ought not to have said that! It is a secret, you know."

Honor stared at her ladyship in blatant disbelief.

"Well, it *is* a secret. If certain people should learn of Tyrel's true identity, the man would be hanged on the instant. Not that he deserves to be," Lady Whitshire added thoughtfully. "Garrett has always said that he did never deserve to be hanged. Well, actually, Garrett says that had he been Tyrel, he would have killed Harry Davenport as well and never thought twice about it."

As Prudence began to play the pianoforte again and Justice and Miss Patterson to sing a most beguiling duet, Honor could do nothing but sit openmouthed, staring at Lady Whitshire, the conversation she had long ago overheard between her brother and the earl repeating itself inside her head. "He—he—collects murderers," she managed at last in a hushed voice.

"Do you mean to say that Garrett has already explained to you about his dreadful hobby horse?" asked the dowager in surprise. "Oh, but that does bode well. And you do not find him distasteful because of it? Better and better. I knew I was not mistaken."

Honor did not quite follow this bit of conversation, her

mind being centered instead upon the fact that the earl had not been hoaxing Justice that evening. Not at all. In fact, he had told the absolute truth. How she wished she had not gone off into consideration of his broad shoulders and trim waist and had instead listened to that quiet discussion in its entirety. "His lordship collects murderers like other people collect butterflies," she murmured, stunned.

"It is his passion," nodded the dowager Lady Whitshire. "He takes great delight in it. He studies them." Lady Whitshire shifted a bit upon the sopha, her blue silk whispering. "Actually, he catches them and then he studies them. Or is it the other way 'round? I am not quite clear on that, for it seems to me that he must study them in order to catch them in the first place, do you not think?"

Honor nodded silently.

"Yes, so do I. Really, it is the outside of enough to have a son with such a hobby horse as Garrett's. One would think that he could have developed an interest in—in—raising pug dogs! Not that everyone would not think him eccentric for doing precisely that, because they would. Gentlemen are not generally fond of pug dogs. But it would be preferable, I think, to his jauntering about London and the countryside in search of murderers and murderesses. It is so very difficult to explain to one's friends."

"I—I should think it would be most difficult."

"Yes. It is."

"Did he actually capture Mr. Tyrel?"

"Yes, indeed. Mr. Tyrel was his very first. He and Mr. Millard were still at Eton when they captured Mr. Tyrel. But Garrett could not be convinced to turn the man over to the authorities. Andrew and I both pleaded with him to do so, but he would not. Garrett can be exceptionally bullheaded, let me tell you. But he has allowed Sir John Fielding and his Runners to take possession of the rest."

"The rest? How many have there been?"

"Oh, several since Mr. Tyrel—whose true name, I assure you, I have long since forgotten. There was Arthur Chalmers and Ben Topley and Cyrus Oxen and that great beast

who did away with four young women and strewed their
bodies along the banks of the Thames. Jonathan Partridge,
I believe that villain was called. And, of course, there was
Cordelia Oates. She poisoned three of her employers and
was about to poison the fourth when Garrett at last divined
that she was indeed the culprit and brought her to justice.
That is the thing that sets him off."

"What?" asked Honor, her hazel eyes losing their lost
look and beginning to brighten with interest. "Justice?"

"Just so. They are hanged, you know. Every one of them
that he has captured to this very day has been hanged
except for Mr. Tyrel. Oh, you should hear him rant and
rave when that happens. Well, it necessarily puts an end
to his study of that particular person," Lady Whitshire
explained in defense of her cub. "After all that he goes
through to obtain these people for his studies, I expect it
is most upsetting for the poor boy to lose them one after
the other."

"Have they not yet dispersed, Tyrel?" asked Whitshire,
pacing his bedchamber impatiently.

"They are just now leaving the saloon, my lord. I should
wait another ten minutes at the very least."

"And what if he is not there in ten minutes?"

"He will be there, my lord. He has been leaning against
the oak or pacing across the verge or sitting upon the
bench since first you arrived home from the Promenade."

"Indeed?" Whitshire twitched the draperies aside the
merest bit and stared down into the night. "I can see his
shadow in the lamplight even now. But who the devil can
he be? And why spy upon Whitshire House?"

"I could not say, my lord. Unless—Oh, my lord, you do
not think that at last Bow Street has come looking for
me?"

The sudden fear that dawned in Tyrel's eyes and the
panic that spread across his face sent a stab of sympathy
through Whitshire. "No, no, Geoffrey, do not think such

a thing," he said, placing one strong hand bracingly upon the valet's shoulder. "You are in no danger from Bow Street or anyone else. It has been near twenty years. I doubt anyone so much as remembers your name."

"But if they have? If at last they have discovered that Geoffrey Tyrel is truly Arnold Snapp—"

"Balderdash! How could they? It would be nigh impossible at this late date."

"But if they have?"

"Then I shall take up sword or pistols or whatever else may be required of me and defend you to the death, you gudgeon, even against Sir John's Runners. You are the best valet I have ever had and I cannot afford to have you go off and be hanged. Who else would allow me to dress so unfashionably and yet manage to make me look acceptable regardless? It is more likely someone from Longbourne House," he added thoughtfully.

"The murderer?"

"Well, perhaps. I took the boy with me this morning to fetch the landau. Someone may have recognized him and taken it in mind to keep an eye upon me. They may not assume that it was I broke into the place simply because I have taken the brat up, but then again, they may suspect just that. And if one of them at the house is the murderer we seek—Are they not all settled in yet? Go and see, Tyrel. I cannot wait much longer."

The valet departed on the instant and returned in a matter of moments. "All gone to their chambers; the ladies in their nightrails, Martha says. And Mr. Virtue is ringing for me, my lord."

"Good. Go to him, Tyrel, and keep him well occupied, eh? I cannot risk having the cub notice me and thinking to follow. His sister would never forgive me should he come to any harm."

"Yes, my lord. Immediately." And with no more than that, Tyrel was gone.

Whitshire waited until he heard Justice's chamber door open and close and then stepped quietly out into the corridor. He made his way as quickly as possible along the hall to the servants' staircase where he disappeared from sight behind the green baize door. His boots made the slightest tapping as he descended the stairs, but he could not think that such a minor sound—and on the servants' staircase at that—would arouse the least curiosity on Justice Virtue's part even should he hear it.

And he was perfectly correct. Justice, in the midst of having Tyrel tug off his boots, heard the door to the rear stairway swing closed, heard as well the slight tapping as his lordship descended, but he merely assumed that one of the servants was returning to the servants' quarters. Honor, on the other hand, assumed no such thing.

Her mind a considerable jumble after her conversation with Lady Whitshire, she had declined Martha's assistance in disrobing and had sent her to wait upon Prudence and Miss Patterson. And then she had spent a good ten minutes pacing the little sitting room, attempting to understand how such a seemingly sane and generous and truly kind gentleman as the Earl of Whitshire could take such an inordinate interest in murderers. "Jonathan Patridge," she had murmured to herself. "Cordelia Oates. I have read of them both. Father has spoken of them. They were no better than savage animals." And then, when she had at last decided she could not calm herself, she had gone to bid Prudence and Julia good night, hoping that a brief conversation with each of them would have a calming affect upon her. She had just stepped out into the corridor from Julia's chambers when she caught a glimpse of the earl's broad shoulders as they disappeared behind the green baize door. Those shoulders had been covered in the same russet coat he had worn to the Promenade, and on through their celebration, and dinner and afterward. He had not departed the saloon, then, to go up to his bed. He had not been bound for bed at all. He had been in his chambers waiting for them to take to their own beds so that he might—so that he might—so that he might what?

Why would he tell the entire household a bouncer? she

wondered. And why sneak down the back stairs when he thought everyone safely in their chambers? What can he be thinking to do?

And then the word echoed in her ears as though her mind had whispered it aloud. "Murderers."

"Oh, he cannot be," she muttered. "He cannot be going out now to search for some murderer? Without a word to anyone?" But he had said a word to someone, she remembered. He had whispered something to Mr. Millard. Something that had caused that gentleman to cease playing in the very middle of a composition.

With a most serious frown upon her face and not a thought past that of dismissing her sudden suspicions by proving to herself that Lord Whitshire had merely gone down to the kitchen to fetch himself a snack and certainly nowhere else, certainly not in search of a murderer, Honor twitched the skirt of her muslin a bit higher and hurried toward the servants' staircase herself.

Chapter 7

Whitshire slipped silently through the kitchen door and out into the night. Streamers of fog nipped at his ankles as he made his way through the garden toward the mews. He moved soundlessly, a shadow amongst shadows, until he drew up short at the far corner of his own stables. Inside horses nickered and stamped, sensing his presence. "Hush, my dears," he murmured lowly. "Do not betray me." And then he peered around the rough stone building toward Hyde Park corner. No one. The park lay silent and eerie, patches of fog like vague white ghosts hovering here and there among the trees. Whitshire's muscles grew taut for the sprint to come—through the remaining mews, around the corner and across to where the man stood on the very edge of the parkland. He took a deep breath, leaned forward and then a hand grasped his right shoulder and he jumped, spinning about, his left fist jamming forward.

"Do not you dare," hissed a voice, dodging that fist. "I have not the least doubt that Miss Prudence Virtue would be greatly put off by a suitor with a blackened eye."

"Millard. Did you see the fellow?"

"Indeed. Rather unprepossessing, I think. But he moved back into the shadows when I rode past, so I could not see him well. I did not wish to be thought to be looking for him, you know, Whit."

"Exactly so. But he is not a giant, eh?"

"Not."

"Good. Will you circle or take the straight-on?"

"Circle. But you must give me time to get behind him."

The earl nodded and Millard slipped silently away.

Miss Prudence Virtue? thought Whitshire as he waited. Suitor? Now what the devil does Andrew mean to suggest by that? And then he dismissed thoughts of Andrew and moved forward, stepping out from between his stables and his neighbor's and gliding quietly up the alley that lay between his land and Artemor's—the alley that led directly into Park Lane.

If he had not been concentrating so intently upon gaining the advantage of surprise over his quarry Whitshire might have heard Honor's cautious footsteps and the quiet rustle of her skirts as she made her way along the alley behind him. Had he heard those footsteps and that soft rustle, he would have turned about and lay in wait for her, and upon discovering who she was, he would have called the entire thing off. But he had not the least notion that Honor was anywhere but in her own chambers.

Across the cobbled street the man stood with shoulders resting against the trunk of an ancient oak, his collar pulled up against the dampness and his beaver low on his brow. Through the mist and the fog he stared up at Whitshire House, scanning the windows one by one. The earl halted for a moment, muttered under his breath, and then burst from the alley. For a moment he was most visible as he bolted beneath the lamplight, but in seconds he was across Park Lane and back in shadows again, dashing straight toward the fellow. At the sound of Whitshire's boots pounding along the verge the man straightened, looked once in the earl's direction, then turned and darted into the murky gloom that was Hyde Park.

Honor lifted her skirts higher and ran as best she could. Her slippers were not the least protection against the rough ground of the alley or the rocky unevenness of the cobbled street, and her heart pounded and her face grew flushed and her breath came in uneven gasps as she fought against the drag of the wind against her skirts. But at last she gained the verge at the edge of the park and there her feet flew, carrying her off into the fog-riddled gloom of the trees a full ten yards behind Lord Whitshire. She could see him emerging now and again into moonlight or out-lined eerily against streamers of fog. She could see enough of him to know she was not terribly far behind. With a grim set to her lovely lips, she continued on.

Whitshire closed on the man where the flagstone path emerged from the lower gardens and crossed the bridle path. With a curse, he flung himself at the villain, stretching out in midair and landing hard upon the ground, his arms locked tightly about the man's legs. And then a booted foot landed solidly upon the earl's jaw and a second caught him along the side of the head and the devil of a spy was wriggling free and getting to his knees.

With a muttered oath Whitshire shook off the pain and gained his own knees. He flung himself forward again, this time catching the villain around the waist and wrestling the dastard to the ground. The man writhed and twisted beneath the earl's weight and then a fist pounded into Whitshire's stomach and something cold and hard bit through coat and waistcoat and shirt and slid along his lordship's ribs with an exquisite sting. Whitshire jerked away; the man rolled from under him, gained his feet and ran—straight into Andrew Millard's fist.

"Careful, Andrew, the blackguard has got a knife," shouted Whitshire, rising quickly from the ground and dashing back into the fray. He grabbed at the man from behind, hoping to catch hold of shoulders, neck, some-thing. And he did grab something. Something that came off damp and limp just as the knife flashed toward Millard and sent that gentleman stumbling in reverse into a rabbit hole. Andrew went down, the villain ran like the devil, and the Earl of Whitshire stood, entranced, staring down at his palm.

"Damnation but we ought to have had him. I am sorry, Whit," Millard sighed, picking himself up and brushing at his inexpressibles. "What have you got?" he asked, approaching his friend and squinting down into his outstretched palm. By the vague light of the fog-dimmed moon the object was hard to recognize. Millard squinted more. "By Jove, it's the blighter's nose! You have pulled the blighter's nose right off his face!"

A horrified gasp met this observation and both gentlemen spun about to gaze upon the most unlikely vision. Millard's jaw dropped. Whitshire's left hand searched urgently for his quizzing glass. "What the devil?" he muttered, holding the glass to his eye and taking an unsteady step forward.

In the dim, ethereal glow of moonlight off fog she stood panting in her much disheveled pink muslin gown. Her matching slippers were stained and torn, and her hair tumbled about her face and shoulders, damp and stringy and bedecked with twigs and leaves. Her breasts heaved with the attempt to breathe easier and her hands waved oddly before her as though she were beating aside some annoying bugs. Whitshire, quizzing glass to eye, took another step forward. "Miss Virtue?" he whispered in the greatest amazement. "What the devil are you doing here?"

Tears began to roll down Honor's cheeks and she swiped angrily at them with the backs of her hands. "I—I—You collect murderers," she accused breathlessly. "Do not deny it. Even your mother says that you do. And I thought that you were going to try to catch one tonight. And I could not let you do something so dangerous alone. And you are stabbed!" she added on a sob. "And you have torn a man's nose right off of his face!"

She was so incredibly bedraggled and overwhelmed. The quizzing glass dropped from Whitshire's hand and he went to her, fitting a strong left arm bracingly about her shoulders. He felt her take a deep breath and then shudder. "It is not a real nose, Miss Virtue," he said softly, slowly opening his right hand before her eyes. "It is a nose made from putty."

"P-putty?"

"Yes, my dear. The sort of putty that actors use when they wish to change their appearance upon the stage," murmured the earl. "I am not strong enough to tear a real nose from someone's face."

"You are v-very strong," said Honor on a tiny sob. "No one thinks so because your coats are all so large they cannot see your muscles. But when you take your coat off—"

"I am still not strong enough to rip a person's nose off," chuckled Whitshire, drawing Honor close against him and bestowing a most tender kiss upon her disheveled curls.

"Ought to get back," Millard harrumphed. "Chilly out here."

"Yes, just so," nodded Whitshire. "Here, Andrew, carry this for me, will you?" And without the least hesitation he tossed the nose into the air in Mr. Millard's direction, then swept Honor up into his arms.

"What are you doing?" Honor whimpered softly. "Put me down at once. You are stabbed."

"Yes, but it is a scratch merely and, once it is bandaged, no one will be able to tell a thing. Whereas you, Miss Virtue, will be hobbling about like a grandmother for the remainder of the Season if you walk back to Whitshire House in what remains of those slippers. Hush now. Do attempt to cease crying, will you not, my dear? It was very sweet of you to think to protect me."

"It was purely stupid," mumbled Millard.

"Well, yes," chuckled Whitshire. "But sweetly stupid."

"I am not stupid," protested Honor, resting her head comfortably upon the earl's shoulder as he began the trek home. "It is the both of you who are stupid to run about chasing dangerous murderers in the middle of the night."

* * *

"I cannot think why you are whistling," sighed Tyrel, fastening the bandage about Whitshire's ribs. "You have run yourself ragged and been beaten and stabbed besides."

"No, I have not run myself ragged, Tyrel. And I gave as good as I got, believe me. Whoever it was, he will be feeling quite as sore as I am at this moment."

"But he does not have a knife wound across his ribs."

"Which is nothing more than a scratch. But you do have a point, Tyrel. Next time, I shall take a weapon with me."

"Next time, my lord? Certainly you do not expect to see the man again? Most certainly you and Mr. Millard have discouraged him from whatever criminal considerations were in his mind."

"Another good reason to whistle," smiled Whitshire, pulling his nightshirt over his head.

"What?"

"You are convinced that the man had criminal intentions and was not a Bow Street Runner in search of yourself."

"A Runner would have used his rod, my lord, not a blade."

"Exactly so. And I doubt he would have taken off at a run at the first sight of me either. So you must not be worried any longer, eh, Tyrel? No one is after you. As far as Bow Street is concerned Arnold Snapp is dead and gone. I am certain of that. Go to bed, Tyrel. Morning will come extremely early for us both."

Whitshire grinned as Tyrel exited the chambers and continued to grin as he pulled back the counterpane. The incredible Miss Honor Virtue had followed him in darkness through the mews and across into the park. She had watched him give chase to a man whom she thought to be a murderer and she had wholeheartedly given chase herself. "Never once giving thought to her dress or her hair or her slippers," the earl murmured as he slid between the sheets. "I did not think there was a woman in the world who would not first give thought to her dress and her hair and her slippers before she became involved in anything. By Jove, Miss Virtue must truly have been worried about me.''

It was the first time that any woman had been worried about Whitshire since his mama had expended a great deal of worry over his lack of inheritance and had thrown her heart into restoring the family fortunes. But he had been merely four years old then and had not had the sense to appreciate how grand a thing it was to have a woman worry over one. The earl closed his eyes and pictured Miss Honor Virtue, her hair bedecked with twigs and leaves and tumbling everywhere, her nose smudged, her dress enticingly disheveled and her eyes red and puffy from those oh, so angry tears. "I do not think I have ever seen anyone so beautiful," he murmured. "I know I have never seen anyone so beautiful."

Honor was quite certain that she would not be able to face his lordship at the breakfast table that morning. He must think her such a fool—an interfering fool at that. What was it he had said? That she was sweetly stupid? Well, she was. At least stupid, if not the sweetly part. Mr. Millard had been correct.

She thought the soft knock upon her door to be Martha coming to help pin up her hair. She did not need the help. Her hair was already quite snugly pinned into a most becoming Grecian knot. "Go off upon your other duties," she called. "I am not in need of you this morning, Martha."

The knock sounded again.

Not Martha then. Honor sighed and rose from before her looking glass. Perhaps it was Lily come to make up the bed and do her dusting. Honor turned the knob and opened the door wide—to discover his lordship standing there, staring down at her with one hand upon the door frame and the other dangling by a thumb from a waistcoat pocket. He was dressed most fashionably this morning—

at least for him it was most fashionable—in a morning coat of deep claret, cut quite precisely to his form, and buff breeches and shining Hessians. If it were not for the brightly striped black and white waistcoat and the red cravat beneath the high white collar, Honor would have thought Lord Whitshire had gotten his clothing from some other gentleman's clothes press.

"Are you never coming out again for as long as you live, Miss Virtue?" he asked quietly. "It is already noon, you know."

"Y-yes. I know. I am not feeling just the thing, I fear."

"Balderdash!"

"Pardon?"

"I said balderdash, Miss Virtue. If you will permit me to make an observation, you are the picture of good health."

"I have a vile headache."

"No, do you? I have a headache as well. And my jaw aches. And my ribs. In fact I ache all over. How odd we should both come down with a case of the aches at one and the same time."

Though he spoke in the most serious tone, his fine violet eyes sparkled with laughter and their influence alone coaxed the slightest of smiles to Honor's lips.

"In a matter of an hour or so there will be innumerable ladies and gentlemen flocking into our drawing room to further their acquaintances with you. Morning callers, you know. And if you do not appear I shall have the devil of a time to explain to Mama why you do not. Pardon me, I did not mean to say—"

"Devil," giggled Honor softly.

"Exactly so. And believe me, you do not wish to face a drawing room filled with virtual strangers without a large breakfast. At least, I do not. And I have been waiting forever."

"To meet a drawing room filled with virtual strangers?"

"No, to eat breakfast, Miss Virtue. Please come. I find I am not inclined to break my fast without you. I have grown accustomed to your bright and shining face at table and cannot be hungry without I see it there."

"Balderdash!" declared Honor.

"Yes," grinned Whitshire, "but well-intended balderdash, I assure you. I admit I am always hungry. But I have not eaten and everyone else apparently has. And I would enjoy your company."

"How can you after I behaved in such an outlandish fashion last evening? How can you even wish to set eyes upon me?"

Whitshire's hand came down from the door frame, and one long, lean finger touched her cheek gently and traveled down it and along her jaw before it moved away to be dangled with the rest of his fingers as his thumb found his other waistcoat pocket. "It is the most devilish thing, Miss Virtue, but I find myself wishing to set my eyes upon you constantly."

Footpads in Park Lane! Whoever would have thought such a thing possible? London was fast becoming a place for decent Englishmen to avoid. Adrian Carpenter dragged his aching body from his bed in one of the corner rooms at Grillon's and sighed. Thank goodness he had taken his knife with him yesterday or this morning he might well be dead. The nerve of the fellow, rushing at him from an alley along a perfectly respectable street! One might expect such harassment in St. Giles but in Park Lane? Unforgiveable! Well, he would be doubly certain to carry his knife with him from now on!

He would stand watch again today and into the night if need be, for it was certainly she who had entered that remarkably large old house in Park Lane. The largest house in the entire street, he thought. Most likely it belonged at one time to a duke or an earl. But to whom does it belong now? As he slipped into his shirt and his breeches, he pondered over it. While he stood before the looking glass tying his cravat, he gave it deep thought.

Even as he fashioned himself a new and most admirable nose, and set bushy eyebrows in place to accompany it, he could not help but ruminate upon the thing.

Three gentlemen and four ladies had entered that house and only one gentleman had departed from it. Which meant, of course, that she was residing there now along with the other ladies. His heart fairly quaked at what *that* might mean. But no, such a thing as he was thinking could not possibly be. Even if robbers did attack one in Park Lane, the neighborhood could not have sunk to such a depth as that. Never. Why if it were so, every decent family in the neighborhood would have moved away years ago.

Unless it was kept most secret. Unless no one knew of it but a small number of select gentlemen. And she *had* ruined herself by riding so outrageously in tunic and spangled tights at Astley's. His heart still quivered with anxiety at the memory of that spectacle. But surely there would be opportunity to cover up that particular scandal. Surely she knew that he would not forsake her because of it. She would never, never sink so far into despair as to think to become a—a—lightskirt! Yet, quite by chance he had gone walking through Hyde Park yesterday at the height of the Promenade and there she had been, dressed to the nines and riding pretty as you please in a most dashing landau overflowing with beautiful women. And all the gentlemen in the park, it seemed, had paid extraordinary attention to the lot of them.

"And the landau did deposit her and the others at that house and none of the women and only one of the gentlemen came out again," he murmured as he studied his new nose with a certain degree of pride in spite of the jitters his ruminations were sending through him. "I watched as all the lamps were turned down and the household closed up for the night and no one else exited that establishment. No more gentlemen and not one of the ladies.

"Phah! Foolishness," he told himself as he adjusted a white periwig over his own short brown hair. "She would never do such a thing as to think to make her living in a

brothel! It is too outrageous even for a gel with her flair
for the dramatic.''

But if she has, he thought, slipping into a coat of rough
brown tweed, there will be blood spilt because of it. A great
deal of blood.

Justice could bear it no longer. The drawing room at
Whitshire House was filled to overflowing with young ladies
and gentlemen. And a goodly number of the gentlemen
insisted upon conversing with Miss Patterson. And Miss
Patterson smiled at them in such a way and appeared to
find their attentions so welcome that Mr. Virtue wished to
strangle each and every one of them. Though any number
of young ladies twittered and twitched and batted their
eyelashes playfully in his direction, Justice was determined
to take no notice of any of them. In fact, he found them
all most annoying, the ladies and the gentlemen alike.
Even his friend Mr. Donnering was setting his teeth on
edge. And Mr. Millard—truly, anyone would think that
Mr. Millard in his tight white collar and perfectly tied cravat
had lost his senses completely the way he sat staring across
the room at Prudence who had become surrounded by a
bevy of gentlemen.

With a most determined step, Justice made his way
through the blathering mob and out into the corridor. He
descended the staircase in a most unseemly manner, swung
around the newel post at the ground floor landing and
stomped down the hallway as far as Whitshire's study where
he knocked once upon the door, then pushed it open,
not waiting at all for an answer.

''Batten the hatches!'' squawked Ferdy on the instant,
fluttering about and jerking his feathery head up and
down.

''What a tremendous bunch of birdbrains!'' Justice
exclaimed, ignoring the parrot and turning one of the
wing chairs to face the earl before flopping morosely down

into it. "I have never heard such—such—frivolous blatherings in all my life. You are correct to hide yourself away."

"Keelhaul 'em," muttered Ferdy. "Keelhaul 'em."

"I expect Justice would like to do exactly that, you mangy bird," grinned Whitshire, leaning back in his chair, his feet planted firmly upon his desk top. "I did not reach the age of thirty-two without learning a thing or two about morning callers. I have been one, you know, from time to time."

"You?"

"Yes, me. When I was your age any number of fathers lured me into paying morning calls upon their daughters. Dreadful business. And I have a distinct fear that Mama intends for me to take it up again. But she will not succeed."

"I should hope not," muttered Justice. "Of all the inane, witless ways to spend one's time."

"Awwk," agreed Ferdy, holding a piece of melon between his talons and taking a peck at it.

"Little Miss Patterson has acquired a following, eh?" asked Whitshire, tapping a silver-backed hairbrush against his knee.

"What?"

"Little Miss Patterson. Acquired a following."

"What makes you say that?"

"Because she is upstairs in the drawing room, Cub, and you are down here moping in my study. I do not flatter myself that my sparkling personality drew you here."

"They are buzzing about her like bees about a honeycomb."

"Just so."

"Well, and they are doing likewise with Prudence and Honor."

"I suspected as much. And I suspect any number of older gentlemen are buzzing about my mother, eh?"

"Yes. Have they all lost their minds, Whit? Even Alex is set upon making a fool of himself. And Mr. Millard—"

"Andrew is here?"

"Sitting near the front window and staring at Prudence while totally ignoring Miss Bethany Sims."

"Oh. Well, everyone ignores Miss Bethany Sims, I am told. Because she never notices that she is being ignored and so one does not feel guilty in doing so. Andrew is staring at Miss Prudence?"

"In the most peculiar fashion."

"Mutiny!" squawked Ferdy. "Mutiny! Mutiny!"

"Ferdy, cease and desist," growled Whitshire. "I cannot think that Andrew will remain abovestairs much longer, Cub. I happen to know that Captain James Furbough of the Guards plans to pay a call upon Miss Prudence this afternoon and, once he arrives, Andrew will be joining us here. Buck up, Virtue. It is not the end of the world, you know. They will all of them be gone by five and we are bound for the theater this evening. You will have little Miss Patterson all to yourself then."

"I am not the least concerned with having Miss Patterson to myself," protested Justice. "I am not concerned with Miss Patterson in the least. It is merely the sheer inanity of it all that sets my teeth on edge."

"Indeed," nodded Whitshire. "Just as it will be the vapidity of Furbough's conversation that will bring Millard stomping down the staircase to us. What is Miss Patterson's first name, Cub? Remind me of it."

"Julia. Why?"

"Because I have here a silver-backed brush with red hairs in it and it bears the initials JP."

"What are you doing with Miss Patterson's hairbrush?"

"Is it Miss Patterson's hairbrush? That is the question. I have not the least doubt that she has a brush upon the vanity table in her chamber even now. Did she buy that one to replace this one? This one, Virtue, I discovered abandoned behind the armoire in Longbourne's bedchamber. And it is an odd coincidence that it should have Miss Patterson's initials engraved upon it, is it not?"

Chapter 8

Adrian Carpenter arose from the hip bath, toweled himself energetically and began to don the very best clothes he had thought to bring with him. He told himself that he had quite enough time to deck himself out properly. After all, he had no wish to appear out of place among the crowd of fashionable theatergoers who would fill the boxes at Covent Garden. And it was merely six. If the traffic were not outrageous, the Royal Opera House could be reached from Grillon's within a quarter hour. White silk stockings and fine pearl pantaloons, white waistcoat, white collar, magnificently tied white cravat and a perfectly fitted double-breasted black coat all contributed to Carpenter's feeling of pampered well-being, a feeling he had not enjoyed for months now. He slipped his feet into jeweled evening slippers and shrugged an evening cloak of shining black satin with a magnificent rose silk lining about his shoulders. He would even have time for a peaceful, unhurried dinner. He took chapeau and cane in hand and with a relief born of knowing at last what was and what was to come next, he took himself downstairs to Grillon's public room. He was smiling.

Never in his life had he been so relieved. The great old house in Park Lane was not a brothel! This very morning he had been literally quaking in his boots as he had seated himself upon a bench midway down the street from the house and watched the comings and goings there from behind a copy of the *Daily Mirror*. Beginning at one o'clock, vehicle after vehicle had stopped before that particular establishment to disgorge—thank you, God—members of Polite Society! Not that he had actually recognized any of them. He had been gone from London much too long to actually recognize any of them. But several of the coaches had had coats of arms emblazoned upon their doors and many of the visitors had been ladies dressed in the height of fashion—and most of them had been mothers with daughters. It was not a brothel! His heart still leaped in his breast with the joy of such knowledge.

And then the most fortuitous thing had happened. Just as a glance at his pocket watch had informed him that the hour of five was close upon him, a small boy had come whistling up to the bench upon which he sat. "Be waitin' on someun, gov'?" the tyke had asked. And upon being told that he waited for no one in particular, the child had sat down beside him and had proceeded to inform him, in the most conversational manner, all about the establishment he had spent yesterday and today watching. It was called Whitshire House, the boy had said, and belonged to his lordship, the Earl of Whitshire, and he was the lad lucky enough to be picked as his lordship's tiger.

Carpenter actually grinned as the waiter poured him a glass of wine. How very lucky that he had wondered aloud that anyone should take up such a young fellow to be a tiger. It had been the very best thing to say! The boy had scowled at him. And then, as if to prove that he was indeed his lordship's tiger, he had announced with great pride that his lordship and Mr. Virtue and the ladies were all bound for the Royal Opera House in Covent Garden this very evening at eight o'clock and that he, Spider, was to ride upon his perch on his lordship's new curricle and to look after his lordship's blacks during the performance because there were too many people in the house to all ride in the coach, so his lordship must take Miss Virtue in the curricle.

The lad had been a font of information. Carpenter thanked God for the tiger's having happened by and cut himself a piece of the beef from the plate the waiter had set before him. It was coming on to six. He would eat his meal slowly and without the least anxiety and perhaps even enjoy another glass of wine. Because there was nothing at all to be anxious about this evening. He knew precisely where the girl would be and with whom. And when he had finished his leisurely dinner, he would have one of the grooms flag him down a hackney to carry him to Covent Garden and deposit him at the Royal Opera House well before the party from Park Lane arrived.

"His face done lit up like a hunnerd candles altogether," announced Spider proudly. "I did niver seen no human man look so very 'appy an' pleased wif 'imself, lor'ship. Not even me pa when he founded 'imself a shillin' under Mr. Sidel's pantaloons. 'Course 'e be dead now, m'pa. But 'e were that happy he were ta be afindin' of a shillin', I tell you."

"And you told him everything, Spider?"

"Jus' like ye said for ta do, lor'ship. I told 'im how I worked fer the Earl of Whitshire what lived in this 'ere house. An' how I was goin' ta be awatchin' over yer blacks when you all went ta Covent Garden. I even tole 'im as how me an' John Coachman was ta be ready at the fron' door at precisely eight o' the clock."

"And did he tell you anything in return, Spider?" asked Whitshire, one foot propped upon a mounting block at the side of the stables. "He did not mention his name, did he? Or his place of residence, perhaps? Or whether or not he had ever been to the Royal Opera House in Covent Garden?"

"Nothin'," frowned the tiger. "Only said as 'ow he had been awonderin' who lived in sich a fine 'stablishment as ours an' that 'e was pleased ta know it were in'abited by ladies an' gen'lemen. Now don't that beat all? Who did 'e think was in'abitin' the place, I ask you, dogs an' cats?" Spider giggled at his own words and then looked up at Whitshire thoughtfully. " 'E don't be no gent, lor'ship," he offered, "if that be what ye be wishin' ta know. 'E be tryin' fer ta look like one, but 'e don't be no true gent. 'E be the likes o' Mr. Curbridge, I thinks."

"Mr. Curbridge? The man in Longbourne's study? The one you said was the butler? You think this fellow on the bench was someone's butler, Spider?"

"Aye. 'Tis what I thinks."

That gave Whitshire pause. A butler? Nonsense. Why would someone's butler be keeping watch day and night practically outside his front door? Of course, he was not entirely certain that the man on the bench today had been the same person as the man under the oak tree last night, but he had a good idea they were one and the same. Still, a butler? No, Spider was mistaken in that. If it had been someone's butler, he would not have been wondering who lived in Whitshire House. Every butler in London knew that. And then it occurred to Whitshire that if the man were keeping watch upon him, for whatever reason, the man ought to know his name as well. He had simply been having Spider on then, about being pleased to know who lived in such a fine house. That was it.

With a shrug of his broad shoulders and a wink of his eye, Whitshire called Spider a remarkably quick-witted little scoundrel and thanked him for a job well done. Then he gave the boy a congratulatory pat on the shoulder and produced from his coat pocket a snuff box filled with candies. "Which you are to keep in your waistcoat pocket, Spider, in case you find need of sustenance tonight while you are waiting upon us."

"Gor, lor'ship! Fer me? An' the snuffin' box as well?"

"Indeed. And when the box is empty, you are to come directly to me in my study and I shall fill it up again."

The wide smile upon that small face and the manner in which the little hand tightened around the box made Whitshire wish to whistle. So he did just that as he strolled off toward the house to dress. They were actually going to Drury Lane and not the Royal Opera House. And they would not leave at eight but at seven, putting off their dinner until after the performance, when the entire party would dine in one of the private parlors at the Clarendon. All in all, if the man had believed every word, they would be free of him for the evening. Until they arrived back home tonight, of course, by which time the dastard would have deduced that he had been duped and would likely be standing about in the park somewhere, waiting for them to reappear at Whitshire House.

"I knew it was the same bloke," mumbled Tyrel. "And what business he has to come lounging about upon the park bench for an entire afternoon, setting everyone's nerves on end, I cannot think. Even Mr. Donnelly was upset. And who the villain thought he was fooling in that stupid periwig—"

"Now, now, Tyrel. It was not a stupid periwig. It was a very elegant periwig, if a bit outdated. You do not think that I ought to take to wearing such a . . . ?"

The sudden shock upon his valet's face sent Whitshire into whoops of laughter. "No, no, I am merely teasing, Tyrel," he managed after a moment or two of pure merriment. "I have not the least desire to go prancing about in a periwig. As a matter of fact, I have been seriously thinking about what I ought to wear to the theater tonight, Tyrel, and I have decided upon—"

"Not the yellow, my lord," murmured Tyrel.

"No, not the yellow."

"Not the violet."

"Be quiet, will you. You are making yourself more anxious by the moment. Next you will be thinking that I have chosen to wear my father's knee breeches and great-grandfather's tricorn.''

"And you have not?"

"No. I have decided that I shall wear the midnight blue coat at the very rear of the armoire and all the folderols that go with it. That is what a fashionable gentleman would wear to an evening at the theater, is it not?''

"Precisely," Tyrel beamed. "That is precisely what a fashionable gentleman would wear." The midnight blue coat had been tailored for his lordship by the incomparable Weston under the eyes of Beau Brummell himself. Of course, it had only been made because his lordship had lost a bet to Mr. Brummell. And his lordship had worn it only once, two years ago, at the Bradleys' ball, but the mere thought that he was to dress the earl in that remarkable form-fitting garment and all the niceties that accompanied it made Tyrel's heart leap with joy. He began on the instant to lay out his lordship's white waistcoat and a stack of white neckcloths, for there was no telling how many might be ruined in tying the perfect *orientale,* and his saffron pantaloons and black evening shoes and his chapeau and cape and cane.

"Do me one favor, Tyrel," the earl muttered as he stepped into his bath. "Do attempt not to look so thoroughly pleased."

Lady Whitshire and the Misses Virtue and Miss Patterson entered the earl's box at Drury Lane like a rainbow of flutterbys floating on a summer breeze. Every eye fell instantly upon them, and then, most amazedly, upon the gentlemen who accompanied them. Honor noted the stares and the great buzz immediately afterward. "Whatever can they all be discussing?" she wondered aloud as Whitshire seated his mother and then came to help her to her seat as well. "Is there something amiss with our gowns?"

"Not at all. You are all quite beautiful," the earl answered with a beguiling grin. "In fact, you are likely the most beautiful group of ladies in the entire theater. The buzz has nothing at all to do with you. It concerns me, I fear."

"You? But why should practically an entire theater be abuzz because of you, my lord?"

"Because I have only appeared once before in public looking the perfect dandy, Miss Virtue. And that was when I lost a wager to The Beau. I wagered that I could shoot the pips out of a playing card at twenty paces by candlelight using my left hand and he, of course, wagered that I could not."

"Heavens, what a thing to wager! Of course you would lose."

"I did hit the pips, Miss Virtue. I lost the wager only by reason of a minor detail."

"What detail?"

"The candle blew out before I had finished."

"You shot them out in the dark?" asked Honor, flabbergasted.

"One of them. But it was to be done entirely in candlelight and so I lost. I ought to have waited until the candle was lighted again. But I had had a deal too much to drink and was impatient."

Honor stared at him, her eyes large with wonder. He was not only more powerfully built than he generally appeared, and had an odd interest in violent people, but now it appeared that he was a crack shot as well. How much more might there be to him? How much more that she did not imagine?

"Do not stare at me so, Miss Virtue," Whitshire murmured. "It was a simple wager and merely involved my dressing to Brummell's specifications or he dressing to mine. I did not gamble away any of my inheritance, I assure you, so you need not begin to lecture me upon that point again."

"I—It is not your gaming confounds me, my lord."

"What then?"

"To—to shoot foxed, and left-handed—and in the dark—more and more I think you are a most dangerous gentleman."

Abruptly, the warm glow that had lingered in his lordship's eyes since first he had escorted her to his curricle, vanished. The charming smile which had met Honor's every bit of conversation faded. And with the loss of them, the glamor and excitement of an evening at Drury Lane seemed to dissipate for Honor. She felt herself thrust most suddenly into a cold, dark, and very sad place. What had she said to make such a thing happen? Flustered, she turned from him to stare out over the audience, to attempt to bring herself back into the exhilaration and bustle going on all about her, but it did not the least bit of good. Without the glow in Lord Whitshire's eyes to warm her and the smile upon his face to send her spirits soaring, all she saw was an enormous group of overdressed, noisy people who talked much too loudly and inanely and desperately beneath a sky of plaster and before a platform of wood.

What have I done? she wondered as she heard the earl remove his cape and slip into the chair behind her. I said merely that I am coming to think him a dangerous man and in a wink he ceased to smile and his eyes grew sad and in that same moment all the world about me became transformed.

"You *are* a dangerous man," she said, turning in her chair to face him. "I cannot think otherwise. I am not some goosish miss, my lord, who refuses to believe what is right before her eyes. I know about your hobby horse and have seen you fight. And now I learn that you are likely unmatched when it comes to pistols."

"Just so, Miss Virtue," murmured Whitshire.

"Yes, it is just so. But I did not intend my observation as a reproach, my lord."

"You did not?"

Honor smiled her most inspiring smile at him. She

wanted nothing more than to make him smile in response
and to bring that warm glow back to those wonderful eyes
so that all the world might be as it had been when first
they had entered the box. "Of course I did not intend it
as a reproach. I am most sorry if that is how it seemed. It
was an observation upon your tale of the wager united with
what I have learned of you in the little time we have had
to know each other. That was all. What would you have
had me say, my lord? Tell me and I shall say it."

"You will?"

"Yes, for I wish you will smile at me again, and quickly
too."

"Do you always speak so plainly, Miss Virtue?"

"Upon subjects that are important."

The earl cocked an eyebrow. "And my smile is
important?"

"Yes. Now tell me what I ought to have said."

"Well, what I would have had you say when I finished my
tale," he began, a remnant of his engaging grin flickering
across his countenance. "What I had hoped to hear you
say, after I muddled my way through that lengthy explanation, was that you were well pleased that Brummell had
won the wager because I look quite elegant in these togs."

"Oh!"

"Well, I expect I do not—look elegant—but that is what
I wished to hear you say, Miss Virtue, because—because I
donned the dratted things only to impress you."

The most diffident look overcame him and his violet
eyes lowered the merest bit allowing him to stare up shyly
at her from beneath those thick, dark lashes. Really, Honor
thought, he is the most confounding gentleman. To admit
that he has abandoned his unfashionable manner of dress,
to which he has apparently clung for years, in an attempt
to impress me, and to do so without the least roundabouta-
tion! And now he bestows upon me the most timid and
yet utterly seductive look! Oh, he is much more dangerous
than any gentleman has a right to be!

"Well, Miss Virtue? Did you mean what you said a moment ago?"

"You look most elegant, my lord. Truly you do."

"Thank you, Miss Virtue. I feel a deal better now about having allowed Tyrel to squeeze me into this devil of a coat. Pardon me," he said with a chuckle in his voice, "I did not intend to say—"

"Devil," finished Honor, her own quiet laughter joining with his. And at that precise moment the glitter and glamor and the excitement of the evening was back to surround them both and carry them off into the magical world of the theater.

Prudence glanced in their direction and wondered what made them laugh so charmingly together. She wished most heartily that she were laughing in a like fashion with Captain James Furbough. She was not, however. The gentleman who sat behind her was not the captain, but Mr. Andrew Millard. And of all the dreams Prudence had dreamed of London, attending a play at Drury Lane in the company of a bishop's son had not been one of them.

"I can buy a scarlet coat," murmured Millard under his breath.

"I beg your pardon?" Prudence turned slightly in her chair.

"I said," declared Mr. Millard more loudly, "I can buy myself a scarlet coat."

"Why would you wish to do that?"

"You are fond of scarlet coats, are you not, Miss Prudence? Most young ladies appear to be. Apparently scarlet is a most invigorating color."

"It is?"

"Very. What do you think of Drury Lane?"

"I like it quite well," replied Prudence, gazing about her with some impatience.

"He will most likely be in the pit."

"What?"

"I said that Captain Furbough will most likely be somewhere down on the main floor before the stage. It is Captain Furbough for whom you are searching, is it not? You did remember to tell him that you planned to attend this evening?"

"Yes, I did."

"I thought as much. Merely look down over the rail then, Miss Prudence, and I expect you will discover Jamie looking up, searching the boxes for you. It is most likely, you see, that he has no idea which box you are in because Whit so seldom attends Drury Lane that no one remembers which box belongs to him."

"Oh! I had no idea!" exclaimed Prudence, standing immediately to peer down into the crowd of people, primarily gentlemen, stomping about in the pit.

"Prudence, whatever are you doing?" cried Lady Whitshire on a little gasp, turning away from a conversation with Lady Eldridge in the adjoining box.

"I am looking for Captain Furbough," explained Prudence, without once taking her gaze from the pit. "Oh, there he is!" And Prudence waved happily down at the gentleman in the scarlet coat who waved back at her, laughing.

Lady Whitshire stood and gazed down over the railing as well and glared directly into the opera glasses that Captain Furbough held before his eyes and lifted one perfectly arched eyebrow the merest bit. Captain Furbough lowered his glasses on the instant, turned about, sat down and began to take great interest in the empty stage before him.

"It is not the thing, my dear," the dowager said, stepping around Miss Patterson to come up beside Prudence, "to be seeking out gentlemen in the pit. People will think you are forward."

"Oh! But Mr. Millard said that Captain Furbough would not know which box we were in and I only thought to—"

"Yes, well the captain knows which it is now," sighed Lady Whitshire. "Certainly no one will hold it against you to have acted in such a manner this once, but now you must be seated and pretend to enjoy yourself." And with a most intimidating glare at Mr. Millard, Lady Whitshire returned to her own seat and her conversation with Lady Eldridge.

"I do apologize," whispered Mr. Millard in Prudence's ear. "I did not think. Gentlemen may stand and wave at each other without causing the lift of one eyebrow. I did not remember that young ladies may not. I am sorry, Miss Prudence."

"It is not your fault," sighed Prudence. "I ought to have known. Young ladies can do nothing but sit and smile and flutter their fans in London without being thought forward or a hoyden or some such thing. It is very hard to adjust, let me tell you."

Little Miss Patterson overheard and smiled at Prudence consolingly. "Men," she agreed, "have the very best of everything and are free to enjoy it, while we must sit about demurely and pretend to be interested in nothing but fashions and folderols. It is most distressing, is it not?"

"You were not required to sit about demurely," offered Justice from immediately behind her. "You, Miss Patterson, were quite free, I think. And you did not much like it."

"Free?" cried Miss Patterson quietly. "I think not, Mr. Virtue. It is not freedom to be forced into a livelihood because one has grown accustomed to eating."

"No, it is not," agreed Mr. Millard. "You are correct about that, Miss Patterson. But it is wrong to think that gentlemen may do whatever they wish. Not many of us are free either. There are any number of rules we must follow as well."

"Like what?" asked Prudence, eyeing both her brother and Mr. Millard suspiciously.

"Oh, any number," Justice assured them both heartily.

"Name one," persisted Prudence.

"Well, we are expected to be—to be—"

"Honorable," offered Mr. Millard, "in all things. Especially in gaming and with the ladies. And if a gentleman is the heir to a title, he is responsible to produce heirs of his own so that the title does not leave the immediate family. And if a gentleman's family is courting disaster, he must marry money regardless of the wrapping the fortune comes in. And a gentleman must be fearless and fashionable and informed and maintain a position at the very top of society. And if he is proved to be dishonorable he is cast out and most lucky if he does not meet his end eating grass for breakfast."

"Grass for breakfast?" asked Prudence.

"Dead on a dueling ground," Justice murmured.

"Dueling is outlawed," protested Miss Patterson, "and has been for centuries."

"Ha!" exclaimed Mr. Millard.

"Ha!" echoed Justice.

"Balderdash," muttered Prudence. "Honor or not, you are still free to go where you will and do what you wish. You have everything and we have nothing at all."

Both gentlemen opened their mouths to protest, but upon the stage *Richard II* was beginning and the young ladies turned away to pay attention to the entertainment.

Chapter 9

"Any sign of him, Tyrel?" asked Whitshire as his valet helped him out of the form-fitting coat.

"None, my lord. Mr. Donnelly did think to have a glimpse of him near ten o'clock."

"He did?"

"Indeed. And so we decided it might be worthwhile to take a stroll, Mr. Donnelly and I."

"You ought not to have done that, Tyrel. There is not the least need to be placing yourselves in danger."

"Well, but we did not, my lord, for the park was quite empty at this side and no one at all lounging about the lane."

"Good. That, Tyrel, is a relief. Though I expect he has not given up on us. He will return in the morning, no doubt. If I could merely discover who the man is, I would likely be able to deduce why this house has come under his intense observation. I did think, you know, that he had discovered I am involved in the investigation of Longbourne's murder and is determined to learn what I might or might not have discovered concerning it. But how the man expects to find out anything by standing about outside or following me to the theater, I cannot imagine. So I begin to think he wishes something else entirely. But what? And do not say that he is after you again, Tyrel, because that is pure balderdash."

"Yes, my lord," nodded Tyrel certain that this was truth. "You do not think that perhaps the man intends to rob us?"

Whitshire tossed his cravat to the valet and grinned. "No, I do not think that. It would be most forward of him to be letting us see his face day in and day out if that were the case."

"But we have not seen his face. Not actually, my lord. Even Spider did not, for the man was once again wearing a false nose."

"He was? The lad did not tell me that."

"False," nodded Tyrel. " 'Not quite fittin' ta 'is face like,' was what Spider said at dinner, my lord. Though the lad did not know why it looked so odd. And he mentioned that the man had great bushy eyebrows as well."

"Yes?"

"Did he have great bushy eyebrows when you accosted him?"

"I have no idea. It was very dark. I only know his nose was putty because I pulled it off. Are you telling me that you think his eyebrows false as well?"

"I do."

Whitshire deposited his waistcoat over Tyrel's shoulder, undid his collar and set that upon the nightstand, then wandered off into his dressing room and poured himself a brandy. He wandered back and stared at the valet with the most bemused expression upon his face. "You do not think, Tyrel, that this man could be Donnelly's burglar who breaks into my house to bestow plates and statuettes, snuff boxes and footstools upon us, do you?"

It was the oddest rattling, thumping, clanking sound. Honor's eyes popped open. "What on earth?" she mumbled sleepily. "It cannot be Whit setting the house afire again?" She fumbled for her lamp, turned up the wick and then paused to listen. All had gone quite still. Dreaming, she thought. I was merely dreaming. Whit? Oh, my goodness, I called his lordship Whit. What a thing to do. Thank goodness there was no one about to hear me. A slow smile mounted to her eyes. "I should like to be allowed to call him Whit," she admitted to herself. "I should like to say, 'Whit, dearest, what are we to do about the children? Garrett put a frog in Nanny's bed, you know. And Loyal climbed to the very top of the oak tree and would not come down and little Melinda has taken to running about with your old beaver upon her head and declaring that she is going to grow up to be exactly like her papa.'"

Honor grinned widely. I wonder what his lordship would do if he heard that, she thought. Run to the country as fast as he could manage, I expect, and remain in hiding there until I became safely betrothed to someone else.

It was puzzling. From all she had been able to glean in the past few weeks, his lordship had never attempted to cultivate his interest with any of the young ladies presented to him. Apparently he was not at all interested in marriage. Even his mama had mentioned his lack of attention to the necessity of saving her from some black villain known as Cousin Freddy whom Honor had deduced was next in line to inherit if Lord Whitshire should die without a direct heir. But if he were not interested in marriage, why had he told her that he had dressed to the nines simply to win her approval? If he was not interested in marriage, he ought not be tempting her so, and she ought to tell him that without delay, because she was beginning to find him exceedingly tempting. The more she knew of him, the more she was inclined in his favor. Even the way he conversed with that atrocious parrot when he thought no one could hear did nothing but make him more dear to her.

"But he is dangerous," she reminded herself. "And this hobby horse of his must be thought most unacceptable to any woman of sense. Furthermore, to keep a murderer in one's house!'' She had not forgotten what his mama had let slip about his lordship's valet.

And just as she had decided that the attraction she felt for his lordship could be allowed to become nothing more than a sincere friendship and that regardless of what he had said about his clothing at the theater, all he truly desired was her friendship, the *rattle, thump, clunk* that had awakened her sounded again.

It came from above her head in the servants' quarters. No, no, that was not correct. The staff in this establishment did not live upon the third floor as they did in so many townhouses. Their chambers lay at the very rear of the ground floor behind the kitchen. The attics then. The odd sounds were coming from his lordship's attics. Thank goodness, Honor thought, that Prudence is such a sound sleeper or she would be in here shivering and mumbling about ghosts. "Well," she murmured, rising and donning her wrapper, tying it tightly about her and then donning her bedroom slippers as well, "I do not believe in ghosts. It sounds much more to me as if a window has been left open and the breeze is tossing something about. I shall never get back to sleep with all that racket going on."

Perhaps it is his lordship's little footstool attempting to break out and return to the front hall, mused Honor with a grin as she climbed the attic stairs with lamp in hand. The commotion grew louder as she approached the closed door to the third floor. *Rattle, thump, clunk, rattle, rattle, thump, clunk,* almost as if someone were attempting to free himself from chains. With a shake of her head in amusement at the thought of his lordship having some murderer chained in his attic, Honor turned the knob and entered the long and dusty corridor that divided the attics into four separate chambers. She stood very still then, listening, attempting to divine from which of the chambers the racket was coming. The very last chamber on the left. It was a deal louder now that she was so near. The window must be open quite wide and the wind blowing most heartily to stir up such a sound.

Honor padded toward the front of the house, her slippers scuffing softly across the uncovered hardwood floor. The door was latched when she reached it and apparently the latch had not been used in many a month because it was stuck. She could not open it with one hand. With a sigh, Honor set her lamp carefully down upon the floor and used both hands to lift the latch. It resisted a moment, then rasped rustily, then absolutely flew upward and out of Honor's grasp. The door banged open against the inside chamber wall. A most pitiful wail sounded followed by a fluttering of cloth and a most definite *rattle-thunk*. Before Honor could so much as stoop to retrieve her lamp to discover what on earth was going on, a veritable specter rushed down upon her, shrieking and wailing as ghostly draperies swirled around it. Honor's eyes grew wide, her heart thumped, she gasped and then she fainted dead away.

"Miss Virtue? Miss Virtue, please do not be dead," Honor heard a wonderful baritone whisper as she began to regain her senses.

"N-no, I will not be," she whispered in return. "I am— I will be fine, your lordship."

He was sitting beside her on the dusty floor, cradling her against himself. He had removed her ruffled nightcap and was brushing the curls tenderly back from her brow. "No, do not be moving about just yet," he whispered. "Did you fall? You have banged your head upon the boards. There is no blood but a lump is definitely forming. Do you hurt anywhere else, my dear?"

"N-no."

"What happened?" he asked then, quietly. "I heard the dangedest commotion. Made me jump straight out of my bed, let me tell you."

"A—a ghost," breathed Honor, liking very well the feel of his strong arms about her and deciding that she really did not need to recover her wits too quickly. "I saw a ghost."

"What? A ghost?"

"Indeed. You most likely think that I imagined it, but I did not. I do not even believe in ghosts and yet, there it was, flying directly at me. I am ashamed to say that I must have fainted, for I cannot remember anything at all beyond that."

Truly, had the lady in his arms told him she had seen a flying pig in his attics, Whitshire would not have gainsayed her. Her changeable hazel eyes were flecked with a vibrant green now, as he helped her to sit up on her own. He did not wish to take his arms from around her, but he knew he must. Miss Honor Virtue, he was fast discovering, was a dire temptation. So dire that when she was near him he wished nothing more than to hold her in his arms and when he held her in his arms he wished nothing more than to abandon all thought of proper behavior. "May I ask what drew you to my attics, Miss Virtue?" he asked, helping her to her feet.

"Oh! I had almost forgotten. There were the oddest sounds. A rattle and a thump and a clunk one after the other over and over again. I thought a window must have come open and the wind blown something loose. I thought to come up and close the casement so that I could get back to sleep."

Whitshire handed Honor her lamp and lifted his own, turned and strolled into the attic chamber. He held the lamp high and peered about. There was merely one window in the place and it was tightly closed and locked.

"It was a rattling you say, Miss Virtue?" he called to her where she stood upon the threshold.

"Yes, a rattling like chains."

"Chains?" The earl's eyebrow cocked significantly. "Chains, Miss Virtue? I cannot recall that the commotion that woke me sounded like chains. Are you quite certain?"

"Yes."

"Well, there are no chains about that I can see at the

moment. No, wait, what the devil! Pardon me, I did not mean to say devil. What the deuce is this?"

"What?" asked Honor anxiously as he disappeared from her sight behind an old dressing screen. "What?" asked Honor again when he did not answer her. "Lord Whitshire," she said quite loudly, "if you do not reply at once, I am coming in there with a—with a stick."

Soft laughter met this threat. "A stick, Miss Virtue? No need for such a horrible weapon, I assure you." He stepped out from behind the screen, a chain dangling from his hand and trailing back behind him, all of it not visible. "This is likely what you heard. Apparently someone was attempting to stuff it into a trunk—or attempting to get all of it out. I cannot tell which. It is a dev—deucedly long thing and most unwieldy. And your ghost, by the way, had very small feet."

"Small feet?"

"You fainted at the threshold, did you not? You did not actually enter this chamber?"

"N-no, I did not enter. The ghost flew out at me."

"Just so. Your ghost then, had very small feet. Look down, Miss Virtue, at the floor. There are my footprints in the dust and yours, which come just so far. And there are your ghost's."

It was true. Honor stooped to bring the lamplight nearer the floor. Between herself and his lordship and going off behind the screen just beside the place his had gone were a series of footprints. Small footprints.

"A lady or a child," mused Whitshire aloud. "I doubt I have ever seen a man's footprint so short and narrow as that."

"But—who? Why?"

"I cannot imagine. Come downstairs now and allow me to put some ice upon that bump. I think we actually do have some ice left in the fruit cellar."

"But what about the gho—whoever was here?"

"Whoever was here is not here now, my dear. And it is

very late," he said, placing the chain upon the floor, then moving to take Honor's arm and escort her from the place.

He held to her all the way down the back staircase to the kitchen, where he went about lighting candles and stoking up the oven fires until the room was alive with light. And then he took his lamp in hand and descended into the cellars, returning in but a few moments with a large chunk of ice.

"This will do some good," he said, wrapping it in a piece of muslin and applying it gently to the back of Honor's head.

Honor reached up to hold the cold compress herself and Lord Whitshire, freed from the task, began to wander about the kitchen, opening and closing doors until at last he had assembled a plate of strawberry, cherry and apple tarts, three lemon creams, two glasses and a bottle of rata-fia. "I would make tea," he smiled down at her as he set his bounty upon the table, "but then we must wait for the water to boil."

"And you are much too hungry to wait?"

"Starving."

"Are you always starving at night, my lord?"

"Um-hmmm," he nodded, dividing the ratafia between the glasses and taking a bite of a cherry tart at one and the same time. "And always when I am in the midst of a mystery," he added when he had turned one of the chairs about, straddled it, finished chewing and swallowed. "Do you not think it particularly odd, Miss Virtue, that we are the only ones awake? You heard chains rattling loud enough to wake you from your sleep. And I heard something and then a shriek and a thump—the thump was you falling to the floor, I gather—but apparently no one else heard anything at all. Why do you think that is?"

"You ought to have heard the chains for they were at the very front of the house, right above your bedchamber," offered Honor. "You must have been sleeping very deeply."

"If they were above my bedchamber when they were

doing all that rattling and thumping about, I would have heard them, Miss Virtue, and I doubt that you would have been at all disturbed. They began to rattle in the chamber over yours, I think, and then were carried to the chamber at the front. Did you not notice any footprints when you opened the attic door?"

"No, but I was not thinking to look for footprints."

"Nor was I," sighed Whitshire. "I opened the door and saw you lying at the end of the corridor and—well, if there were footprints, the two of us will have trod over and over them by now. Does your sister sleep so soundly that she would not be likely to hear such a commotion as woke you or the shrieking or my rushing up to your aid?"

"Indeed. It is almost impossible to wake Prudence once she has fallen completely asleep and Justice is the same."

"And Miss Patterson? Do you think she slept through it all as well? Her chambers are directly across from yours."

"I have no idea."

"No. Neither have I. But my mother—I cannot believe that Mama slept through all this activity. I shall peek in on her, I think, when we return upstairs. Could you, do you think, peek in on Miss Patterson? Just to be certain she is not huddled beneath her bed frightened near to death?"

"Indeed, I most certainly will," agreed Honor. "What of your servants? Do you not think that they—?"

"No, they would not have heard a thing. The attics do not extend out over the servants' quarters. Have a tart, Miss Virtue, do. I have eaten two already and I really ought not eat every one of them. Your eyes are gold now," he added as Honor took a strawberry tart from the plate.

"My—my eyes?"

"In the attics they had the most incredible green flecks all through them. But now they are the most beautiful gold."

"*My* eyes?" Honor nearly choked on a bite of the tart. "My eyes are boring hazel," she managed once she had swallowed sufficiently.

"No, never say so. They dance and flash and change with your every mood. I know. I have been keeping a close watch upon them."

"You have been—? Lord Whitshire, do you have the vaguest idea what you are saying?"

"Yes. And you may depend upon it, Miss Virtue. I am not mistaken. Your eyes will send any number of gentlemen's hearts spinning. They cannot help but do so."

Honor felt very warm of a sudden and her cheeks flamed. "I—we—I ought to go up to bed now."

"Yes, you ought," nodded the earl, placing both elbows upon the table and resting his chin upon his fists. "They are turning dark now," he added, staring directly into Honor's eyes. "It is passion, I think, turns them dark and sets them to boiling."

"Well, of all the—!" exclaimed Honor, wriggling under his avid gaze. "I have never heard such—such—"

"Balderdash?"

"Yes! I have never heard such balderdash in all my life. Passion, indeed!"

"Do you realize, Miss Virtue, that we are once again alone together in the middle of the night. And both of us again most improperly dressed."

"I like your robe," murmured Honor. "It is quite handsome."

"Do not change the subject, Miss Virtue. We are being most uncircumspect, you and I. I fear I have compromised you again."

Honor could not help but giggle despite the rapidity with which her heart beat and the most suffocating feeling that crept into her lungs. She had the oddest sensation that her ears were beginning to burn and that the back of her head perspired despite the melting ice she held there. "Do not," she giggled.

"I must. Will you marry me, Miss Virtue?"

Honor opened her mouth and closed it again without a sound. She set the dripping muslin upon the table, took the last bite of her tart and chewed it very slowly.

He had never seen anything like the way her eyes danced in the candlelight at that moment. Whitshire felt every vestige of control falling from him. He watched her chew, studied the movement of her jaw, wished more than anything to follow the line of it with his index finger and then to extend the line downward to that tiny indentation in her throat and across her collar bone and farther into that valley hidden so heartlessly beneath her robe and nightdress and onward—What the devil was he thinking! His ears turned a bright red and perspiration broke out upon his brow. And still she chewed.

"*Will* you marry me?" he croaked around a sudden and very desperate lump in his throat. Devil it, but he thought he was going to spring across the table at her any moment and he could not do that. He could not do anything at all. She was his guest—his mama's protégée—and he was responsible for her happiness and her safety and— "*Will* you, Miss Virtue?" he gasped.

Honor swallowed at last and with a shaking hand lifted the glass of ratafia to her lips. The violet of his eyes was no longer that of the dew-covered flowers she picked in the spring. No, not soft and dewy, but rather an exciting, even violent color. A deep, desperate almost-purple that set her to aching for him, for his touch, for his kiss. For the least little whisper of his breath upon her cheek. Great heavens! What was she thinking? He was her host and his mama was her sponsor for the Season and—Honor set the glass of ratafia aside. "Marry you because I was dull-witted enough to think I had seen a ghost and fainted dead away and you were forced to come rescue me and so we are alone together in a kitchen? I think not, my lord. We must need be Bedlamites to marry for such a reason as that. Who is to know, after all, that we are alone together? This time not even your feathered friend Ferdy."

"No," muttered Whitshire, the unbearable tension rushing out of him, leaving him most exhausted. "Not even Ferdy. Will you allow me to escort you back up the staircase, Miss Virtue?"

"Thank you, my lord," Honor replied, wondering why she suddenly felt so very drained and could barely seem to keep her eyes from closing. "It is very late, I think, and I shall be most happy to climb back into my little sleigh bed. But I will peek in upon Miss Patterson first," she assured him, as he rose and came around the table to pull her chair back for her. "Do you truly think that she will be huddled under her bed in fear?" she asked as he went about the kitchen snuffing the candles.

"No, Miss Virtue, I do not. Not truly. It is just that it seems odd that no one else should be aroused but we two and that your ghost should disappear so handily without being forced to leap from a window," he responded as he banked the fire.

"Oh!" Honor followed his thought at last as he took both of the lamps and offered her his arm, leaving her one hand free to keep the skirts of her nightrail out of her way. "But it cannot be. Why would Miss Patterson be rattling chains about in your attics in the middle of the night? No, I cannot think it was she."

"Perhaps not," Whitshire murmured as he escorted her up the staircase. "But it was someone, Miss Virtue, someone, I suspect, in residence. Someone with very small feet. I doubt it was Martha, or one of the tweenies or Spider crept in from the stables. But perhaps I am mistaken and some gypsy woman bent upon stealing the silver managed to find entrance. If so I doubt not she has given up the attempt and departed by way of an unlatched window or an open door. Or," he added as they reached the second floor, "it may have been my mama. Though why she should be running about rattling chains and shrieking in the middle of the night, I cannot think."

He escorted her to Miss Patterson's door and waited as she entered. When she returned and assured him that that young lady was fast asleep upon her bed, he stood staring down at her for the longest moment, then leaned down and placed the gentlest kiss upon her cheek. "Go to sleep

did you think him to be? Has it anything to do with why you wished to go home in the first place?"

"No, nothing. At least, I do not think it has. It is merely that I thought—Justice, he was so close behind us, almost upon our heels. He could hear every word we said. I am certain of it. And yet we did not so much as notice him."

"Indeed," grinned Justice. "Someone's butler, I should think."

"Why do you say so?"

"Well, because butlers are forever just behind you or just around the corner, or just crossing the hall, or standing somewhere quite within sight, yet you never actually notice them."

Mr. Donnelly, who had been kind enough to fetch it from the corner of the music room to which it had been banished, handed the little footstool to Honor, then bowed and departed.

"We came rushing home because of a footstool?" asked Justice incredulously.

"But it is not just a footstool," murmured Honor, staring at the pretty needlepoint top.

"What is it then? It looks just like a footstool to me."

"Well, it is a footstool, but not just a footstool like any other footstool. There is something quite unique about it."

"Indeed there is," agreed Lord Whitshire, his voice crossing the threshold to the summer parlor a mere second before he did likewise. "Good morning, Miss Virtue, Cub. Everyone has gone off to Sunday services it seems, except for ourselves and Donnelly. Been out for a stroll have you?"

"Indeed," nodded Justice. "A rather lively one."

"Yes, so I see."

Honor looked up at him, puzzled, and he and Justice laughed.

"You forgot to remove your bonnet, Miss Virtue. And it is most becomingly askew."

"Oh. Oh!" Honor quickly reached up to untie the pretty green ribbon that held the bleached straw confection covered with bright green leaves in place and set the hat aside. "I was in such a hurry," she murmured, patting at her hair, several strands of which had come loose from the knot at the back of her neck. "I must look a sight."

"Actually, you look quite beautiful," murmured Whitshire, causing Justice's eyebrows to rise the slightest bit. "May I join the two of you?" Without at all waiting for an answer, the earl crossed the room to take a seat immediately beside Miss Virtue upon the striped settee. "What is it, Miss Virtue, that is so unique about that footstool?" he asked, his gaze intently upon her and not the tiny piece of furniture at all.

"I—it is—it is the needlepoint. The design. It is quite out of the ordinary."

"It is?"

"Indeed."

"How so?" asked Justice, leaning forward to see the thing better. "And why do we care that it is out of the ordinary?"

"We care, Cub, because the thing does not belong in this house and we have no idea where it came from or how it got here," murmured Whitshire, his eyes still fastened quite intently upon Honor's wind-flushed cheeks.

"It is the shadows of the flowers," said Honor, squirming the merest bit under his lordship's gaze. "Do you see? Here. Any number of flower designs exist, but these, these are flowers seen in sunlight, and they cast this perfect shadow. See how the shadow falls just so." Her fingers moved slowly over the needlepoint. "Only someone most skilled could produce such a spectacular effect."

"That," murmured Whitshire, at last condescending to look at the thing, "is a spectacular effect?"

"Indeed. For needlepoint it is most spectacular. It is so very detailed and so very beautiful. There cannot be two precisely alike in all the world."

"There cannot?" asked Justice.

"No, I do not think so. Some lady of the house has done this herself, I think. And her work will likely be displayed throughout the establishment."

"I see," murmured Whitshire. "And all we need do is to go about looking for similar perfection of needlepoint in all the residences of London."

"Do not tease," Honor grinned, giving his lordship a most forceful poke in the arm which made Justice's eyebrows rise even higher. "The reason I came rushing home was to learn if what I remembered was correct. And it was. But if Justice had not mentioned Lady Eldridge, I should never have thought of it."

"My godmother? Do you mean to say, Miss Virtue, that you believe this footstool to belong to my godmother?"

"Yes, indeed I do. We shall take it to her, shall we, and be certain? And perhaps she can tell us how it left her premises and came to reside in Whitshire House."

All thought of the man in the park had faded from Honor's mind. Justice had said he must be a butler and though she was not at all certain that was the case, still, the man had not followed them. Since he had settled upon a bench, she had assumed that he was not the person with whom his lordship had fought, the gentleman who had been keeping a confusing watch over the establishment. If she *had* given him one more thought, Honor might have set the footstool aside and strolled to the window and peered out from the summer parlor to the verge of the park across the street. Had she given him one more thought, she would have noticed Carpenter, no longer upon the bench but standing with his hands in the pockets of his breeches, gazing up at the windows of Whitshire House.

Lady Whitshire sat straight and stiff in the pew and stared quite properly forward. Beside her, Prudence and Julia gazed about in wonder at St. Paul's Cathedral and its patrons. Row upon row of elegant and exquisite ladies and gentlemen scanned other pews, hoping to notice someone in particular of their acquaintance whose presence in church together or more importantly alone might produce a ripple in the scandal broth the following week. Prudence and Julia were most impressed by the array of notables in attendance and murmured together quietly, noting first one person and then another. "There is Captain Furbough," sighed Prudence of a sudden. "Is he not the most handsome gentleman you have ever seen?"

"No," Miss Patterson responded after a moment. "I do not believe he is. There is something—scurvy—about him."

"Scurvy?" cried Prudence, quite forgetting where she was.

Five entire pewsful of eyes swiveled in her direction.

"Limes," declared a deep voice loudly from two pews ahead of them. "Lemon and orange and lime. Cure the scurvy every time."

Prudence's eyes widened and her cheeks flushed. She put her hand quickly over her lips to keep from giggling right out loud.

Julia hid her face in her prayer book and her shoulders shook.

"What? What did he say?" asked Lady Whitshire as though rising from a trance.

"He said, 'limes'," giggled Prudence.

" 'Lemon and orange and lime. Cure the scurvy every time,' " whispered Julia, her eyes tearing with glee.

"Well, of all things to be muttering about in church," declared Lady Whitshire. "They ought never to have allowed him to join the navy in the first place."

"Who?" asked the girls together.

"Clarence," responded Lady Whitshire gravely. "That is William, Duke of Clarence, the Regent's brother. You must just ignore his mutterings. He is a very kind sort of person, but he does often say the most inappropriate things at the most inappropriate times." And she returned to staring once more straight before her and lost herself in thought.

It was not that she had done anything wrong. How could it be wrong to wish to secure her own future and to lead her only child into the most divine happiness at one and the same time? If only Garrett were not so very obdurate—and thick-skulled—and inept!

No, that is not at all just, Lady Whitshire chided herself. Garrett is none of those things. He is just very, very odd. How he can spend day after day in Miss Honor Virtue's company and not fall madly in love with her I cannot imagine. She is quite perfect for him. There is not another young lady in England with whom he could make a more perfect match. Why, she barely blinked an eye when I explained to her about his murderers. I should like to see him find any other miss who would barely blink an eye at that. She is so very much like her papa. And I did so love Loyal. I loved him with all my heart. I would have married him, too, if it had not been for Anthony and that frightful duel.

The mere thought of that frightful duel brought tears to Lady Whitshire's eyes and she took a little lace handkerchief from her reticule to wipe them away. Then she looked at the little lace handkerchief. And then she looked at it again. The flowing initials embroidered upon it in a delicate rose stared back at her. D C H they said most daintily. "Delilah Cordelia Hart," Lady Whitshire whispered under her breath and hurriedly stuffed the handkerchief down to the bottom of her reticule, then looked up attentively at the parson who had already reached the middle of his sermon.

"I have wondered where it got to!" exclaimed Lady Eldridge as she took the footstool from Whitshire's hands. "I was most afraid that Aunt Sophy had dropped it out the window upon some poor defenseless passerby or set fire to it or stuffed it up into the chimney to keep out the drafts. One never does know what she will do these days." Lady Eldridge bestowed a most innocent smile upon

Honor and Justice as she said this and waved them both to a seat. "You will have some refreshments, will you not? Of course you will," she answered for them. "Garrett, do ring for Simms. No, do not. Simms is right here. Tea, Simms, and cakes and some brandy for the gentlemen. And do take this footstool off to the blue saloon. Why did your mama and your other houseguests not accompany you as well, Garrett? I should have been most pleased to see them."

"They are at services, Aunt Adeline," the earl grinned boyishly, depositing himself and his long legs upon her short floral settee where his knees came almost to his chin. "Miss Virtue and Justice and I are apparently the only sinners in our entire household. Is Uncle David not at home?"

"No, no, your uncle has gone off to the midlands to watch some sort of horse race. You know how he is. Sporting mad. I tell him he is much too old to be so mad for racing, but he will not listen. Men rarely do," she added with a wink at Honor. "Listen, that is. Now, tell me, Garrett, how did you come by my footstool?"

Whitshire waited until the refreshments were served and the footman gone before he responded. That long pause gave him time to think of a suitable answer. Except that he could not think of a suitable answer. "I have not the least idea how I come to have it," he confessed with a shrug. "I simply tripped over it in the front hall one night."

"It was the night of the afternoon of your rout, Lady Eldridge," provided Honor quietly, accepting a cup of tea from her hostess's hands.

"It was?" asked Whitshire in surprise.

"Yes. I remember precisely. You escorted us home from the rout and then you said you must be off again at once and you did not return until very late." Honor's changeable hazel eyes had become a teasing topaz as she focused them upon his lordship. "You do remember, my lord, how very surprised you were."

"Indeed," the earl grinned in return, remembering

quite well the commotion in the front hall and what had followed afterward. "I was so very surprised that I quite forgot myself and said devil any number of times."

"You are always saying devil this and devil that," laughed Lady Eldridge. "That is nothing new, Garrett. But how it came to be at Whitshire House that evening when it was here that very afternoon is most puzzling."

"Unless," provided Justice, sipping at a glass of Lord Eldridge's brandy and enjoying it immensely, "one of us stole the thing and bundled it into the boot and then smuggled it out once the coach reached the stables."

"Who the devil would do that? And why?" frowned his lordship. "You did not do it, Justice, nor one of your sisters, and Miss Patterson—were you not with Miss Patterson the whole time, Cub?"

"Yes, I was," scowled Justice. "I was merely joking about bundling it into the boot. And if you do not cease and desist from always suspecting my—Miss Patterson—every time something untoward happens, Whit, I shall be forced to call you out."

"Ho!" exclaimed Whitshire with a most enticing twinkle in his eyes. "I should like to see the day! So you consider her to be your Miss Patterson, do you, Cub? Well, and I do not always suspect her of everything. It is merely that I know so little about the girl and yet everywhere I turn something leads me back to her. But that is neither here nor there. She did not, obviously, steal the footstool, or you would certainly have noticed. Which leaves us with— Andrew or my mother?"

"Well, neither Andrew nor your mother would have stolen my footstool," protested Lady Eldridge merrily. "Why in heaven would either of them wish to do so? No, I do recall seeing Aunt Sophy walking about with that footstool at one point during the afternoon. That is why I feared she had done something dreadfully foolish with it, you see. Because she had it in hand. Perhaps she gave it to your coachman, Garrett, and he, thinking it to be something that belonged to you put it in the boot and carried it home. Now that is a most definite possibility.''

"But why would Aunt Sophy give your footstool to my coachman?"

"Why does Aunt Sophy do anything that she does?" asked Lady Eldridge. "It is a most amazing adventure living with Aunt Sophy, let me tell you. Well, and now that I think on it, I am quite certain that is exactly what must have happened. The whole episode is solved. And I am most pleased to have my footstool returned to me. I thank you very much for bringing it."

Honor could not think why, but the solution did not quite fit. She smiled readily at the conversation as it continued among Lady Eldridge and Lord Whitshire and Justice, and she did her very best to offer a word or a comment here and there, but something nibbled at the back of her mind and refused to be gone. Something was wrong about the readily accepted explanation.

It was only after they had taken their leave of Lady Eldridge and their landau was turning into Park Lane that it came to her. Why would Lord Whitshire's coachman carry the footstool into the house and set it in the front hall? He was a coachman and would not think to set foot inside the house without being requested to do so. He would have gone 'round to the kitchen door and called for Mr. Donnelly and given the care of the thing over to the earl's butler. And Mr. Donnelly already suspected burglars of bringing the footstool. Obviously the coachman had not given it to him.

"You have not said a word all the way home, Miss Virtue," Lord Whitshire observed from the box. "Is something amiss?"

"No. Nothing. I have been enjoying the beautiful day and the lovely drive, that is all."

"Exactly. And so have I," drawled Justice, giving his sister a most peculiar look. "We have been dull company for you, eh, Whit? Well, but you had fresh cattle to contend with. What is going on?" Justice murmured as he helped his sister from the carriage and escorted her toward the front door. "You have not the least idea if it is a beautiful day or not and the drive was not particularly lovely. You did not take note of one thing all the way home."

"I cannot tell you now," whispered Honor, as Lord Whitshire tossed the reins to one of his grooms, leaped from the box and came dashing up the walk after them. "I have thought of something, but I do not wish to speak of it in front of Lord Whitshire." And with that she turned and bestowed a most delightful smile upon the earl, tucked her free hand into the crook of his arm and allowed both gentlemen to escort her up the steps and into the vestibule.

Chapter 11

Whitshire cursed, tossed the stack of papers into the air above his head and slumped back in his chair, sticking his boots, in spite of his spurs, up onto his desktop.

"Stow it!" cried Ferdy raucously. "Danged son of a sea—"

"Do not you finish that sentence, Ferdy!" exclaimed Whitshire.

"—witch," finished the parrot and picked at his toes.

"Oh, witch." Whitshire's angry scowl vanished, and he chuckled. "Somehow I was expecting something else, Ferdinand."

"Awwk! Hee, hee, hee."

"I taught him that, Andrew," declared Whitshire with a definite tinge of glee.

"You taught him hee, hee, hee? I am impressed."

"Yes, well, I thought it might make him sound like a pirate, Millard. A regular swashbuckler, you know?"

"It makes him sound demented."

"Stiff-rumped fribble," mumbled Ferdy.

"I taught him that, too," grinned Whitshire.

"I am so very happy that the two of you are getting on

so well," Millard replied, crossing one knee over the other and leaning back more comfortably into one of the wing chairs. "And that he is so adept at cajoling you out of your foul humor."

"I am not in a foul humor."

"Not now, no."

"Well, but, Andrew, we have nothing. The papers are useless, the ring is ten years old and the hairbrush—"

"I never thought to see the day," Millard interrupted.

"What day?"

"The day you would sit there and deny evidence that is right before your eyes. The papers are not useless. They tell us that Longbourne was part owner of a schooner called *The Jewel of the Orient* which has made eight most profitable trips to India in the past ten years and that his partners' names are William and Charles Paxton. And they tell us that Longbourne lost a veritable fortune in a bank failure over forty years ago. And one of them is a map, for goodness' sake! If he did not trust banks, and he had good reason not to, that map may well lead to every cent the old man had in the world. Getting hold of that map alone would have been reason enough for someone to murder the old coot!"

"Yes, I know all that."

"But you are choosing not to combine any of that with what we have already discovered and refusing to draw one conclusion from any of it," protested Millard, leaning his chin upon one fist and studying his friend seriously. "Why?"

"I am not choosing not to do it. I have done it."

"Recite it for me then."

"Bedammed, Andrew, I am not a schoolboy!"

"Bedammed!" echoed Ferdy. "Bedammed!"

"Stow it, Ferdy," grumbled his lordship. "You do not know one thing about it."

"No, and neither do I," sighed Millard. "If you have taken to distrusting me after all these years, Whit, tell me so straight out and I shall quietly walk away or else, tell me why you are so reluctant to go forward on what we know. And that man, in case you have not heard, is once again keeping watch upon this house."

"He is? From where? Tyrel has not seen him since the night Spider sent him on that wild-goose chase to Covent Garden."

"I came through the park. He is sitting upon a bench just across the bridle path from the lower gardens. He can see the house from between the trees if he leans at just the right angle. That, however, is not what bothers me. Is it that you do not trust me, Whit? Or have you simply lost interest in collecting murderers?"

"Neither. It is—well—it is the ring and the hairbrush and the fact that Justice is in love with little Miss Patterson."

"Pardon me?"

"Justice is in love with little Miss Patterson. Do not stare at me, Millard, as if I am a complete Bedlamite. Justice is in love with Miss Patterson and it is not calf-love either. At least, I do not think it is calf-love. And if what I suspect is correct, any further efforts on our part will involve Miss Patterson in this murder and that sort of knowledge might well destroy the Cub. He has already threatened to call me out if I continue to suspect Miss Patterson of so much as pilfering a footstool."

"But—"

"The ring, Andrew, was in Sir Nathan's desk drawer among his ledgers, where one might expect a ring to slip off unnoticed if the wearer were attempting to locate certain of Sir Nathan's papers without being caught at it. And the ring was purchased by a gentleman named Paxton—one of the partners most likely—close to the time of the first sailing of *The Jewel of the Orient*. And it is a lady's ring, designed for a very small lady, someone the size of Miss Patterson. And then there is the hairbrush which bears the initials JP and has strands of red hair in it which are precisely the shade of Miss Patterson's hair. JP—Julia Patterson—or most likely, Julia Paxton."

"All perfectly true. But not necessarily correct, you know. You are making logical connections but there well might be both a Julia Paxton and a Julia Patterson who both have red hair."

"But it is Julia Patterson who has one of Longbourne's horses. I cannot cease to suspect her, Andrew. I suspect her more and more. But I cannot be the one to destroy the Cub by setting Sir John Fielding upon the young lady he loves. I like Justice. I grow more and more fond of him. And you," he added, "are growing more and more fond of Miss Prudence, are you not?"

"Yes, enough to wish to try my luck at courting the girl, but I doubt I stand a cricket's chance in catland against Furbough."

"Regardless, you cannot wish to hurt her by hurting her brother. And I—"

"And you what, Whit?"

"I . . ."

"Yes?"

"I—Devil it, Millard, do not look at me like that. I cannot help myself. I have lost my heart entirely to Miss Virtue."

"Aha! I knew you would when first I saw her standing all dirty and disheveled behind us in the park. She knows about your hobby horse, does she not?"

"Yes."

"And she does not object to it."

"She has not as yet. But I think she might object strenuously to my being responsible for the breaking of her brother's heart. Do not you agree, Andrew?"

"I have the answer then."

"Corkbrain," muttered Ferdy.

"No, Ferdy, I do have the answer," declared Millard. "We shall set about not to discover the murderer or murderess, but to prove Miss Patterson innocent of any involvement in the crime."

"Do you think we can?"

"If she is innocent. And that way you may tell Justice

that you suspect her of nothing but are merely attempting to lay all speculation about her to rest."

"And we can enlist his aid in doing so! Except, if she did murder Longbourne—"

"Then perhaps she had a most excellent reason. It would not be the first time that someone had an excellent reason for murder. And it would not be the first time that you and I kept a murderer safe from the gibbet either. Tyrel would have been hanged, Whit. You know that is so."

Honor paced the drawing room with short, quick steps. Her garden dress of checked muslin swept about her ankles, and her hands fluttered from folded at her breast to fisted at her hips to tightly clasped behind her back. Should she say something to Lord Whitshire or should she not? No, she should not. She should speak first to Lady Whitshire and between them—No, that would not work because what would she say to Lady Whitshire? Most certainly Lady Whitshire knew all and did not intend to stop.

"Whit is in his study with Mr. Millard, and Prudence and Miss Patterson and Lady Whitshire are beginning already to primp for the ball this evening," announced Justice, entering the chamber. "You promised Sunday to tell me what was bothering you, Honor, and it is already Monday afternoon and you have not said a word yet."

"Only because I was not certain at first and then I could not get you alone. Oh, Justice, I cannot think what is best to do! Whit's mama is a thief!" Whereupon a virtual torrent of tears came flowing from Honor's eyes against all of her wishes, and Justice, amazed, stepped forward and wrapped her in his arms.

"Do not cry, Honor," he urged softly. "You are not generally a watering pot."

"I know," sobbed Honor. "I know I am n-not."

"No, of course you are not. Here let me get into my pocket so that I can get you my handkerchief. Yes, that's better. I can reach now. Please do not cry, Honor. I cannot think that there is anything at all to cry about. You cannot be correct, you know. Why would Lady Whitshire be a thief? It is not as though she needs the money," he mumbled, fishing his handkerchief out and pressing it into his sister's hand while keeping one arm still firmly about her. "Blow your nose and dab at your eyes and take a very deep breath," he urged. "And then we will sit over there upon the sopha and you will tell me everything."

Honor did the best she could, though tears continued to wend their way down her overwarm cheeks as she allowed Justice to settle her upon the sopha and to sit close beside her with one strong arm comfortingly around her shoulders. "Now," he said as she hiccuped forlornly, "tell me what nonsense has got into your head."

"It is not n-nonsense. L-Lady Whitshire took the footstool."

"No. Why would she?"

"I d-do not know. But she did. And she has taken other things as well. Th-that snuff box and the statuette upon the mantel. They were b-both at Rundell and Bridges when we visited there. And Mr. Donnelly let me see two p-plates that m-magically appeared. And one was from G-Gunter's where we stopped for an ice and the other is P-Papa's and M-Mama's."

"One of our plates is in Whit's pantry?"

"Yes. One of the plates Mama painted herself. The one with the yellow r-rose. Oh, Justice, Lady Whitshire must have stolen each and every one of the things that have appeared mysteriously here. She was present at each place and saw each one of them and—and—no one else could have stolen Mama's plate, not anyone from this establishment."

"Well," murmured Justice. "Well, I expect we ought to say a word or two to Whit about it."

"No, we cannot! Oh, Justice, it would break his heart to know his mama has been s-stealing! And I c-cannot bear to break his heart because I l-love him so!"

"You love him? Whit?"

"Y-yes. With all my heart."

Justice stared down at his sister in amazement. "Whit?" he asked again. "Are you certain you mean Whit, Honor?"

"What is wrong with my loving Lord Whitshire?" Honor asked, a sob catching in her throat. "He is a g-good and h-honest gentleman and k-kind as well."

"Yes, he is that," nodded Justice, a most bemused smile creeping over his countenance. "But he is very odd."

"You s-said he was a great gun."

"He is a great gun, but he is also very odd. I do not know how to tell you this exactly, my dear, but Whit has never been deadly serious about any young lady. He told me so. And it is because he cannot think that any young lady would care to abide in the same establishment with him unless he ceases to engage in his hobby."

"I care to abide in the same establishment with him."

"Well, yes, you do now, but—"

"I do not care a fig that he collects murderers!" declared Honor roundly, surprising her brother no end.

"You know about—?"

"I know all about it and I know that Mr. Tyrel is a murderer. And I do not care."

"Mr. Tyrel is a—Who told you that? I did never know that Mr. Tyrel is a murderer. Thunderation!"

"Lady Whitshire told me. She told me everything. And I shall marry Whit regardless. We shall chase after murderers together if that is what he wishes to do. But that is neither here nor there," mumbled Honor angrily, swiping at her nose with the handkerchief. "It is Lady Whitshire we must deal with. And quickly, too. Because if his lordship discovers what she is doing, it will be like a knife thrust through his heart."

"And I know just the thing!" announced Justice, giving Honor's shoulder a reassuring pat. "Are you quite certain where all of the things have come from?"

"Yes."

"Good. We shall enlist Prudence and Miss Patterson and together the four of us will return everything. Except for

Mama's plate. We shall not worry about Mama's plate for a while yet."

"Return the things? But how can we? They have been stolen, Justice. How are we to explain to people where we got them? We cannot say that—"

"We will not say anything," proclaimed Justice. "We will smuggle the things back to the places they belong. It will be like stealing in reverse. And most likely the people will merely think they were misplaced. But we must have a word or two with her ladyship about it, Honor. We cannot allow her to keep on stealing things or we will never finish returning them."

"I will speak with her," promised Honor solemnly. "I shall confront her about it the very first thing tomorrow morning."

"Why not now?"

"Because we are to attend the Ripleys' ball tonight and she is so looking forward to it. She and Mrs. Ripley are very old friends. I do not wish to upset her now by telling her that we know all. But I will keep a close watch upon her, I promise."

"Yes, all right. But we will speak with Prudence and Miss Patterson now. And we will all keep a close eye upon her ladyship tonight so that she cannot steal anything else."

In low-cut, high-waisted gowns of glimmering satin with overdresses of Brabant lace, whose skirts flared so widely with their flounces and ruffles that no more than one lady and one gentleman could sit upon a banquette without doing damage to the gowns, the ladies from Whitshire House had to divide themselves between the earl's town coach and Lady Whitshire's traveling coach for the drive to the Ripleys' ball. Lord Sandsquire, a most intriguing gentleman numbering a good many years over fifty had been invited to join them for the drive out, since the Ripleys' establishment lay a good hour to the west of London. He and Lady Whitshire shared the oldest of the coaches with Justice and Miss Patterson while Lord Whitshire and Honor joined Prudence and Mr. Millard in the town coach.

"I do not know how it is," said Whitshire softly as the horses stepped out, "but I cannot feel easy about my mama."

Beneath the street lights, Honor could see Prudence's eyes grow large and she did, in fact, feel a rather large lump of fear rising in her own throat in equal reaction to the statement.

"What do you mean, my lord?" she asked, holding tightly to the strap as the coach passed over the far end of the lane which was missing several cobbles.

"Well, she is in that coach with Sandsquire with only Justice and little Miss Patterson to chaperon. That does not bode well. But no matter how I tried, she would not let me be the one to accompany her."

Millard chuckled. "The Incomparable Melinda rises again, eh, Whit? I knew it when I saw her descend the staircase. My lord, but she is beautiful, your mama."

"Indeed," agreed Prudence, the fear that Lord Whitshire had learned of his mama's unsavory propensities gone as quickly as it had come. "I cannot believe that any woman could look so beautiful and still have a son as old as his lordship."

"Prudence!" hissed Honor.

"No." Whitshire laughed. "Do not go hissing at your sister, my dear Miss Virtue. She is quite right."

"She is not. You are not so very old as she makes you sound."

"But old enough to make my mother's appearance amazing."

"Well, perhaps," conceded Honor.

"Sandsquire was once one of her most dedicated beaux," his lordship continued, "and I do not know that I ought to trust him up there with only the Cub and Miss Patterson to make him toe the line. He is an old rascal if ever there was one."

"I should never have guessed it," Prudence responded.

"Which? That he is old or a rascal?"

"A rascal. Anyone can see he is old. He dresses in the most ancient style. Oh! I ought not to have said that precisely. I do beg your pardon, my lord."

"Not at all, Miss Prudence. I do admit that this particular coat is not precisely up to snuff, but it is not quite as far out of the realm of possibility as Sandsquire's."

"It is a lovely coat," Honor offered. "I do not think I have ever seen a more beautiful coat in all my life."

"Unless it was on the wax figure of Charles the Second at Madame Tussaud's," Millard finished for her. "I do think it is the same coat as a matter of fact, Whit. Did you steal the thing? By gawd, he has hired himself a horse," added Millard, staring from the window. "And a dashed fine horse it is, too. How the deuce did he know that he would require—?"

"His lordship sent Spider to him again," murmured Honor.

"And he believed the lad? After last time?"

"Must have, for he is back there," muttered Whitshire, peering from his window as well.

"Who?" asked Prudence. "Do you mean to say that someone is following us?"

"No," responded Whitshire and Millard and Honor simultaneously.

Prudence, with her gleaming yellow curls and her wonderful blue eyes, was quite as beautiful as any Belle to enter the London scene since Lady Whitshire's time, but she was not brainless. She told them all so quite loudly on the instant. "And if you can none of you trust me to know the truth of the matter, not even my own sister," she added with a most pointed glare at Honor, "then I shall cease to think of any of you as my friends from this moment forward. You may depend upon that!"

"I expect she is as brave as you are, is she?" asked Whitshire with a questioning glance at Honor.

"It has nothing to do with being brave," protested Mr.

Millard. "I cannot think he follows us for any sensical reason at all. The man is most likely dicked in the knob."

"Someone is following us!" exclaimed Prudence, and pressed tightly against Mr. Millard to peer out his window. "The one upon the bay with the blaze?"

"Indeed," Millard whispered hoarsely, growing exceedingly warm of a sudden, but not wishing her to move away for an instant.

"Prudence, do sit back or he will see you," ordered Honor.

"Very well. But you must tell me all about him. Everything. And do not think I shall faint dead away," she added, glaring first at Lord Whitshire and then at Mr. Millard. "I am not such a peagoose as to be frightened by such a fribble as he looks to be."

Prudence listened in complete silence as first Lord Whitshire, then Mr. Millard, then Honor related the tale of the night in the park when they had attempted to catch the man. "And you did not say a word to me?" she asked Honor, disappointed to have been left out.

"I requested her not to say a word to anyone, Miss Prudence. I am sorry, but I had no idea what to think about him. I still do not. I had never seen the man before and then suddenly he began to spy upon Whitshire House. And of late, he appears to wish to follow us about whenever he can."

"Well, of course he follows us about."

"Of course he does? What do you mean of course he does?" asked Mr. Millard in surprise. "Miss Prudence, do you know this man?"

"No. But I can guess who he is and why he is suddenly lounging about on Park Lane."

Honor groaned. "Do not, Prudence. You know your imagination is your greatest failing. It has gotten you into trouble time and time again. You cannot possibly guess who this man is. You have never seen him before in all your life."

"No, I have not, but I think you have not looked back

to see him, Honor. The man is wearing a cape with pea green lining.''

Honor sat up quite straight and then pounced across Whitshire to peer back at the rider before they should leave the lights of London behind them. "Great heavens, he is!''

"Just so. And you know as well as I, Honor, that there are very few gentlemen who would run about with such an ugly lining to their capes.''

"What the devil are you talking about?'' asked Whitshire, reluctantly helping Honor off of him. "What has the lining of the man's cape to do with anything?''

"The piggy-eyed villain,'' gasped Honor.

"The piggy-eyed villain,'' nodded Prudence.

"Who the deuce is the piggy-eyed villain?'' asked Millard in exasperation.

"Devil!'' shouted Whitshire elatedly. "It was not a bouncer, Andrew! Miss Patterson was telling Justice the truth! There actually does exist a piggy-eyed villain who has been following her about, and he is even now astride that bay with the blaze following us to the Ripleys'!''

It did occur to Honor that Prudence might be mistaken. But she did not think so, not this time. The pea green lining was most singular. She could not quite understand why the existence of a piggy-eyed villain should make Lord Whitshire so very happy. But she did not at all care. Just to see him so, filled her heart with sunshine and her head with fancies. What an extraordinary gentleman he was!

In his happiness Whitshire leaned across and thumped Mr. Millard heartily upon the back, took both of Prudence's hands into his own and kissed the back of each separately and then sat back and put his arms around Honor and tugged her close to him and kissed her most resoundingly upon her brow and her chin and nose and cheeks.

"Enough, you gudgeon!'' Mr. Millard laughed at last, pulling his lordship away. "You are compromising the girl, Whit, and right in front of her sister and me! What a bit of scandal broth it will make should word of it get out. And all because there is a piggy-eyed villain. At least, we think there is."

"I am not compromised," protested Honor, straightening her cloud of a shawl and her gown and her hair. "Not in the least. It was merely a celebration. But I do hope you are going to tell us why it is such a great celebration."

"Of course they are going to tell us," declared Prudence with a most quizzical look at Mr. Millard. "And then we are all going to pretend that no one did the least thing improper inside this vehicle tonight."

"No one did the least thing improper inside this vehicle tonight," Mr. Millard grinned. "We have all been stiff-rumped and self-righteous as the Bishop of Canterbury himself."

Chapter 12

The young people discovered quickly that keeping one's eye upon Lady Whitshire in the midst of a ball was not going to be as simple as they had expected. It was the responsibility of a chaperon to be always within sight of her charges, and most of the mamas and companions and dowagers settled into the gilded chairs that lined the edges of the ballroom while their charges danced. But Lady Whitshire had not the least intention of doing anything so very staid. She procured a dance card for herself and let it dangle about her slender wrist, and gentleman after gentleman approached to request this gavotte or that contredanse. And though at first Honor and Justice and Prudence and Miss Patterson applauded this as a great help to them—for how could that lady possibly steal anything while in the midst of a dance—they soon discovered that simply because a gentleman signed his name to a card, it did not mean that his intention was to lead Lady Whitshire onto the floor.

Lord Davenport led her out into the Ripleys' garden to wander among the roses for the length of the gavotte. And Viscount Aberdeene thought to escort her through the gallery when his dance came around, and Ball Hughes, the fabulously wealthy Golden Ball, petitioned her to wander with him through the open saloons, sampling hors d'oeuvres and sipping champagne and conversing upon any number of subjects, some of them exceedingly naughty.

That was when Honor's turn came to keep watch upon her, and Honor's ears burned as she followed Ball Hughes and Lady Whitshire from chamber to chamber while attempting to remain unnoticed by either. But so far her ladyship has behaved perfectly, Honor thought. At least while I have been on watch. Perhaps I was wrong to think she has stolen all those things. Perhaps someone else is responsible. Perhaps Papa gave her our plate to remember Mama by. And just then Lady Whitshire exclaimed over a most elegant presentation of Turkish figs surrounded by Russian caviar and Spanish olives, and Honor watched in horror as her ladyship took up a little silver fork, speared one of the olives and placed it between her lovely lips and, directing Mr. Hughes's attention to another dish behind him, slipped the fork into her reticule.

Honor, who at that moment was peering out from behind a strategically placed potted palm, felt her heart thump inside of her. She had not been mistaken. But she had been most naive. Oh, horrendously naive to think that if the lady did steal something, she and the others would be capable of returning whatever she stole. Why had she not given the matter more consideration? Of course Lady Whitshire was not going to steal things and then carry them about in her open hands so that anyone might see them.

How in thunderation am I going to get my hands upon her reticule? Honor wondered.

"Lose something, Miss Virtue?" asked a melodious baritone.

"My lord!"

"I have been looking all over for you. You did promise me the first of the waltzes and it is about to begin. Or have you changed your mind?" Lord Whitshire gazed down at her with the most quizzical expression upon his handsome face.

"I—No, of course I have not." Honor looked anxiously about her. Her nose brushed a palm leaf; it made her sneeze.

"Are you spying upon someone in particular, Miss Virtue?"

"S-spying? Why would you think that I am spying? Of all the things to say!" The previous dance had concluded. Then where was Justice? Where was Prudence? Where was Miss Patterson? Someone was to come to relieve her of her vigil. They had been trading off the responsibility after every dance for the entire evening. Perhaps not one of them had been able to locate Lady Whitshire this time around. And then Honor heard a deep cough and recognized a most familiar figure upon the opposite side of the palm.

"Are you quite certain you will not have a taste of the caviar, Miss Patterson?" asked Justice loudly enough for his sister to hear. And for the briefest moment he turned to study the palm and his eyes met Honor's through it reassuringly.

With a relieved sigh, Honor took his lordship's arm. "To the ballroom?" she smiled. "Must I have someone's permission to waltz? I have heard that a young lady may not waltz unless one of Almack's patronesses has given her the nod."

"Never fear, Miss Virtue. I have pried permission out of Queen Sarah who has been bending my ear for the past ten minutes. And I do believe that Mama has pried vouchers out of her for Almack's for you and your sister as well."

"Oh! Are you quite certain? Papa is only a baronet after all and I did not think—"

"Yes, but Mama is The Incomparable Melinda and more than a match for the likes of Sally and the rest, let me tell you."

* * *

The Incomparable Melinda had exchanged partners on her way through the saloon, giving Ball Hughes a chaste kiss upon the cheek as he handed her over to Lord Sandsquire who escorted her from the chamber and down the corridor into the music room and then out onto the music room balcony.

"How the deuce are we to follow them out there?" asked Justice, leaning against the flowered wallpaper of the hallway. "There is no possible excuse for us to be here alone in the corridor much less to go barging out onto that balcony."

"Yes, there is," nodded Miss Patterson, stooping down to grasp the hem of her gown and ripping it with abandon. "Now you must simply lead me to her. She is my chaperon after all and will most kindly accompany me to the ladies' room to repair my hem."

"She will?"

"Of course. And it is a very large tear so it will take some time. I shall discover a need to fuss with my hair as well and, oh, any number of things. I shall keep her there until this dance is over. You need simply send Prudence down to us."

Justice led Miss Patterson into the music room and out onto the balcony, where they discovered Lady Whitshire just as she turned away from Lord Sandsquire and toward them while depositing something very tiny inside the bodice of her gown. Justice felt his face flame red on the instant. Up until this very moment, he had not noticed the lady take one thing and had begun to doubt Honor's conclusion. Now, of course, he was convinced, though flustered.

"Oh, my lady," cried Miss Patterson in a sad little voice, ignoring completely what she, too, had seen and directing everyone's attention toward herself. "I am so very glad that we have found you. I have ruined my gown. Whatever am

I to do? There are not enough pins in all the world to repair it."

Lady Whitshire knelt on the instant to examine the hem and then rose upon Justice's hand. "It is nothing, dearest," she smiled. "We shall have it together again before the next dance begins. Come. You will excuse us, will you not, gentlemen?"

Receiving a nod from both gentlemen, Lady Whitshire whisked little Miss Patterson off toward one of the ante-chambers upon the ground floor that had been furnished for the ladies' particular needs upon this occasion.

"Fond of Miss Patterson are you?" asked Lord Sand-squire conversationally, taking a gold case from his pocket and offering Justice a cigarillo. "I could see it in the coach on the drive here. Devil of a pretty little chit she is with that mop of red curls. Reminds me of someone."

"She does?" asked Justice warily. Had Lord Sandsquire been in the audience that evening at Astley's?

"Indeed. Cannot think whom. But it will come to me. You, my boy, remind me greatly of your father as a young man. I was that surprised to see Garrett lead you into White's that day in February. I never thought to see it happen."

"To see what happen?" asked Justice confused.

"Why, to see a Forester introduce a Virtue around. They were sworn enemies, you know, your fathers."

"They were?" Justice's eyebrows rose and he inadvertently stuck the cigarillo into his mouth and Lord Sand-squire politely lit it for him. Surprised, Justice inhaled and then doubled over in a spasm of coughing. Lord Sand-squire obligingly pounded upon his back with great enthusiasm.

Whitshire took her so gently into his arms that Honor barely felt the pressure of his hand upon her back or the clasping of his gloved fingers over her own. And he led her into the waltz so carefully that she was quite certain he had never performed the dance before in his entire life. She and Prudence, of course, had performed it any number of times in their little schoolroom at Fairmorn, praying for the day when their papa would think to send them to London for the Season.

"We need not waltz if you do not wish to do so," Honor said softly. "You are a deal too tired, I expect."

"Tired?" Whitshire looked down his nose at her with the most arrogant eyes. Honor could not help herself. She had never seen any gentleman look quite that way before. She laughed.

"Is it my nose tickles your fancy, Miss Virtue?" he drawled. "I did warn you that it was a sight too long."

"No, no," laughed Honor. "It is the way you are looking down your nose at me."

"Peering at you from such a great distance, you mean," the earl restated, his eyes glowing with great good humor.

"Hush, you are making me laugh more and I am not to be laughing at all. It is most *mal à propos.*"

"Indeed," drawled Whitshire, and then with the most jaded expression upon his face, he wiggled his ears.

Honor's eyes opened wide. She choked. Then she burst into whoops.

Whitshire tugged her close enough for her to bury her face against his chest.

"Most inappropriate behavior, Miss Virtue," he whispered in her ear. "Everyone is staring at us."

"You are a fiend," Honor hissed, her eyes sparkling with glee as she pulled away to a more discreet distance. "And you do know how to waltz!" she added, for she discovered at that moment that they were floating across the floor without the least hesitancy.

"Well, of course I know how to waltz, you gudgeon," chuckled, Whitshire. "I would not have requested to dance the waltz with you else. I am not a complete beetle-brain. But it was kind of you to suggest that perhaps I was tired."

"You started off like that on purpose."

"Yes, I did. I wondered what you would say. I did the

same once to a Miss Delia McBane and she pretended to stumble and twist her ankle and begged to sit back down.''

''No.''

''Yes. I did not particularly like Miss Delia McBane. I do particularly like you, however, Miss Virtue. But then I have liked you for any number of years.''

''You have merely known me for a few weeks, my lord.''

''Is that so? It seems as though I have known you forever. How very odd. I rarely ever wiggle my ears at people I have not known forever. Should you like to see me do it again, Miss Virtue?''

''N-no,'' giggled Honor. ''I do not think so just at the moment.''

Whitshire dropped her hand, grabbed hold of his quizzing glass and raised it to his eye. He cocked an insolent eyebrow and stared down at her through the glass as they dipped into a turn.

''Th-that is w-worse,'' managed Honor, attempting to hold her breath to keep from laughing aloud again. But she could not do it and an enormous guffaw burst from her. That sent Whitshire into whoops and every gaze in the ballroom fell upon them.

''We are both ruined,'' laughed Honor yanking at the black hair that curled down over his collar at the back of his neck.

''Ow!'' cried the earl on a gasp of a chuckle. ''Do attempt some decorum, Miss Virtue, or the Ripleys will never invite us to their establishment again.'' And with that he swept her out through the French doors and onto the balcony and clasped her in both of his arms. She lifted her laughing face to his and he kissed her.

It was not at all the sort of kiss one would expect from the Earl of Whitshire. The excited assault upon her face that he had executed in the coach was nothing at all like it. Nor was his kiss hesitant or staid or practiced or arrogant or roguish. It began gently as though he were tasting the very essence of her lips, deepened into a caress and then grew urgent and probing until it raised a fire in Honor that made her fight to kiss him back, harder and more forcefully and with deeper passion than he was kissing her. It became a battle between them, that kiss, and Honor was determined to be the victor—until she felt a tap upon her right shoulder.

She spun away from him, right out of his arms, her face red with embarrassment and saw—no one.

"I tapped," murmured Whitshire, folding his arms across his chest and leaning back against the bricks of the house. "The music is about to end and I did think you would rather not be caught in such a compromising position. I am almost certain that one busybody or another is making her way across the floor even as we speak to do just that—catch us in a compromising position. Am I correct, Miss Virtue? You do not wish to be compromised? Or have you changed your mind?"

"No. You are most certainly correct," nodded Honor, tugging and patting at her gown and her hair. "Do I look quite proper?"

"Most proper," smiled Whitshire. "So proper, in fact, that I am tempted to— Good evening, Miss Hartford, Mr. Bailey. You have met Miss Virtue, I think."

As the waltz ended, Prudence clung to Captain Furbough's arm, stars glittering in her eyes and visions of a strong, broad-shouldered, scarlet-coated husband flittering through her mind. "I cannot see Lady Whitshire anywhere," she declared, looking about the chamber. And she could not see Justice either. It had been Justice's and Miss Patterson's turn to keep an eye upon Lady Whitshire, and Prudence had truly expected one or the other of them to come fetch her. "I expect you must take me to Honor," she said, looking up into the captain's dark and most mysterious eyes.

"Was it not your sister began laughing in the midst of the waltz?" asked Furbough, smiling down at her. "And in Whitshire's arms of all things? I do wonder what he said to her. He is not terribly brilliant, Whitshire. A dull dog really."

"Lord Whitshire?"

"Oh yes. Not quite so dull as that bishop's son he is forever running about with, but then, everyone expects a bishop's son to be a dead bore. And Millard does not disappoint. I believe they went out to the garden, your sister and Whitshire. Shall we go and see if we can find them?"

"I thought they went out upon the balcony."

"Well, yes, they did. It was not through these doors, however, but those. There are stairs descending from that particular side of the balcony to the rose garden below."

With a nod, Prudence allowed the captain to escort her from the ballroom. It was very dark upon the Ripleys' balcony and a thick column separated one side from the other. And though Prudence might well have heard Honor's voice if the captain had ceased to murmur at her for a moment, she did not see her sister or Lord Whitshire as she allowed Captain Furbough to help her down the little steps and into the rose garden below, where little paper lanterns did their best to bestow a romantic glow upon the very finest of Mrs. Ripley's rose bushes.

"The Virtue sisters are quite the belles of this ball," murmured Captain Furbough softly, placing an arm about Prudence's waist. "You do not mind, do you, my dear? I only desire to keep you from tripping upon the pebbles."

The very feel of his arm around her, one strong hand resting upon her waist, sent decidedly pleasant ripples through Prudence. She knew she ought not allow him to touch her so familiarly, but she could see no great harm in it. Honor and Lord Whitshire were close, after all, and in a moment they would come upon them. Besides the pebbled paths could be truly dangerous if one were to misstep.

"I have not the least doubt that before the Season ends, you and your sister will be hailed as diamonds of the first water. All the gentlemen of London will be casting themselves at your feet."

"Oh, I do not think so," protested Prudence.

"Ah, and modest as well! What a gem you are, my dear. I knew that would be so the moment I first lay eyes upon you in that landau beside your sister as Whitshire drove you through the park. Of course, I did never think to be so very lucky as to receive the least attention from either of you."

"And Miss Patterson," added Prudence. "Do not forget that Miss Patterson rode with us."

"Ah, yes, the carrot-top. But she is a child compared to you."

Prudence did not fully understand this comparison because though Julia was not as tall as she, she was certainly not any younger and perhaps even as old as Honor, though she did never state her age and Prudence had been loath to ask. "I do not see Honor and Lord Whitshire anywhere," she said, gazing about. "Surely we ought to have come upon them by now."

"I expect they have gone to view the fountain," offered Furbough. "The fountain stands in the very middle of the garden and is lit with lanterns much as the paths. It is quite beautiful actually. Here, we just turn this way and we will be upon it in a moment. Are you chilly, my dear? I daresay I ought to have fetched your shawl. Well, but we both shall be warm again soon."

"What do you mean you cannot find her, Justice?" Honor asked as Lord Whitshire took himself off to fetch her the glass of punch she had requested. "You were to have been here to escort her to her ladyship. It is Prudence's turn to keep an eye upon her. She would not have forgotten that. Not when it is so very important."

"I came as soon as I could," explained Justice. "I was busy choking to death at the other end of the house. But once I ceased to do so I dashed back here and Prudence was nowhere to be seen. Why would she go off without me, Honor, when she don't know where to go? That makes no sense at all."

"Where is her ladyship?"

"She is downstairs with Miss Patterson. Tore a hem," Justice added tersely. "Miss Patterson did, I mean. They are mending it. Miss Patterson thought that would be the easiest way to keep Lady Whitshire from stealing anything else. She took something from Lord Sandsquire, Honor, and popped it into her bodice when the old gent was not looking."

"Oh, dear, and she slid a silver fork into her reticule, too. And there is no way we can possibly retrieve either one tonight."

"I should think not."

"No. But we must retrieve Prudence. Where can she have gone?"

"Who?" asked Mr. Millard, stepping up beside them. "Is someone missing? This is my dance, I believe, Miss Virtue."

"Indeed," nodded Honor, "but I beg you will free me from my promise, Mr. Millard. It appears we have lost Prudence."

"What? Lost Prudence?" asked Lord Whitshire, handing Honor her glass. "Do not say so."

"She has most likely gone in search of your mother." Honor sighed. "I cannot think why she did not wait here until one of us came to fetch her."

They set out, Honor upon her brother's arm, toward the ladies' rooms below, and Mr. Millard and Lord Whitshire to search through all the open saloons upon the first floor. "We shall meet at the staircase just there," Whitshire said, pointing, "once we have finished. Else we will be wandering about all night looking for the girl when one of us has already found her. And do not go putting it about that she is missing," he warned quietly. "The scandalmongers will make some great monstrous story out of it should it reach their ears."

* * *

The fountain bubbled cheerily from an urn held by a charming marble cherub, down over three wide steps and into a crystal clear pool in which shining golden carp swam. Prudence looked at it and then looked away. "They are not here," she said nervously. "I cannot think where they can have gone. We have been through the entire garden, have we not, Captain Furbough?"

"You must call me Jamie," murmured Captain Furbough.

"Oh, no, I could not," protested Prudence. "That would be much too forward. We are not at all that well acquainted, you know."

"No, but I hope we shall become much better acquainted soon, Miss Prudence," he whispered, the hand that rested upon Prudence's waist slipping a bit lower and more to the rear.

"Captain Furbough, what are you doing?" Prudence hissed, attempting to seize the wandering hand and fling it away from her.

"I am doing what any man would do who found himself alone in a dark garden with such a vision as yourself, my dearest Prudence. I am discovering myself to be overcome with desire."

"You—you are?"

"Yes, my angel. Allow me for a moment to taste those trembling lips, and I promise I will do no more. There is no one here will see us, my darling. There is no one to know."

Prudence was almost positive that this was not a good idea. But she had always longed for a knight in shining armor and Captain Furbough did look a good deal like that knight. And he was a Guardsman. Most certainly a captain of the King's Guard would not take undue advantage of a gently bred young lady. That would be most dishonorable.

"Come, my beautiful Venus and let me drink the pleasures of life from those rosebud lips. I shall adore you forever more.''

''Adore me?'' Prudence felt his gloved hand move slowly up and down, caressing her hip. And then he tugged her close to him. Into his arms. And he tilted his head and leaned slowly down to place his lips hungrily upon her own.

And then, his lips bruising hers, he crushed her against himself until she could feel every single inch of his hard, solid anatomy. Prudence, shocked by such proximity and by his roughness, attempted to pull free of him. But he would not set her free. His strong arms were a good deal too strong, and his broad shoulders a good deal too broad and his scarlet coat had gold buttons that hurt to be pressed against too. Prudence was really quite angry and not a little disappointed and abruptly afraid. She struggled against him, but her efforts proved the beating of moth wings against iron.

And just as Prudence thought she could struggle no more, the captain tore himself from her with a howl and spun about. ''Damnation!'' he sputtered and then he howled again. Directly following the second howl, a reticule began to beat him mercilessly about the head.

''Do not stop now, Miss Patterson,'' Lady Whitshire urged as she swung her reticule once more, smacking the captain's ear soundly with it. ''Keep jabbing, my dear. Keep jabbing.''

Captain Furbough flailed and jumped and howled some more, attempting to escape from his persecutors until at last they took pity upon him and allowed him to take off at a run, leaping over rosebushes two at a time.

Chapter 13

Adrian Carpenter leaned his back against the rear of the Ripleys' fountain and grinned. He grinned with relief and with satisfaction and even with a certain amount of grudging pride. He had been lingering about amongst the shadows, keeping an eye upon both the house and the stables so that he would not be likely to miss the Whitshire coach as it was called up when he had noticed what appeared to be a young lady in trouble in the middle of the rose garden. But by the time he had made his way to the fountain, the situation was already being competently handled. Thank goodness for Miss Julia's temper and her ever-present hatpin, he thought, the pride in his grin growing more evident. Never thought to see the day that anyone would be thankful for those two things, but thank goodness nonetheless.

At the front of the fountain Lady Whitshire had dipped her handkerchief into the water and was busily scrubbing away at Prudence's heated and tear-stained face. "You are not to worry, darling," she murmured. "It was none of it your fault. That beast shall pay dearly for thinking to besmirch your honor. You may count upon it. My Garrett will not allow such behavior to pass without notice. He will see to this Captain James Furbough, I promise you."

"I rather think it will be Mr. Millard who sees to him," offered Miss Patterson, busily straightening Prudence's gown.

"Andrew?" Lady Whitshire ceased her ablutions and stared.

"M-Mr. Millard can d-do nothing," sniffed Prudence. "He is the s-son of a b-bishop and a d-dead bore."

"Andrew?" repeated Lady Whitshire taken aback.

"He is in love with you, Prudence," declared Miss Patterson. "I see it in his eyes each time he looks at you. He loves you and he will see that Captain Furbough reaps his just reward."

"What will he d-do?" asked Prudence mournfully. "P-pray over the villain? Mr. Millard will more likely say it w-was my own f-fault to go into the g-garden in the first place."

"Andrew?" gasped Lady Whitshire. "Blame you? Great galloping geese! Andrew? And he is in love with her?" she added with a stare at Miss Patterson. "Andrew is in love with Prudence?"

"Yes," nodded Miss Patterson, kneeling to straighten Prudence's hem. "Hopelessly."

"Two with one blow!" exclaimed Lady Whitshire. "And you do not love him back, Prudence? Because you imagine Andrew to be a dead bore and a coward to boot?"

"I did not say that he was a coward," sighed Prudence. "But he is a bishop's son and his behavior must always be exemplary."

Lady Whitshire's laughter chimed merrily through the garden.

"You jabbed him with a hatpin, Julia?" asked Honor, one arm tightly about Prudence's waist. "And you, my lady, hit him with your reticule?"

"Indeed, and you should have seen him run," whispered Miss Patterson as they climbed the stairs together.

"It was fortunate that Julia's hem tore or we should never have seen them enter the garden together," murmured Lady Whitshire. "As it was, they had to pass right by the outside doors to the chamber in which we were having the hem pinned up."

"Yes, but if we had not been forced to worry about making the other ladies suspicious, we would have arrived a deal sooner and none of it would have happened in the first place," murmured Miss Patterson. "I knew there was something scurvy about that man. I could feel it."

"Are you certain you do not wish to go directly home, Prudence?" Honor asked then. "No one will think badly of you if you do. It must have been a most distressing experience."

"No, I do not. Everyone will wonder why we leave and—"

"Ah, found at last, Andrew. I told you she would be," declared Whitshire as the ladies reached the top of the stairs. "And she was with Mama and Miss Patterson all along." He was smiling at them, Honor noticed, but the smile did not at all light his eyes. His words were for anyone who might overhear them. And well-chosen words, too, because Prudence would be ruined if anyone discovered that she had been alone in the garden with the captain.

"They are playing a waltz again," added Whitshire, taking Prudence's hand into his own. "Come waltz with me, Miss Prudence." And without another word to anyone, Lord Whitshire escorted Prudence back to the ballroom and swept her out onto the floor.

"Smile, my dear," he whispered down at her. "Whatever has occurred, you will deny it best by smiling up at me now."

Prudence's chin lifted and her eyes met his and she forced her lips to turn upward.

"Now tell me about it," he said. "But you must make it seem as if we are merely having a pleasant conversation."

As Prudence began to inform Lord Whitshire of what had happened, Captain Furbough entered the ballroom, bold as you please, with a young lady upon his arm, both of them conversing with another couple. Prudence wished to walk straight over to him and scratch his eyes right out, but his lordship held her tightly, instructed her to mind her steps and urged her to complete the tale she had begun. "He said that you and Honor had gone there," she finished, her smile wavering. "I would not have gone else."

"Of course you would not. Do not upset yourself any longer, my dear. Captain Furbough is a dead man."

"Oh! Oh, no, you cannot! He did me no great harm, your lordship. Her ladyship and Miss Patterson routed him before he could do more than kiss me. I am sure he needs be taught a lesson, but you must not kill him."

"I do not intend to kill him, Miss Prudence. Ordinarily I would, but I merely intend to inform Andrew of all you have told me. It is Andrew will kill him."

"Mr. Millard?"

"He is in love with you, my dear. Top over tail. Do you mean to say that you have not noticed? Well, even if you have not, he is in love with you regardless, and he would not thank me for taking the privilege of defending your virtue away from him."

"But he would not call the captain out? Dueling is a crime and should the captain die, Mr. Millard would be hung for murder. And he is a bishop's son besides. He cannot possibly think to do violence to someone."

"Ho!" exclaimed Whitshire, the light of laughter abruptly reaching his eyes. "Andrew not to think of doing violence to someone? Still, I shall attempt to convince him not to call the rogue out if that is your wish, Miss Prudence, though I doubt I shall be able to get him to ignore the thing completely. Andrew not to think of doing violence! What a peculiar idea you have of bishop's sons. I expect you think they must all be stiff-rumped and self-righteous and holier than anyone. You truly ought to get to know

Andrew better, my dear. I hope you will. He is my dearest friend and I cannot but wish for you to set aside your notions and at least grant him as much opportunity to win your heart as you will grant the other beaux who come a-courting."

They remained for supper, Prudence's determined good cheer and Captain Furbough's languid presence putting to rest any speculation that might have lingered about the two who had been absent from the proceedings at one and the same time. And Honor's plan to keep watch over Lady Whitshire became a deal easier because Lady Whitshire did never wander out of sight of any of the girls from then on. Which was why it came as such a shock when Lady Whitshire, after the coach had been summoned and their wraps fetched, excused herself and hurried back up the staircase, leaving all of them behind her in the vestibule.

"Tyrel, what the devil is this?" asked Whitshire, holding up a sapphire stickpin for his valet's inspection the next morning.

"It is a sapphire stickpin, your lordship."

Whitshire groaned and turned his eyes to the ceiling.

"There is no use to pray for patience, my lord," remarked Tyrel in the midst of cleaning his lordship's razor. "It *is* a sapphire stickpin and that is all I know about it."

"You have never seen it before?"

"Never. It is not one of your lordship's; it is not one of Mr. Virtue's; it is not one of mine. Mr. Donnelly discovered it upon the long table near the front door this morning, and sincerely hoping that it was yours, he sent Marlborough up with it."

"Devil! You do not think we have been accosted by Donnelly's burglar again?"

"Yes, I do. The fact is, my lord, that not only was that stickpin upon the long table, but a tiny silver fork of exquisite design has appeared upon the sink in the butler's pantry and a most elegant vase has taken up residence upon the pianoforte in the music room. Mr. Donnelly has taken to his bed, my lord."

"I do not think that I blame the poor man."

"No, my lord. You ought not. Mr. Donnelly has had quite enough mysterious occurrences to last him for the rest of his life."

"Yes, well, they are about to cease. I am almost decided to pay a call in Bow Street. Damnation, but I cannot tie this thing in any style whatsoever," grumbled Whitshire, undoing his fourth neckcloth and tossing it angrily to the floor. "Anyone would think that my hands were made of solid wood! If this is what it is like to be in love, I shall need to take drastic action, let me tell you. I cannot be forever fumbling about before a looking glass for the rest of my life."

Tyrel juggled the razor in midair, could not bring it under his control and it clattered into the basin. He quickly scooped it up and dried it hurriedly upon the piece of muslin he kept especially for that reason. Then he walked most sedately across the carpeting and put the straight razor away inside his lordship's jewelry box.

Whitshire, watching in the looking glass, chuckled.

Tyrel turned toward him. "Is there something humorous I am missing, my lord?"

"Only yourself, Tyrel. The razor does not generally reside in my jewel box, does it?"

"Well, of course not! Of all the things to think."

"You just put it there, Tyrel."

"I never——" began Tyrel, and then he peered into the jewelry box and lifted the razor out, his face a study in astonishment.

"There is not the least thing to be upset about, Tyrel."

"No, your lordship."

"No. I am in love with Miss Virtue, you see. You do like Miss Virtue. You have told me so any number of times since she came."

"M-miss Virtue?"

"Yes, Tyrel."

"I—I expect she does not yet know about—"

"She knows everything."

"Everything, my lord?"

"Well, perhaps not everything, for there are a good many things I have yet to tell her. But she knows well enough about my hobby horse, Tyrel, and about you."

"About me!"

"Well, I do not think she knows all about you. Mama does not know all about you, and she is the one let it slip. But Miss Virtue does know that you are a murderer, I am afraid."

Tyrel paled noticeably as he turned and carried the razor back across the room and placed it in its leather case. "Do I understand that you intend to marry Miss Virtue, lordship?" he asked quietly.

"I have proposed that idea to her twice and she has turned me down flat both times, but she did let me kiss her on the balcony at the Ripleys' last evening, so I expect there is still hope that she will have me."

"I shall begin seeking a new situation directly, my lord," murmured the valet, his hands shaking as he stowed the case of shaving gear away upon the shelf above the basin and pitcher.

"No. Why?"

"A young woman of Miss Virtue's upbringing cannot like to have a person of—a violent nature—about her house, my lord. It is only sensical. There will be children and she cannot know—"

"Planning to decapitate our children already, are you? How do you know they will be that annoying, Tyrel? Perhaps one or two of them will take after their mother. Have you thought of that?"

"Do not tease, my lord," replied the valet, his voice rasping with pain. "I shall not like to leave you."

"You shall *not* leave me. If Miss Virtue and I do marry, Tyrel, you shall remain my valet and that is that. You will not seek a new situation because you have no need of one, and if you do, I shall write your new employer the most scathing letter about you—so scathing that he will turn you out on the spot."

"But, my lord."

Whitshire crossed the chamber, put a strong hand upon each of Tyrel's shoulders and faced him squarely. "Miss Virtue will not think to so much as ask if I would consider sending you away."

"You cannot know that, my lord."

"I can. I do. Miss Virtue is not some missish peagoose with a backbone of jelly. Miss Virtue has heart and soul and considerable bottom, Tyrel. Count upon it. If she does consent to be my bride, she will not balk at my keeping you on."

"You cannot go to Bow Street!" Honor exclaimed, fairly leaping up from the wing chair as Whitshire entered his study.

The earl's eyebrow cocked inquisitively. "Pardon me, Miss Virtue?"

"I said that you cannot go to Bow Street," repeated Honor, her hands twisting agitatedly together before her.

"Danged rumpot!"

"Ferdy, do be quiet," ordered Honor, beginning to pace the chamber. "Martha has told me that she heard from Marlborough who heard from Mr. Donnelly who heard from Tyrel that you intend to stop in at Bow Street about—about—the little things that keep appearing in the house, and you cannot!"

"Do you realize that you are in my study, Honor?"

"What? Yes, of course. I came to wait precisely because I knew this is where you would come after breakfast and that here we could be alone."

"I see. And there is something of consequence that you wish no one else to know?"

"Well, well, not exactly. We all know. That is to say, not

all of us. Mr. Millard does not know. And the staff, of course. And—and—you. I did never wish for you to know at all, but if you are determined to go to Bow Street, then . . ."

Whitshire could not help but think her the most beautiful woman he had ever seen. Even now with her hair falling from a hastily pinned topknot and her voice raised an entire octave by her obvious anxiety, he knew he loved her. He closed the distance between them in three long strides, took one of her hands in his and led her to the matching wing chairs. "Let us sit down, Honor. You must simply tell me what it is that I do not know. I gather it is about Donnelly's burglar who so kindly breaks into this house to bring us presents."

Honor nodded. "There were a condiment fork and a stickpin and a vase."

"I know," he murmured, having turned his chair to face her directly and sitting so far forward in it that there was barely room for a worm to wiggle between their knees. He gazed at her expectantly, his head tilted the merest bit to the side and his wonderful violet eyes filled with attention.

"Why must you go to Bow Street?" Her words were a plea. He recognized that immediately.

"It is someone in this establishment. Someone dear to you. I shall not turn them in to the Runners, Honor, in that case, but it cannot continue. People will begin to notice that their possessions are missing, you know. And besides, we have no right to keep them."

"I know that. And we tried very hard last evening to keep her from—but we were not quick enough or smart enough—and we can none of us think of how—"

"Trust me, Honor. Tell me the truth and trust me to make everything right again."

How could she? Honor stared at him, the fever of anxiety that had racked her since she had heard of his plan to stop in Bow Street finally lessening with the assuredness and gentleness of his tone. But it was his mama! How could she say such a thing to him? Whit, your mama is a thief.

How could she say that when anyone who had seen them together knew that he loved his mama with all his heart?

"If you do not tell me, Honor, I cannot be of any help at all," he whispered then, gently massaging the backs of her hands with his thumbs. "Let it come, darling. Let the words slip out and all will be well, I promise you."

"It is your mama," she managed at last in a breathless whisper. "Your mama has been—"

"Mama?" Whitshire's eyebrows rose but his voice remained low and soft. The terrible, heartrending sadness she had expected to see in his glorious eyes did not appear, only a most curious light. "Are you quite certain, Honor? You do not mistake?"

His reaction was not at all what Honor had expected and she grew brave. "I am most certain. I saw her take the little fork, and Justice and Miss Patterson were there when she took the stickpin and I expect she went back upstairs to purloin the vase." In a rush of words Honor told him all that she knew.

"Well, I'll be da-deuced," he murmured when she had concluded her tale. "I never thought to see the day. Does Mama know?"

"That she is stealing?"

"Um-hmmm. You did not confront her with it, I mean."

"I was going to speak to her about it today, but you said—and I could not let you—"

"Exactly so," nodded Whitshire. "Are you feeling better now? I have never seen you so terribly upset."

"I thought—I thought such news must break your heart and I did not wish to be the one to bring it to you."

Whitshire's eyes glowed with a warmth Honor could not fail to see. "You are the dearest, strongest, most determined woman I have ever met. As a matter of fact, you are amazingly like Mama."

"Me?"

"Indeed. But you ought not to have taken this particular problem upon your shoulders, my dear. Though I appreciate the intention, the problem is mine, and I shall be the one to deal with it." He freed her hands and stood and crossed to the bellpull. "Donnelly, you are back on your feet again, are you? Send someone to ask Lady Whitshire to join us here as soon as she is able."

"Close the door, Mama," Whitshire said, "and come sit down beside Honor, eh?" He offered her his arm, escorted her to the chair he had abandoned and stood before them both with his long arm stretched out along the mantel.

"Mama, there is something I must tell you."

Lady Whitshire looked up at him with triumphant eyes. "Oh, Garrett, it worked! Oh, I am so very happy for you both! I did think it was rather a muddleheaded thing to do, to be rattling chains in the attic. But I knew Honor would come to investigate and I knew you would as well. I could not think of any other way to get the two of you to realize how perfect you are for each other."

"It was you in the attic?" asked Whitshire and Honor simultaneously.

"Yes. I borrowed the chains from Nev in the stables and Spider helped me to carry them up the stairs that afternoon. It was the only way I could think of to bring the two of you together without Andrew or Justice or Prudence or Julia tagging along. You are both of you light sleepers, you know. And you are both inordinately curious. And you are both brave and fearless and stubborn as mules. But I am not at all sorry that I had to sneak about in the middle of the night. It was all worth it to think that you have discovered each other at last and that you are to be married!"

"Married?" asked Whitshire and Honor simultaneously.

"That is why you have called me here, is it not? To ask my blessing? And you have it, children. You most certainly do!"

For the longest moment Whitshire could not think of a word to say. He stood there studying the joyous look upon his mama's lovely countenance and the blood rushing up to set Honor's cheeks aflame, and his heart fairly swelled with love for the both of them. Then, most unaccountably, he burst into laughter.

"Stow it! Stow it!" squawked Ferdy. "Danged rumpot!"

"I—I am sorry," managed his lordship awkwardly around his grin as his laughter ceased. "It is just that—I cannot—Mama, we did not ask you here to give us your blessing. We are not betrothed. Do not redden even more, Honor, or I shall go off again."

"You did not? You are not? Oh, Garrett, what is wrong with you? Are you totally witless?"

He did go off again at that and Honor could not help but laugh herself simply because of the infectiousness of his laughter.

"It is not at all humorous," declared Lady Whitshire when at last they both came to a giggling halt. "I have done everything I can think of to get the two of you together. And only look how well you suit. You are both doubled over with laughter because you, Garrett, did not propose and because you, Honor, did not accept. There are not two other people in the entire world who would be laughing about such a thing!"

"Enough, Mama," smiled Whitshire. "Are you very worried that I have not married anyone as yet?"

"Worried?"

"Yes, worried, Mama. Do you think because I have not yet settled down and produced an heir that Freddy is going to inherit and you are going to be poor all over again?"

Honor looked from one to the other of them in surprise, but Whitshire merely shook his head a bit at her to urge her not to speak and so she held her tongue.

"Freddy is a monster," declared his mother roundly.

"I know you think so. But it is not his fault that he is next in line, Mama. And I am quite certain if there were some way in which you could inherit the title, Freddy would be pleased to step aside. He is frightened to death of you, Mama."

"I do not wish to inherit the title. I only wish for you to

be happy, Garrett. And perhaps you will produce an heir," she added on a tiny breath.

"Because if I do not . . ." Whitshire murmured.

". . . everything will be lost," sighed Lady Whitshire. "You are as brave as you can stare, dear heart, but you have not a thought in your brainbox except to catch murderers. One day you will be discovered steeping in your own blood upon the cobbles because of it. But I will be still alive. And Freddy will inherit. Then I shall be right back where I started when your papa died and must live in that frightful house in Suffolk and be pensioned off like an old servant!"

"Miss Virtue," the earl said then, stepping toward Honor and giving her his hand, "I must ask you to await me in the summer parlor if you will. There is something I must say to my mother privately and—"

"Of—of course, my lord," murmured Honor, allowing him to lead her from the study and close the door behind her. He has decided that it would be too embarrassing for her to speak of her stealing things before me, she decided as she wandered toward the staircase. That is why he has sent me off. Oh, the poor lady! To think that she believes that she must lose him to a murderer before his time! And to fear that that dreadful Freddy will put her out because of it! I never once guessed that she worried about anything at all behind her delightful smile. Once she learns that Whit knows all about her stealing things, she will be in despair! Oh, I do wish I had not told him, but if he had actually gone to Bow Street . . . He called me Honor, she thought then, most abruptly. Great heavens, in the midst of all this worry about his mama, he called me Honor over and over again. And I did not so much as notice until this very moment! Why would he call me Honor when up until this very morning I have always been Miss Virtue?

Chapter 14

Whitshire entered the summer parlor an hour later to discover Honor alone and still waiting upon him. "It is most difficult to explain, Honor," he sighed. "I shall attempt it, but I doubt you will believe a word."

He had called her Honor again! Honor's eyebrow lifted the slightest bit, but he did not appear to notice and simply lowered himself onto the sopha and stretched his long legs out before him.

They sat in silence for a very long moment. A soft breeze entered through the open casements, tugging at the summer draperies and whispering through the room. Bright sunlight gave a warm glow to the reds and greens and golds of the carpeting and made the satins of the upholstery shimmer. It painted rainbows upon the papered walls and warmed the woodwork to a mellow rose.

"When my father died," the earl began, "I was merely four."

Honor gazed at him attentively, but he stared at the wall behind her and did not continue.

"You were four," she repeated when it began to seem as though he would not continue without her urging.

"Yes, I was four, and— You will pardon me for asking, I hope, but what I am about to say, you will not hold any of it against my mama, will you? Because it is not as though she ever in her life actually planned to— No, never mind. I mistake you for some Society Miss. You are Miss Virtue, and you would never be so cruel as to— You are fairminded and forthright and will hear what I say without holding the past against Mama or myself. No, do not look at me as though I am mad, Honor. I am merely— This was not at all what I had planned to discuss with you this morning and I am the least bit afraid that perhaps— But I digress."

"You certainly do," smiled Honor.

"Yes, well, it is because I do not know what you will think about the matter, I expect. This is not the first time that my mama has stolen things."

"It is not?"

"No. She took things that did not belong to her once before. It was shortly after my father died. I have told you already, I think, that my papa was an inveterate gamester. He was a gentleman prone to bad investments as well. And, unfortunately, he took no interest whatsoever in his lands or his tenants. When he died—he did not expect to die so soon, you understand; a hackney ran him down in Little Bridge Street—well, when he died he left Mama all alone with a child to raise, Whitshire House, three estates that were mortgaged to the hilt and produced nothing but debt and the dreaded house in Suffolk. You have heard Mama speak of the house in Suffolk. It was the only country establishment in the entail which possessed a decent roof to keep out the rain and so was the house in which we lived after Papa's death. Mama would have much preferred to live here in Whitshire House, but we could not possibly. Because in Town, the cent per centers and the tailors and the modistes and the haberdashers and the greengrocers and everyone else to whom Papa owed money were forever at our door."

"How dreadful for her! She must have been so very

distraught when she learned how sadly off he had left the two of you!"

"Yes, I expect distraught is a fine enough word as any. Mama was quite accustomed to wealth and coddling, you know, and it was a most shocking change for her. But she did not wish me to grow up with no hope but to sell my title upon the marriage mart for a fortune that smelled of the shop, you see, so she determined to get Papa's fortune back, or at the least to build up a new fortune in my name. And she did a great many things to achieve her goal, too.

"She studied the newest techniques in agriculture and learned to manage the estates and pestered solicitors and bankers and every single gentleman she knew for information and assistance in improving our position until they all did, in fact, improve our position. Some gave her tips on likely investments and provided her with capital. Some took time to explain to her passages in the books she constantly read—passages about improved drainage or rotation of crops which she could not quite understand. Others taught her the best ways to economize and explained what could not be economized upon.

"My mama is not called The Incomparable Melinda for nothing, Honor. She has always known that she holds a particular power over gentlemen and when the need arose, she made extraordinary use of that power to gain knowledge and suggestions and out-and-out free labor.

"Once, I remember, we traveled to the estate at Freeman's Hill in the company of a duke, a marquis and an earl and all three of those gentlemen rolled up their sleeves along with the tenants who remained and set about repairing the tenants' cottages and readying the land to plant."

Honor could not imagine such a thing. Even her own father, who was merely a baronet, would not think to roll up his sleeves and actually perform hard physical labor.

Whitshire grinned. "You do not believe me, but for Mama's smile and a word of gratitude, there were gentlemen who would do anything. Her ambition to provide for me was so strong and her personality so compelling that they could not, once she confronted them, say her nay."

"But what has this to do with her stealing things?"

"Nothing. Except to explain how it was then. How strong Mama was, but beneath that strength how thoroughly frightened she was too. She did not actually need to steal, Honor, that first time, because things did improve. More money began to come in than went out and—I am making a total botch of this, am I not? I am sorry, and I beg your pardon for it."

"No, do not. It is just that I am having a very hard time—"

"Yes, I am making a total botch of it. I am making it all much too complicated for one thing. The truth of the matter is that my mother has stolen things now and she has stolen things once before, but she has not the least notion that she has ever stolen anything in her life. I know that she has, but she does not."

"What?"

"She has no idea, Honor, where these things have come from. None. Not an inkling. She is as amazed about the jewels and statuettes and other folderols as we have been. And she came here intending to tell me that such happenings had occurred at Freeman's Hill—that odd pieces of jewelry had come to visit her—and to ask my advice on the matter."

"She does not realize that she steals?"

"No. And I am not ever going to tell her that she does, either. But you are not to worry, Honor. I will set about to discover to whom all the wandering trinkets belong, and I will see that they are returned—every single one of them. But I have not told Mama that it is she who is responsible for their appearance and I cannot. Nev was quite certain that I ought never—"

"Nev? Your groom, Nev?" interrupted Honor.

"Yes, my groom, who was my mother's groom before she married and stayed on with her through all her good times and all her bad as well. Nev said, when I caught him with his hand in my Aunt Caroline's reticule years and years ago, that he was putting in, not taking out. And he explained to me that my mama was in sheer terror of going under and that it was the terror made her steal and then guilt followed right behind the terror and made her forget that she had stolen anything. And he said then, all those years ago, that it would not be at all the thing to tell her what she did, because that would frighten her all the more and there was no telling what she might do if she became even more frightened. We had a most interesting year, Nev and I, back then, attempting to return everything that Mama had acquired, let me tell you."

"She stole things for an entire year?"

"Two, two years, but the first year I did not know anything about it. I caught Nev returning my aunt's cross and chain on my fifth birthday. And after that he and I were both constantly at work. It was a game for me, actually, to attempt to slip things out of Mama's reticule and get them to Nev, who would take them back where they belonged. Nev would be forced to ride all over the countryside slipping things into people's houses at night through open windows or setting them in the most unlikely places about the grounds. Once our nearest neighbors, Squire Wilkins and his wife came to dinner and I heard him telling Mama that he had discovered his pocket watch dangling from the pump handle in his kitchen garden. He was so amazed to think that he could have lost the thing in such a place. I thought I should die laughing. I had to run upstairs to the nursery so that no one would hear me."

"You listened at doors when you were a child?"

"All the time. I knew everything that went on about the house. I did not have a nurse or a tutor, you know, to keep me on a leash because Mama could not afford one after Papa died."

Honor envisioned the curly-haired boy with the wide violet eyes peering through a keyhole and then resting his ear against a door, and she grinned. "You were a rascal, I think."

"A pure rapscallion. But Nev put me to good use."

"And your mama has not stolen anything since? Not until now?"

"Not that I know of. She started again, I think, because of my birthday. I was thirty-two at the end of January."

"Why should that make her begin to steal?"

"I was thirty-two at the end of January and not married, Honor. Not married and therefore still not doing anything at all about producing an heir and securing our estates and fortunes into the next generation, and I was still involved in, well, looking into murders. Meanwhile Cousin Freddy was waiting in the wings as was the house in Suffolk. I think Mama panicked."

"Do you know," murmured Honor thoughtfully, "it was just at the end of January that your mama came driving up to Fairmorn and sent Justice to you and then convinced Papa that Prudence and I should come with her to London?"

"She did that? I thought perhaps your papa had called upon her to give you a Season. A widower does generally require some lady's aid in the matter when there are daughters involved."

"No, Papa was totally amazed to see her."

"As amazed as I was?"

"What?"

"I had not the least idea she was coming to London. And I was purely flabbergasted to learn she had brought two young ladies with her. Almost as flabbergasted as I was when your brother first appeared upon my doorstep. She sent Justice first to soften me up, by gawd. Devil it, but she is devious, my mama. Pardon me, I did not intend to say devil."

"Of course not," grinned Honor. "You never do."

"Well, I do sometimes, when there are not ladies present. Mama had it in her mind all along that I was to marry you, Honor. Of all the sly, shrewd, cunning things to do— to select a bride for me herself, bring you to London without giving me the least inkling to expect you and then when I did not immediately jump to her tune, to rattle chains in the attic to get us alone together so that we might discover ourselves a perfect match. She is a veritable Machiavelli, my mama!"

"He is bleeding all over the vestibule and Mr. Donnelly's heart is having palpitations and Prudence has fainted dead away into Miss Patterson's arms—which knocked Julia down, Honor, because she is not at all large enough to catch Prudence—and Whit has gone off to Russell Square and Lady Whitshire has gone with him, so you must come!"

Honor stared at her brother, mystified. "And the footmen?" she asked, thinking that these were the only likely sources of help Justice had not accounted for as she set aside the book she had been reading and rose from the window seat.

"The footmen are no help at all. Marlborough is simply standing there staring at Mr. Millard and turning white, and James has run out onto the front steps to be sick to his stomach."

That made Honor move a deal faster than she had at first intended. "Then Mr. Millard is truly bleeding all over the vestibule?" she asked, hurrying toward the staircase. "I know you said as much at first, Justice, but you do tend to exaggerate."

"No, no, I am not exaggerating. There is blood everywhere!"

Honor rushed all the way to the ground floor with Justice upon her heels to discover Mr. Millard—certainly bloody—lifting Prudence up into his arms so that little Miss Patterson might get out from under her.

"Where shall I take her, Miss Virtue?" he asked, as Honor descended the last step.

"You must give her to Justice, at once."

"No, I can carry her. You must only tell me where."

"Do not be obstinate, Mr. Millard. Justice do take Prudence away from him this minute and carry her up to the striped saloon. And then come right back here and carry Mr. Donnelly to his room."

"No, no, I shall recover," gasped Donnelly clutching at his chest as he sat upon one of the ladder backed chairs in the vestibule. "A bit of Daffy's Elixir and I shall be fine, and James and Marlborough will have some as well. But it was a shock, Miss Virtue. I am a deal too old to see such a specter upon my stoop."

"Yes, you most certainly are," agreed Honor. "Are you all right, Julia?" she asked without once taking her gaze from Mr. Millard. "You did not twist an ankle?"

"I am only a bit sore," replied Miss Patterson breathlessly. "James is being sick upon—"

"I know," interrupted Honor. "Mr. Millard, should you like to lean upon my shoulder and come with me to the kitchen?"

"I can walk perfectly well," announced Millard. "I take it Whit is not at home."

"No, he and his mother have gone to Russell Square."

Millard, who had started toward the rear of the establishment, pulled up short. "Why have they gone to Russell Square?"

"I am sure I do not know, Mr. Millard. Now off with you. Julia and I shall see what we can do to patch you up."

"No," Millard said then, hesitantly.

"No?" Honor came to a standstill.

"Whit and Lady Whitshire cannot have gone to Russell Square unless they plan to stir up a nest of hornets. I cannot take time to be patched together now, Miss Virtue. I must go after them."

"What?" asked Honor, staring at Mr. Millard and not at all noticing the very real look of fear that had come over little Miss Patterson's face.

"Longbourne's," Millard said. "They have gone to Longbourne's. Whit don't know anyone else in Russell Square. Not upon a visiting basis, he does not. And if he has taken his mother to Longbourne's, it is because he has thought of something to bring the broth to a boil and requires her help to do so. If they are not careful, they will both get themselves killed."

"You know that is not so, Mr. Millard," managed Honor quietly, her heart thumping hard against her ribs. "You know how fond his lordship is of his mama. You cannot truly think that he would be so careless as to place her ladyship in mortal danger."

"Well, no, I cannot truly think that. But—"

"No buts, Mr. Millard. He would never place his mama in danger. And besides, you cannot go rushing about town with blood pouring from your nose and your eye blackening and your chin and knuckles all bruised and torn and bleeding. Someone will take you for an escaped madman and capture you and carry you off to Bedlam. His lordship would never forgive me should I send you out into the street in such a condition." And grasping Mr. Millard's elbow, Honor urged him down the corridor and into the kitchen.

Soap and water and towels appeared as did a silver knife for the back of Mr. Millard's head to stop his nose from bleeding, a cut raw potato to place on a steadily blackening eye, and basilicum powder and sticking plaster for his cuts. In almost the blink of an eye, Andre's kitchen became a hideous mess, but Mr. Millard grew steadily more presentable.

Shortly after his nose ceased to bleed, Prudence appeared in the kitchen upon Justice's arm and was seated in a chair directly across from the gentleman. She looked rather shaken and was most definitely pale. Honor stopped her ministrations to give her sister's arm a pat, while Miss Patterson turned toward the sink to empty out the water they had used to clean Millard's wounds.

"Are you better, Millard?" asked Justice, hurrying to catch Miss Patterson and take the heavy basin from her. "I thought he had you that last time. But you came back like a veritable demon."

"I have never lost a brawl in all my life," mumbled

Millard through stinging lips. "I should like to think I never will."

"A b-brawl?" asked Prudence. "You engaged in fisticuffs in the street? Mr. Millard, how could you?"

"Well, you did not want him shot, Miss Prudence," mumbled Millard. "And he refused to accompany me to Jackson's. What else was I to do? Allow him to toddle off without facing the consquences of his actions? I do not think so!"

"You ought to have seen it, Prudence!" Justice exclaimed, carrying fresh water back to the table for Miss Patterson. "I vow Furbough thought one punch would do the trick and he would walk away unscathed, but he was decidedly mistaken."

"Decidedly," agreed Mr. Millard.

"Captain Furbough did this?" Prudence's blue eyes turned bluer still. "Captain Furbough beat you to within an inch of your life?"

"I am not beaten to within an inch of my life. I am just a bit bloody is all. I bleed a lot. But I am barely scratched."

"I should not say that exactly," offered Honor with a slowly dawning smile. "And in what shape did you leave Captain Furbough, Mr. Millard?"

"Flat on his face on the cobbles," declared Justice. "His friends had to carry him away! Beat the rogue right into the ground, Millard did, even if Furbough is bigger than he is."

"He is not all that much bigger than I am."

"Yes, he is. He can give you two stone, Millard, and he is at least two inches taller and his arms are longer and that makes a great deal of difference in a brawl."

"You fought Captain Furbough in the street?" asked Prudence as though her mind could not keep pace with the conversation.

"In the middle of Bolton Street, Picadilly," declared Justice proudly. "And you ought to have seen the gentlemen pour out of Watier's to watch!"

* * *

Lady Whitshire took a seat upon the calico sopha in the main drawing room of Longbourne House in Russell Square. She sat stiffly erect on the very edge of the seat and her son stood beside her with his hands clasped behind his back as they waited. Not a word passed between them. In a matter of moments, the late Sir Nathan's housekeeper, gowned in creaseless black bombazine, with a cap of dull black satin covering her head, entered the chamber and stood submissively before the grand presence of her ladyship.

"You are the late Sir Nathan's housekeeper?" asked Lady Whitshire regally.

"Yes, my lady. I am Mrs. Curbridge."

"Your husband is butler here?"

"Yes, my lady."

"So. I have come, Mrs. Curbridge, to discover what has happened to the young lady."

"The young lady? I am afraid I do not—"

"The young lady with the red hair. Her initials are JP, Mrs. Curbridge, but do you know," Lady Whitshire said with a shake of her head, "I can still not remember her name. What a fool I become as I grow old. However," she added, "the child was a guest of Sir Nathan's before—the incident—but I have not seen one hair of her head since and it is most important that I locate her."

The housekeeper looked up to study the lady and the gentleman but a stern pair of blue eyes and an arrogant pair of violet ones and turned her own gaze immediately to the floor.

"Miss Paxton has gone home to the country, my lady."

"Miss Paxton! Yes, that was the name. Miss Jane— Junia—"

"Julia."

"Yes, Miss Julia Paxton! Exactly! There, you see, Garrett. I told you that I should remember if given enough time.

And do you have her direction in the country, Mrs. Curbridge?''

"Perhaps it is among Sir Nathan's things, my lady. Or Mr. Henry Walsh may have Miss Paxton's direction. He was Sir Nathan's solicitor. It is he has taken charge of the will and all pertaining to it."

"Ah, very good. You shall proceed to this Mr. Walsh's office the first thing tomorrow morning, Garrett. He is in the City, Mrs. Curbridge?"

"Indeed, my lady. Mr. Henry Walsh has chambers near Gray's Inn. I do not have the exact direction."

"I shall locate him, Mother."

"Indeed you shall and quickly too," stated Lady Whitshire, for all the world as if Mrs. Curbridge were not present. "You have put this matter off quite long enough, dear heart. To think that you would allow a map—of who knows what importance and belonging to someone else entirely—to lie upon your study desk for months without doing one thing to locate the rightful owner! Did I not tell you immediately, Garrett, that Sir Nathan and I had exchanged prayer books when I dropped mine upon the floor at St. Paul's that Sunday? Did I not show you the map inside of his and impress upon you the need to return the book and map both?"

"Yes, Mother, but I was hard-pressed to find the time."

"But now Sir Nathan is dead, dear heart, and you cannot return either. Such comes with procrastination, which I have been attempting to explain to you for years."

"Yes, Mother," replied the earl, for the world as though he were seven and at his mama's knee.

"Well, now it is our duty to see to it that Miss Paxton receives what is intended for her, just as dear Sir Nathan would wish. I am certain it is she whose initials he placed upon that map and she shall have it and his *Book of Prayers* as well."

"Yes, Mother. I shall take the prayer book and the wretched map directly to this Mr. Walsh tomorrow morning."

"Indeed you will, for if I discover it lying at the corner of your study desk tomorrow afternoon, I shall be highly displeased, you may believe me! It is likely the map is of something quite important and the poor child looking all over for it. Thank goodness he thought to write 'for dear JP' upon the thing so that Mr. Walsh cannot have the least doubt to whom it belongs." And with that Lady Whitshire rose from the sopha, placed her hand upon her son's waiting arm and left the room, her aristocratic nose quite high in the air.

"Desmond, did you hear?" called Mrs. Curbridge down the staircase as the carriage carrying mother and son pulled away.

"Every word," growled Curbridge, closing the door upon the empty street and stomping up the stairs. "No wonder we could not find the thing. The old despot lost it himself. Whoever would have guessed. Well, at least we know whatever thief sneaked into this establishment that night had no better luck than we."

"Yes, a great consolation that is. Mr. Walsh will send it to the girl, Desmond, and all of our opportunities will be lost. We will have murdered the old gentleman for nothing."

"Never you worry, Janie. We have got the monies from the selling of the old despot's stickpins and studs and the like. We have got nearly eight hundred pounds, Janie, from that. And we shall have our pensions what you convinced him to add into that will. And then there are the jewels the old gent gave you."

"Yes, and they are nothing, Desmond! Nothing compared to what lies hidden! I know it to be so. How many nights did he tell me how he mistrusted all of the banks and how his fortune lay safe and tidy and ready to hand at all times? How often did he brag when he was in his cups about how all of his late wife's jewels—diamonds and sapphires and rubies—lay hidden among his savings? And now that spiteful child is to have everything."

"Never," growled Mr. Curbridge. "That map belongs to us and we shall have it too."

"But how?"

"Why, I shall go and fetch it, Janie. I know perfectly well where Whitshire House lies. In Park Lane across from Hyde Park. Yes, and I know what it looks like, too. There are sketches of it in all the guidebooks. First of the houses ever built upon that land. Aye, I shall find the house. And then I shall discover the map, my dear, and take it away with me."

"It will be waiting in the gentleman's study in the prayer book upon the corner of his desk," Mrs. Curbridge murmured. "And you must go for it this very night, Desmond. Tomorrow the gentleman will carry it to Mr. Walsh and all will be lost to us."

"This very night," nodded Mr. Curbridge in agreement.

"How will you gain entrance to the place?"

"Why, any way I can, love. Any way I can. Though I have not been forced to make use of it for a number of years, I am not without talent, Janie."

"You always did have a way about you," nodded Mrs. Curbridge, gazing proudly up at him.

"Indeed. A way with a lock and a pick like no other. I did not study at grandfather's knee for nothing. No, I did not."

"But you will be very careful, Desmond. Promise me that you will be very careful. And if someone should see you—"

"I will slit his throat from ear to ear," promised Mr. Curbridge with a smile. "I surely will, Janie. And you will have the map and all that goes with it. Every blinking thing."

Chapter 15

Mr. Millard eased himself carefully into the chaise longue in the summer parlor and leaned back. Of all the incomprehensible things! He felt a good deal worse now that his injuries had been attended to than he had when he and Justice had left the scene of battle. His arms and legs ached. His stomach ached. His head ached.

And I am holding a raw potato to my eye, he thought dismally. What a fine sight I must make. But at least Furbough will not think to play his games with Prudence ever again. Why is it, he wondered, that Furbough forever has all the ladies in an uproar over him and I cannot get a one to look upon me with the least favor? It is not as though I am misshapen or I smell badly or my teeth have rotted out. Who the devil is James Furbough to stroll into a room and set all the ladies' hearts to pattering? "It cannot be merely that scarlet coat," he muttered in despair.

"Scarlet coats are notoriously appealing," replied a soft voice from the doorway behind him. "There is something about a gentleman in a scarlet coat that makes young ladies believe them to be—to be—"

"Miss Prudence?" asked Millard, struggling to turn about on the chaise longue.

"No, do not attempt to look at me. I do not wish for you to look at me. I am so heartily ashamed."

"What? But why? You did nothing. You trusted a gentleman to take you to your sister, that is all. It is he should be ashamed. He betrayed your trust."

"I do realize that. That is not my particular shame."

"Miss Prudence, do come over here where I can see you. We cannot hold a conversation with you standing behind me."

"Not just yet, Mr. Millard. There is something I must say first, and then, if you still wish it, I will remain and we may speak together like civilized human beings."

"I cannot think of one reason why I would not wish you to remain," mumbled Mr. Millard, readjusting the potato upon his eye.

"That is because you are so very kind and understanding," responded Prudence, her voice growing the least bit quivery. "And you are more. You are brave and honorable as well. But—"

"Here it comes," murmured Millard to himself, his heart constricting with pain. "But, Miss Prudence?" he urged when she did not continue.

"But when a young lady is searching for a knight in shining armor, Mr. Millard, she does not think to so much as look in the direction of a quite proper and polite bishop's son."

Mr. Millard's poor heart attempted to shrink itself down to an even smaller size. "I understand—" he began and then stopped abruptly. "No, I do not. I do not understand anything," he growled. "I am not some fribble mincing about on high-heeled shoes and spouting gibberish. No, I ain't, and never have been. I am as much a man as Whit and more a man than Captain James Furbough who has proven himself a dastard time and time again."

"Time and time again?" asked Prudence breathlessly.

"Yes, time and time again. Do not think that you are

the first and only pretty miss to fall into one of his traps, for you are not. And if I had not feared to offend your sensibilities, I would have called the fellow out and put a ball through him right at the place where it would do him the most good. But Whit said that you would be lost to me entirely if I did that, so I beat the stuffings out of him with my bare fists instead!''

"Right at the place where . . . ?" Prudence's face began to flame. "Oh, Mr. Millard, for shame."

"I do not care. How dare he betray your trust? How dare he attempt to take advantage of you? Captain Furbough is not a knight in shining armor, Miss Prudence. He is a wolf in sheep's clothing. Well, no, that is not precisely correct. He is a wolf in wolf's clothing wandering among the sheep and having his way with them. But why the sheep are so constantly taken in, I cannot conceive.''

"Because we are blind," murmured Prudence. "Because we read and dream and imagine people to be what they are not. Th-that is what I am so very ashamed of doing, Mr. Millard. It is my greatest failing, my imagination. We met and you were so very sweet and polite and dressed to perfection and then I learned that you were the Bishop of Allerton's son and immediately I imagined what a— dull dog—a bishop's son must necessarily be.''

"A dull dog? Me?"

Prudence's voice sounded quite faint. "Y-yes."

"Well of all the . . . !" Mr. Millard's heart was constricted no longer. Not a bit of it. "And I expect because Furbough was a member of the Guards, you imagined him to be— What did you imagine him to be?"

"Courageous and adventurous and dangerous but noble.''

"Prudence Virtue," ordered Mr. Millard, "step around here to where I may see you at once!''

Prudence did as she was told, each slow step increasing the rhythm of her heartbeat. Her cheeks were red and blotchy and tears stood in her eyes and her head was bowed. She absolutely could not look Mr. Millard in his one good eye.

"Am I to understand that to win your heart a gentleman must be courageous and adventurous and dangerous but noble? Are those the requirements?" Millard asked, surveying her.

"Well, yes, I did think they were. But now I find there are more requirements. The gentleman who wishes to own my heart must also be kind and understanding and totally outrageous."

"Totally outrageous? Thunderation!"

"You do not think it was totally outrageous of you to confront an extremely large gentleman and to engage that giant in fisticuffs in the middle of Bolton Street?"

Mr. Millard took the raw potato from off his eye and peered up at her suspiciously. "I am a dull but outrageous dog?" he asked uncertainly.

"No," replied Prudence, lifting her eyes to meet his at last and discovering that the very sight of the left one so dark and swollen made her wish to throw her arms around him and kiss it to make it better. "You are not dull. I ought to have known that simply from being around you, but I did not give you the least opportunity to be anything but what I imagined you. And you are certainly not a dog. You know perfectly well *that* is merely an expression. But you are totally outrageous," she added, her sweet lips quivering upward. "You are the most outrageous gentleman I have ever met. And if you do not cease to be so outrageously familiar with my name, I shall be forced to address you as Andrew, you know, for that is how it is done when two people become close."

Andrew Millard felt as though he might well rise up from the chaise longue and fly around the room picking the painted roses from the ceiling cornices. "Are we— becoming close?"

"If you should like to do so, my brave and outrageous hero," smiled Prudence, clasping her hands demurely before her.

"As if I would not!" exclaimed Millard, struggling to disentangle himself from the chaise longue.

"Andrew, do not you dare," ordered Prudence. "You are injured and anyone can see you are not feeling at all the thing. You must stay right there and rest for at least an hour or you will be of no use to anyone for the rest of the day. And look, just as I promised," cried Prudence, the abruptness of her change in tone quite jarring Millard's sense of reality. "Here is Mr. Donnelly now with our tea and Honor as well!"

She had quite disappeared after assisting Honor with Millard. Justice had hunted all over the house before thinking to take himself off to the stables to look for the girl.

"Here you are, Miss Patterson," he smiled, having reached Jasper's stall to discover her seated upon a pile of hay in the farthest corner. Jasper's enormous nose was almost in her lap as she stroked him tenderly, smoothing the hairs that formed the star upon his brow. "Are you very upset?"

Miss Patterson gazed up at him through eyes shimmering with unshed tears and did not say a word.

"Jupiter! And you did so well, too. I did not think the sight of blood more than a bit discomposing to you. Honor has grown accustomed to it from nursing my mama through her final illness."

"Your mother is dead?"

"Yes."

"And your father?"

"Oh, he is in fine form. He would not come to London, though. He is not particularly fond of London." Cautiously, Justice stepped into the stall and made his way around the big gelding. He lowered himself to the hay beside Miss Patterson.

"It was most brave of Mr. Millard to attempt to teach Captain Furbough a lesson," murmured the young lady.

"Yes, well, he did much more than attempt it. Captain

Furbough will think twice before he approaches another young lady in such a manner, let me tell you."

"He is very brave, Mr. Millard. And honorable."

Justice nodded. "You are not in love with Millard, are you?" he asked tentatively. "Because if you are—"

"Oh, no! Mr. Millard is very much in love with Prudence. I could tell that from the first."

"Good. I mean, it is good that you are not in love with Millard because . . ."

Miss Patterson lifted her pixie's face to stare up at him. "Because?"

"Well, because, ah, I have discovered that I am growing most fond of you, Miss Patterson."

"And I of you, sir," she replied. "No, that is not at all true. I do think I am in love with you, Mr. Virtue, and have been since you first caught me at Astley's and were so kind as to bring me here and arrange for his lordship to give me sanctuary."

"In love?" Justice gasped.

"I know it is terribly forward of me to say so straight out," sighed Miss Patterson. "But it is the truth, and I am so very tired of attempting to hide it. You do not despise me for speaking the truth, Mr. Virtue?"

"No!" exclaimed Justice and then hastily lowered his voice. "But there are any number of beaux, Miss Patterson, who—"

"Not now. I do not wish to discuss the subject any further at present, if you do not mind. Mr. Virtue, do you know why his lordship has gone to Longbourne House?"

"I expect it has something to do with Sir Nathan's murder."

"Why should that be of interest to Lord Whitshire? And so many months after it has occurred? I expect it was the talk of the *ton* when first it happened, but any number of scandals have driven it from most people's minds by now. I expected that only the Bow Street Runners would be concerned with it by this time and even they have likely given up."

"No, they have not. The Runners are still searching. But Whit thinks they are searching in the wrong places and has decided to go about discovering the murderer for himself."

"Oh! But he cannot! It is—it must be most dangerous!"

"Never fear, Miss Patterson, Whit has experience," bragged Justice proudly. "It is his hobby horse—catching murderers. He has caught any number of them. And he will catch this fellow, too. I have not the least doubt."

Miss Patterson smiled a watery little smile at that. "His hobby horse? I have never heard of such an outrageous hobby horse as that. The earl is very brave, is he not?"

"Whit? I should think so."

"And honorable as well."

"Most certainly."

"Does Lady Whitshire know about his hobby horse?"

"Indeed. And even though she speaks against it, m'sister, Honor, says that it is quite obvious that Lady Whitshire is proud of Whit for capturing those dastards that he has already captured. I think Whit has gone to Russell Square to lay a trap and that Lady Whitshire has agreed to help him do so."

"Lady Whitshire is the most wonderful of women, even if she does steal a bit here and there," Miss Patterson sighed. "And she is most courageous as well. But truly, she and Lord Whitshire ought not to have gone to my uncle Nathan's."

Justice stared at the girl. "Your uncle Nathan's?" he asked in shock. "Sir Nathan Longbourne is—was—your uncle?"

"Not truly my uncle, but I have called him that since I was a very little girl because he and Papa and Uncle Monty— Oh, Justice, I must do something! I cannot let such kind people as his lordship and Lady Whitshire put themselves in danger. If they have gone to stir up a nest of hornets in Russell Square, then I must think of some way to protect them. I must! Because it is most obvious that the hornets in Russell Square have nasty stings indeed."

* * *

They began to gather in the summer parlor before dinner, a contemplative lot who spoke little but paced a great deal. Whitshire paced diagonally from the northeast corner of the chamber to the southwest. Millard paced the opposing diagonal, from the southeast corner to the northwest. Justice paced up and down the room in the very center. And Honor paced from corner to corner to corner to corner, forming a perfect square of the chamber.

"If merely one of you missteps there is going to be a frightful accident," offered Lady Whitshire, looking up from *Le Beau Monde* through which she was paging without reading one word. "Do cease fidgeting, children, or you shall drive me to my grave."

"Yes, and you are making me terribly dizzy," sighed Prudence. "Mr. Millard, do come and sit down beside me."

"Yes, do, Andrew," urged the earl. "You have had quite enough exercise, I should think, for one day. I shall add some steps, eh, and pace for you as well as myself?"

"It is not humorous, Whit. We must be certain to be prepared. If someone of Longbourne's household is the murderer as you suspect and word of the map reaches that someone—which it must, because the housekeeper will certainly speak of your visit—he will come tonight. You have not left him any other time to come. He will assume you are going to take it to the solicitor's tomorrow. We must decide how to handle the situation and how the ladies are to be kept safe and we must do so at once."

"You do not think, Andrew, that after dinner will be soon enough?" asked Lady Whitshire. "I doubt, dearest boy, that Garrett's murderer will come rushing into our dining room along with our truffles and our kidney pie."

"I doubt it as well," conceded Millard, continuing to pace. "But what if we are wrong?"

"We are not wrong," Whitshire stated flatly. "Our villain will wait until the house is closed up for the night before he risks entering. And the ladies will be in no danger if they merely retire to their beds a bit earlier than usual and lock their doors behind them. If our fish rises to the bait, he will not go searching about on the second floor for the map. Mama said quite clearly that it was in the prayer book upon the corner of my desk in my study, and no one can imagine a gentleman's study to be upon the second floor of his establishment."

"Yes, and most certainly whoever it is will enter by one of the ground floor windows and so search the ground floor first," added Lady Whitshire. "And they will discover Garrett's study and the prayer book and the map without ever needing to set foot above stairs. We shall all be perfectly safe in our chambers."

"Is Julia never coming down?" asked Honor, worriedly. "I have not seen her since she helped me to care for Mr. Millard. You do not think she is ill? Perhaps I ought to go up and check upon her."

"No," murmured Justice. "That is to say, I spoke to Miss Patterson only a bit ago and she is fine. She is merely changing her gown and will be down shortly, I expect."

"Are you certain, Justice?" Honor pressed, noting a most troubled expression upon his face as they paced by each other. Has Justice changed his mind about Miss Patterson? she wondered. Is that why he paces? Did she say something when they spoke to make him suspect her of involvement in Sir Nathan's murder?

Oh, surely not! she told herself then. If that were so, Justice would not hold his peace about it. He would never think to put Lord Whitshire in danger simply because he has grown fond of Miss Patterson. I am grown fond of Julia myself, but I would not think to set her welfare above Lord Whitshire's, not if I had had words with her that might indicate she is truly a murderess.

That hairbrush Justice spoke of might belong to anyone, she added in Julia's and Justice's favor. Julia Patterson is a most innocent young woman who has fallen upon hard times, and that is all. She has not once done anything to make me suspect her. It is Whit who suspects her and even he does not wish to do so.

I ought not to think of him as Whit, she told herself then. There has been not so much as a serious word spoken between us on the subject of—of—Well, he did ask me to marry him. Twice. But that was merely because he wished to do the honorable thing—which is not honorable at all. To marry someone simply because you have been alone with them. Of all the rubbish I have ever heard!

And then her mind abruptly switched back to what had begun her pacing in the first place. That hairbrush might belong to anyone, she thought again. Though it might also belong to Julia. We do not truly know the least thing about her, and she might well have been lying about her uncle Monty and about the horse. But she was not lying about the piggy-eyed villain, Honor reminded herself as the argument in her mind continued. She is being followed about by someone. We all saw him. And Whit was so very happy to think that the man *was* Julia's piggy-eyed villain. But what if the man follows her about because he knows that she—that she—"Oh, this is absurd," she muttered.

"What is absurd, Miss Virtue?" Lord Whitshire asked.

"What?"

"You said that something was absurd just as you paced by me."

"I said that? It is nothing. I am muttering to myself. Here is Julia now," she added all on one breath.

"We are thinking, Julia, to make an early night of it," announced Lady Whitshire. "Garrett and Andrew are concerned over a minor inconvenience that may occur here this evening and, though I doubt it will interfere with dinner, I do think it would be best if we ladies all retired to our chambers by ten."

"The gentlemen are expecting a murderer to sneak into the house tonight," translated Prudence without the least hesitation. "Lord and Lady Whitshire have baited a trap for him, and we are all to lock ourselves into our chambers so that we will be safe."

"Prudence," hissed Mr. Millard.

"Well, everyone else knows the truth, Andrew. If you and Honor had not confided in me about his lordship's interest in Longbourne House and the murder this very afternoon, I should have thought you all crazy to wish me to go to my chambers so very early and to lock the door tightly behind myself. And Julia will think exactly the same if she is not aware of what is going on." Whereupon Prudence proceeded to tell all of the earl's plans to Miss Patterson, heeding not one of the frowns Mr. Millard bestowed upon her.

"Well, damnation," sighed Whitshire, as the gentlemen passed around the port after dinner. "So now Miss Patterson not only knows about our seeking the murderer, but she knows about the map as well. Now what do we do?"

"Do about what?" frowned Justice. "Why should not Julia know? You are not still suspecting her? I vow, Whit—"

"No, do not vow him nothing else, Virtue," growled Mr. Millard, resting his elbows upon the table and twirling his glass of port with the fingers of both hands. "You are not going to call him out. He would not go. He is your friend. And friends do not duel each other. It is all my fault, Whit. I ought not to have told Prudence. But I was not at all thinking logically over tea. And she did ask why I was so worried about you and your mama, which I was because it took you forever to arrive back here. And—I just blurted out all I knew of the thing and when you returned, I urged you to tell her the rest."

"Why should Julia not know all?" persisted Justice, ignoring his wine and leaning forward.

"Because we are attempting to prove that your little Miss Patterson had nothing to do with the thing," sighed Whitshire. "And it would have been wonderful to have someone else come after the map and she prove not to have known anything about a map at all. It is the map, we think, for which Sir Nathan was murdered. But now, of course, Miss Patterson does know about the map."

"Oh."

"Yes, well, I cannot be certain that anyone will come tonight at any rate, Justice. I am merely hoping. Because then, we may have our murderer, or at any rate a definite link to our murderer. Not only did we leave word at Longbourne House about the map, but at Sir Nathan's solicitor's office as well—which is what took us so very long, Millard. Word will get around quickly, I assure you. And if our man is connected with either the household or the solicitor, he will come."

"What is the map of?" asked Justice.

"We haven't the foggiest notion," mumbled Millard.

"Yes, we have," corrected Whitshire. "It is most likely a map to where the gentleman buried his fortune."

"His fortune? He had a fortune?"

"Perhaps. We think so. He was part owner in a trading vessel—a most successful trader from the tale his papers tell—and he had good reason not to trust banks. According to Sir John Fielding's Runners, though the staff reported some jewelry stolen, they also said that there was very little of it to steal. So we are thinking that perhaps Sir Nathan hid his profits away somewhere, and any jewelry worth keeping, and that the map leads to the hiding place."

"Thunderation," muttered Justice. "Why would he bury it? Why not simply hide it away somewhere where he had not got to dig it up every time he wished some flimsies?"

"It would make a deal more sense," Whitshire agreed, staring down into his port, but neglecting to lift it to his lips. "Still, why would he make a map if he did not bury it? At any rate, Cub, you can see how Miss Patterson's proving to know nothing of such a map would have certainly stood in her favor."

"And now we will needs be even more careful tonight," mused Mr. Millard. "We cannot depend upon Miss Patterson not coming for the map herself, and we do not wish to hurt the girl."

Both Whitshire and Millard glanced at Justice, awaiting his angry protestation at their expecting his beloved to come seeking the map, but Virtue merely picked up his port and sipped at it thoughtfully. "Where will I be?" he asked then, quietly.

"What do you mean where will you be?" Whitshire asked. "You will be up in your chambers with your door locked."

"Oh, no! Not on your life! I am going to be right by your side, Whit, or somewhere nearby. And you ought to be glad of an extra hand, too, not glaring at me for offering it."

"I am not glaring. But I can hardly involve you in such an undertaking, Cub. What would your father say to such a thing?"

"He would say two men would be better for a third."

"You ought not deny him the opportunity, Whit," Millard said with a thoughtful frown. "You have never yet denied me the opportunity to join in the fun."

"Yes, but you are a good deal older than—"

"Balderdash! I was a stripling when we began! Younger than Justice. There comes a time when a gentleman needs to prove he has bottom. And I will be damned if I am going to deprive my future brother-in-law of proving that he has bottom when such a likely opportunity presents itself."

"Future what?" gasped Whitshire and Justice as one.

"Well, it is not definite, quite," Millard said with a most beguiling grin. "But it will be soon, I promise you. Now, what will be the best way for the three of us to deploy ourselves in order to take the villain quickly?"

"Four of us," murmured Whitshire.

"What?" asked Justice.

"Four of us. Tyrel has offered to be of assistance as well."

Chapter 16

It was merely ten-thirty in the evening and already the lamps and candles of Whitshire House were winking out. Obligingly upon the second floor, the ladies had each doused all but one lamp apiece in their chambers and drawn the draperies tightly across the casements. "Now no one will so much as guess that we are awake," sighed Prudence as she wandered into the sitting room she shared with her sister. "But I will not go to bed. I will not! How can Andrew even imagine that I would fall off to sleep while he is belowstairs placing himself in the gravest danger?"

Honor's eyebrows rose the slightest bit and the corners of her mouth turned upward. "Andrew?" she said quietly.

"I expect that I may call Mr. Millard Andrew after he was nearly beaten to death for my sake, may I not?" asked Prudence, with the slightest pout.

"Have you forgotten that Mr. Millard is a bishop's son, dearest?" Honor smiled. "Or have you forgiven him for it?"

"All bishop's sons are not alike," declared Prudence. "I should think you could see that quite clearly."

"I have always known that, you goose," grinned Honor.

"You are the one who imagined what bishop's sons must be."

Prudence had the good grace to blush heartily. "I was so very wrong, was I not? And I did apologize to Andrew for it."

"You did?"

"Yes, just before you came into the summer parlor and we sat down to tea. Oh, Honor, I was so very ashamed to admit that I had given Andrew not the least opportunity to win my heart only because I imagined him to be something he most definitely is not. And he roared when he learned of it, too. I did never think to hear a bishop's son roar so."

"I expect he roared because he loves you, dearest, and wished to impress upon you your mistake."

"He must love me, do not you think?" mused Prudence with a shy smile. "Lord Whitshire said he did. He said that Andrew was top over tail in love with me. And to think that I overlooked him in favor of a devious, dastardly rake like Captain James Furbough! I am positively mortified."

A slight scratching at the door interrupted the sisters' conversation and Honor stepped quickly across the carpeting to allow little Miss Patterson entrance. Her arms were stacked with clothing up to her chin. "Some of these must fit," she said, as Honor relieved her of a number of shirts and breeches and boots.

"Fit?" Prudence stared at her, puzzled.

"Yes. Well, we are not actually going to remain up here when the gentlemen we love are belowstairs putting their lives in the gravest danger, are we? I know that I am not! But we cannot go sneaking about in these dresses. They will hear us coming from an entire corridor away and so will Mr. Curbridge."

"Mr. Curbridge? Who is Mr. Curbridge? And where did you come by all these clothes?" asked Honor suspiciously. Had Whit been correct from the first? Had Julia been involved in Sir Nathan's murder? And was she now planning to involve Prudence and Honor in some plan to distract the gentlemen while she stole the map?

"Mr. Curbridge is the butler at Longbourne House," explained Miss Patterson, setting the rest of her burden upon the striped settee and then flopping down beside it in a most unladylike manner. "Spider and I have discussed everything, and we have concluded that if his lordship is correct and Sir Nathan was not murdered by robbers but by a member of his household, then it is likely Mr. Curbridge who did the deed. And it is likely Mr. Curbridge will come to steal the map as well. He is a nasty man."

Honor stared at the girl.

"Spider borrowed these clothes for me from the grooms' quarters on the very spur of the moment. He used to be the fireboy at Longbourne House, Spider was. He was called Diggens there," offered Miss Patterson nonchalantly.

"You admit that you have been to Longbourne House?" Honor queried as Prudence blinked in amazement.

"I have been there any number of times but I did not tell his lordship so. Until today I was not aware that his lordship was attempting to capture Uncle Nathan's murderer."

"Uncle N-Nathan?" stuttered Prudence.

"Yes, Uncle Nathan, who was the sweetest, dearest gentleman in all the world. And if I had had the least idea that his life was in danger, I should never have run off. I should have stayed and protected him. But I did not know. I only knew that Uncle Monty meant to marry me off to one of his horrid friends and that Mrs. Curbridge had betrayed my hiding place and that I must strike out upon my own and quickly too. I failed Uncle Nathan, but I shall not fail Justice. I intend to stand by Justice through this night, and I thought perhaps the two of you might wish to stand by your—"

"Yes, yes, we do!" exclaimed Prudence. "I have been wondering all evening how to sneak belowstairs and keep a lookout for this villain. I do not wish to let Andrew endanger himself while I am tucked safely away up here."

"No, and I wish more than anything to be of help to Whit," sighed Honor, fingering the clothing. "But how do we know we can trust you, Julia? You have lied to us. Perhaps you wish to have the map and this is a plan to get us to help you do so."

"Balderdash!" sputtered little Miss Patterson. "I have not lied about one thing—except Jasper. I did tell the merest tarradiddle about Jasper. And I expect I did rather fib about my name. But no one at all thought to ask me directly if I was ever at Longbourne House or if I knew Uncle Nathan. I did not lie at all about that. I simply did not volunteer the information."

"You lied about your name?" asked Prudence. "You are not Julia?"

"Yes, I am Julia, but I am Julia Angela Patterson Paxton. I did not wish to mention the Paxton part because— because I did not know any of you, you know, and I rather thought that if I said I was Julia Paxton that his lordship might well recognize the name and write off to my uncle Monty immediately."

Whitshire huddled beside his desk in total darkness, pistol in hand, hoping for all the world that whoever the villain might be, he would appear soon. The desk was not tall, and Whitshire was not short. Scrunched down as he was, he was beginning to ache in the most unorthodox places. Ferdy fluttered his wings in the far corner and muttered to himself and then settled back to sleep. Other than that small interruption, all remained silent. Then the casement, which Whitshire had left open a crack, creaked in a rising wind and brought him immediately to attention. But nothing followed the creak. No booted foot appeared upon the sill. No shadow of a murderer crept carefully into the chamber, and so he let his attention wander the merest bit. To the young woman locked safely into her bedchamber upon the second floor. To Honor. The woman I love, he thought with a great deal of happiness.

Mr. Millard stood in the corner behind the kitchen door and prayed silently for the latch to lift. It was likely it would. Whit might leave the casement window in the study ajar, but a villain unaccustomed to housebreaking might not think to prowl about seeking open windows—at least not until he had tried the doors. And the kitchen door would unlatch at his slightest touch. The moment it swung inward and Whit's invited burglar stepped into the kitchen and the door swung closed behind him, Millard would lower his pistol and halt the wretch in his tracks.

At least, I hope I will halt him in his tracks, thought Millard, jiggling his left foot to drive some circulation back into it. I shall need to step between him and the door, I expect, just in case he proves to have the presence of mind to go scooting back out of it. Thank gawd Prudence and the rest of the ladies agreed to remain upstairs behind locked doors. There is no telling how desperate our villain may be. He may force us to chase him throughout the establishment. He may guess that neither myself nor Whit have the least wish to be firing off pistols in a house filled with people. Well, who would? No telling where a ball may end if it misses its mark. Not that I will miss my mark. I have never missed it yet. But if I kill the fellow, Whit will never forgive me.

The glass panes in the kitchen door rattled the slightest bit, bringing Millard's musings to an abrupt end and centering his attention upon the latch. Was it rising ever so slowly? No. Merely the wind rattling the panes and nothing more.

Justice could not think how he could be of any help whatsoever seated upon the floor and peering down into the front hall from the first floor landing. He felt a great deal like descending the staircase and going to demand of either Whit or Millard that they give him a more likely place to stand guard. And that they give him something more deadly than a rolling pin to stand guard with. What the devil were they thinking? That the villain would stroll directly into the vestibule and come to a halt beneath the landing? And then what? That he, Justice, would leap over the rail, drop down upon the devil like a spider and roll the dastard to death?

Thunderation, he thought, if Julia were to see me like this, she would laugh herself silly. "Julia," he whispered, admiring the feel of her name upon his lips. How wonderful it was to know that you loved someone who loved you in return. And he did love her. He knew that to be true. He loved the young lady with all his heart. And there had been no mistaking her words in the stable. She would be his for the asking.

But she would laugh to see me here with a rolling pin, he thought, a smile curving his lips upward. She and Honor and Prudence too. I can see them now. I shall need to be certain not to make the least mention of it when all is over and to warn Whit and Millard not to mention it either. They will all begin calling me The Baker, else, or some such teasing appellation. And just as he began to ponder what other appellations might be applied to him, a shadow flickered across the curtains upon the front door and the quietest tickling of the lock reached his ears. Justice froze. He held his breath. He peered into the darkness below that was lit only by the moonlight filtering through the glass panes beside the door and waited.

Tyrel sat forlornly upon the steps midway to the first floor on the servants' staircase, his elbows resting upon his knees and his chin resting upon his fists. Beside him lay Lord Whitshire's short sword, which he did not wish to touch, not at all. And well his lordship knew it, too. But Lord Whitshire could not have given it to young Virtue. Tyrel understood that perfectly well. A short sword in the hands of someone unacquainted with its use was a most dangerous and deadly weapon. Tyrel's first experience with one had resulted in the death of his last employer and, though now he was well aware of a short sword's efficacy, he was loath to so much as touch the thing.

But I will touch it in defense of his lordship, he told himself. I will use it with deftness and authority, just as Lord Whitshire taught me to do all those years ago. And when this is all over, and Sir Nathan's murderer discovered and taken, I shall go to Miss Virtue and explain myself. His lordship must be telling a tarradiddle to say to me that this young lady knows me to be a murderer and yet will not fear to have me always about. I shall tell her the whole of the matter and if she wishes me to leave, I shall leave. I will not stand in the way of his lordship's marrying the one woman, after all these years, for whom he feels an affinity. That would be outrageously selfish of me. Outrageously!

Tyrel shifted his position the slightest bit. His poor rump was getting sore without so much as a carpet to cushion it. He dangled his arms out before him across his knees and lowered his head. In the darkness of the stairwell he could barely see the step below him. But he knew the strategic importance of his being just there. He was to support Mr. Millard should that gentleman require his assistance and he was to keep the villain from dashing up the servants' staircase to one of the upper floors. If all he managed to do was to frighten him in the direction of the main corridor, it would be enough, for his lordship would come pounding out of the study to engage the blighter. Visions of a terribly young Lord Whitshire, pistol in hand, confronting his own poor self, flittered through Tyrel's mind. But then the faintest of sounds sent them skittering away. What the devil was that? Tyrel strained to hear the sound again. A door above him swishing softly shut!

Tyrel gained his feet; the loathsome short sword leaped into his hand; he pressed himself flat against the staircase wall. The sound of stealthy footsteps descending from high above sent chills up his back. He ran quickly through the servants in his mind. No, not one of them ought to be upon the stairs at this hour. Mr. Donnelly had shooed each and every one of them off to their own quarters more than an hour ago. But someone was upon the staircase.

Someone determined not to be heard. Tyrel's heart pounded and he began to perspire. It made not the least sense for his lordship's murderer to be entering the house from the upper stories. Not the least sense! Doors and windows had been unlatched for him upon the ground floor. His Lordship and Mr. Millard waited upon the ground floor. And the map lay upon the corner of his lordship's desk in the study upon the ground floor!

Beyond the study window Whitshire thought he heard movement, a soft step upon the verge and a hushed breath. The casement creaked again, the merest bit, a gust of air entered the room and swirled the papers upon his desk and then the most ghastly shrieking he had ever heard echoed toward him from the rear of the house. He was on his feet in a moment and dashing out through the study door toward the ungodly sound, his pistol at the ready. But just as he reached the corridor, he heard a great *ka-thump* and Justice shouting and he turned toward the front of the house to see moonlight streaming in through the wide open front door and two men struggling in the vestibule. He hesitated for but a moment. Andrew was in the kitchen and Tyrel upon the stairs. Whatever the screaming, there were two men close to see to it. Virtue was alone at the front of the house. Whitshire dashed up the corridor toward the shadows rolling about on the vestibule floor.

Millard literally jumped away from the kitchen wall at the first of the screams. Thunderation, it sounded as though the house was filled with banshees and all of them upon the servants' staircase. Without a second thought he dashed for the baize door, bounded through it and up the stairs into a darkness writhing with bodies. "Tyrel, where are you?" he shouted. "Stand away."

"No, Mr. Millard, do not shoot. Do not!" cried the valet in harried tones. "Go back. Light candles and bring them here. Hurry!"

"Prudence, do cease screeching," he heard Miss Virtue say then. "It is merely his lordship's valet."

And then a pair of boots was hurrying down the steps as fast as boots could hurry in darkness, and a small hand grabbed at his arm. "We do need candles, Mr. Millard. I think Mr. Tyrel has hurt himself, and Prudence has slipped upon the stairs. Honor cannot see clearly enough to help either one of them."

"Miss Patterson?"

"Yes. No, do not stop and gaze angrily down at me. I cannot possibly see you doing it in this darkness at any rate. Is this the door to the kitchen? Ah, at last a bit of light. Quickly, Mr. Millard, is there not a brace of candles somewhere about? Yes, here. Light them for me at once."

"What the devil!" shouted Whitshire at the front of the house.

"P-picked the l-lock," panted Justice, struggling to stay atop the housebreaker who kicked and pummeled at him from beneath. "Ow! By Jove, but I shall d-darken your daylights for th-that one! Ow! Cease kicking, fool. You shan't escape me and Lord Whitshire is here with a pistol loaded and ready."

"Jiggers!" cried a voice from beneath Justice. "Don't be ashootin' of me, lor'ship. I ain't done nothin'. I swears it!"

"Spider?" murmured Whitshire, crossing to the long table and striking his flints to light the brace of candles that stood there. "Spider?" he asked again more loudly.

"Aye, it be me unner 'ere!" cried his tiger loudly. "Git 'im off me, lor'ship!"

Whitshire gave Justice a hand and tugged him upward, then stared down at the disheveled boy upon the floor. "What the devil made you think to pick my front lock?" he asked, amazed, and then leaned down to pull the boy to his feet.

"I din't be pickin' no lock," shouted the boy, waving his arms up and down excitedly. "I gots a key! I 'ad gots a key," he amended, "until that bugger come achargin' at me! An' now ever'thin' is spilled ever'where," he added in the most appalled voice. "Nev will be aroarin' at me sure!"

Whitshire noticed for the first time that the hall was literally strewn with clothing. A pair of patched breeches had skittered under a ladder-backed chair. A threadbare cambric shirt hung from its top rung. Two high-top boots lay like crossed swords against the wainscoting, and a cat-skin waistcoat clung to the curved railing. Cocked at a jaunty angle upon the newel post was a most recognizable old hat. "These are Nev's things," murmured Whitshire gazing from Spider to Justice and back again.

"Aye. 'Take 'em right up as quiet as kin be ta 'er lady-ship's chambers. They be right at the top o' the stairs the firs' door on yer lef',' he said. 'An' don' be goin' around ta the back, on accounta 'is lor'ship be awaitin' upon someun there,' he said. An' he gived me the key. An' now I 'ave lost it! An' all because this bloke come rushin' at me down the staircase wavin' a hugemendous club in 'is hand and sceared me 'eart inta stoppin'."

"Whit, come at once," cried a voice from the other end of the hall. The very sound of it jerked his lordship's attention away from Spider and Justice both.

"Honor? What the devil?"

"Hurry, Whit, come quickly. Mr. Tyrel is dreadfully hurt, I fear, but he will not allow any one of us to help him."

"Tyrel? Where is Andrew?" Whitshire was already running down the corridor as he shouted the words.

"Mr. Millard is upon the staircase, but Mr. Tyrel will not have his help either. Prudence has twisted her ankle and Julia has cut her hand moving the sword aside." Her voice lowered as he neared. In a moment one strong arm was around her waist, and they were rushing together toward the kitchen. "Are you all right?" he asked her breathlessly.

"Yes, I am fine, but Mr. Tyrel needs you. He is—he is crying, Whit."

Whitshire left her with a quick kiss that just touched her ear and dashed ahead of her into the kitchen and through the baize door and up the servants' staircase. "Tyrel," he said, dropping to his knees beside the valet who sat despondently upon the stairs surrounded by a most ineffectual lot of well-wishers. "Tyrel, what happened? What can I do? You are bleeding. Let me see."

Reluctantly, Tyrel offered his lordship a sight of his injured calf. "It is n-nothing," the valet managed hoarsely. "A s-scratch merely, b-but . . ."

Honor stood upon the stair below them hastily wrapping Julia's cut hand in a piece of clean muslin she had grabbed from the kitchen. But she was paying no great attention to the wound, her mind focused instead upon Whitshire as he sat down beside the valet and put an arm about that gentleman's shoulders.

"But what, Tyrel?" Whitshire asked quietly, taking a handkerchief from his pocket and giving it into that gentleman's hand.

"I did almost kill the ladies," gasped Tyrel, swiping at tears that came streaming down his cheeks. "I thought they were the m-murderers, that there were more than the one you expected, and I almost k-killed them!"

"But you did not, Tyrel."

"N-no, but only b-because the first of them dodged aside and the second s-slipped upon the stairs and then I made out M-miss Honor's voice. Oh, thank God that I made out Miss Honor's voice, d-dressed as she was!"

Whitshire's head turned toward Honor and he stared wide-eyed in the candlelight, realizing for the first time that she was wearing breeches and a man's shirt and waistcoat. "What the devil?" he muttered. His gaze left Honor to rest upon Julia and then he took in Prudence who was wrapped in Millard's arms upon the staircase above him. But he asked no further questions, turning his attention once again upon Tyrel. "Did you stab yourself, Tyrel?"

"I brought the sword back too q-quickly," managed Tyrel on a sob. "And then I d-dropped it. Oh, my God, I d-did almost become a murderer ag-gain but this time a m-murderer of innocents!"

"It is all my fault," murmured Whitshire, drawing the valet into his arms as one would a frightened child. "You would not have been put in such a position had I not thought up this fool plan. I am sorry, Tyrel. I am so very sorry." And with that Whitshire stood, lifting Tyrel, and carried the man down the stairs and into the kitchen where he set about cutting the man's bloody stocking from his leg. Millard, following with Prudence in his arms, set that young lady down as well and, removing the oversized boot she wore, began to examine her ankle. Justice, who came bounding into the kitchen at just that moment, exclaimed at once over Julia's hand and the other injuries and went hastily to pump water and stoke up the fire to heat it while Honor took his lordship's key ring and set off for the still room and the basilicum powder, rolled bandages and sticking plaster. All of them were so very involved with attending to the injured that not one of them gave the least thought to the intruder they had been expecting.

Desmond Curbridge gazed carefully about. No one. Behind him all of Hyde Park lay empty and silent and before him, across the cobbles, stood the vaguely lighted edifice of Whitshire House. With studious eyes he scanned the huge old establishment. A bit of light could be seen through the curtains of the front hall. Most likely a lamp left burning for his lordship, he thought. And a bare flickering of light could be seen playing across the ground at the near side at the very back. That will be the servants' quarters then, he thought. But other than that the house lay in darkness. Curbridge nodded and crossed the street. He would not attempt the front door. Not at once. It was likely that the house was locked up tight and in the end he would be forced to pick the front lock, but he would scout about first. One never knew when the servants would turn forgetful and neglect to check a window here or there.

His leather-soled shoes whispered upon the grass that separated Whitshire House from its nearest neighbor. He was lucky, he knew, that the Whitshire earls had refused to sell the land immediately surrounding the old house. He would be forced to keep an eye out for the neighbors else. With considerable patience, Curbridge moved up to each of the casements upon the north side, searching for entrance. The first four were tightly locked. The same with the next four. It began to look as though he must endanger himself by picking the front lock in plain sight. And then he heard a slight creaking a short distance beyond. The very last of the casement windows was ajar and shuddering in the breeze.

With a smile mounting to his face, Curbridge gazed about himself once more then walked to the window, pried it open further, stepped up onto the sill and entered the establishment. He stood for a moment, hoping for his eyes to adjust to the darkness, but not one flicker of moonlight came through the window to assist him so he decided at the last that he must resort to the candle stub in his pocket. Nervous, his ears catching sounds and murmurs coming up the corridor from what he assumed to be the servants' quarters, he struck his flints and applied the flame to the candle wick.

"Avast, ye scurvy lubber!" croaked a hoarse voice directly behind his left shoulder. "I'll have yer guts fer garters! Hee, hee, hee."

The candle stub shot up out of Curbridge's hand clear to the ceiling, luckily losing its flame along the way and Curbridge himself dove to the carpeting, dropping his flints and drawing his knife as he did. From the darkness outside the window powder flashed and the sound of a pistol shot rent the night. Inside the establishment, a blaze of light appeared outside the study door and a determined voice stated flatly, "Hold. Do not move an inch or you are a dead man." Feet came pounding up the corridor from the kitchen as Curbridge rose to his knees, knife in hand,

and leaped forward. A second pistol shot split the night. "Murder! Murder! Murder!" screeched Ferdy excitedly, his feet holding tight to his perch while his wings flapped wildly.

Chapter 17

"Gor blimey!" exclaimed Spider, peering out from behind Lady Whitshire's skirts. "An' ye din't even need Nev's clothes neither."

"Mama!" yelled the earl, sprinting up the corridor and sliding to a halt beside her. "Are you all right? Devil, you have killed the man!"

"I did not shoot him," declared Lady Whitshire with the lift of an arrogant eyebrow as the rest of the party, minus only Tyrel, advanced upon her. "I would have shot him, but someone else chose to do so first."

"Who?" asked Millard, his eyes pinned upon the figure who lay bleeding upon the study floor.

"Me," answered a deep voice from outside the study window. And with a rustling of cloth and a jangle of spurs, a veritable giant of a gentleman with gold hair streaked with silver stepped over the sill and into the chamber.

"Uncle Monty!" shrieked Julia, and then quickly clapped a hand over her mouth and buried herself against Justice's chest.

"Let us have some more light in here, eh?" suggested the gentleman as a second figure crossed the sill. "Light every candle and lamp you can discover, Adrian. The fellow is not dead," he added, stepping forward to nudge at Curbridge with the toe of a gleaming Blucher. "Aimed for his shoulder, hit his shoulder. Knife must have flown across the chamber somewhere. Dangerous games you play in this establishment," he added, crossing behind Whitshire's desk as more candles flared into life. He sat in the earl's desk chair. "Julia, do cease snuggling against that gentleman in such a hoydenish fashion. And you," he added, gazing at Spider. "Fetch someone a bit taller than yourself and some rope. That villain will require to be tied up and carried away."

Spider took off at a run and Julia turned within the safety of Justice's arms to glare at her uncle. "I am not a hoyden, Uncle Monty," she declared. "And I will not marry Lord Knightsbridge, not if you carry me off kicking and screaming across your saddle bow!"

"Gracious!" exclaimed Lady Whitshire, giving the pistol she held to her son as more light brought the room to a warm glow. "You left this in the front hall, Garrett. William, *is* it you? *You* are Julia's Uncle Monty?"

"Melinda! You are more beautiful now than ever I remember."

Lady Whitshire smiled brightly.

"That is your son, eh?" continued the man. "Ah, yes, I do remember those eyes. You do not remember me, Garrett?"

"No, sir, though I assume you are William Paxton," murmured Whitshire, stepping aside to allow Nev and Spider back into the chamber and watching as they bound Curbridge's arms tightly behind him. "Best stop his shoulder from bleeding, Nev. The kitchen is filled with basilicum powder and bandages."

"Aye, your lordship," nodded Nev, lifting the groaning Curbridge from the floor. "Be we keeping this one?"

"In the stable," nodded Whitshire, "for a time."

"I'll see he's looked after," grinned Nev and began to exit the chamber with Curbridge over his shoulder and

Spider on his heels. "Her ladyship's duke," the groom whispered as he passed between Whitshire and Honor. "I'd recognize 'im anywhere."

"Duke?" murmured Whitshire and turned to peer again at the gentleman who now leaned back in the chair and planted his heels upon the desk top.

"Do not frown so, dear heart," smiled Lady Whitshire. "William, I do thank you for shooting that villain. You have met Garrett. And here are Mr. Millard and Mr. Virtue. And Miss Virtue, Miss Prudence Virtue and— Oh, you know Julia. How very interesting that you should be her scandalous uncle Monty. I do wish I had known. Children, His Grace, William, Duke of Montegraham."

Honor curtsied politely, though she was the only one of the young ladies to do so. Prudence could not with her aching ankle, and anyone could see by the way that Julia stuck out her lower lip that she had not the least intention to do so.

"Virtues?" queried the duke, a smile lurking at the corners of his mouth. "Melinda, Anthony must be turning over in his grave. Julia, since you do not wish to speak to me, go up to your chamber at once. You have no business to be standing about in breeches."

"Oh!" gasped Honor, abruptly remembering her own state of dress. "Prudence," she whispered. "Come away, darling. We are none of us fit to be seen."

No sooner had the three young ladies departed than Montegraham sighed and tossed his gloves onto the desk before him. "Now, Whitshire," he declared, his eyebrows coming together in a frown, "you will explain to me, please, why I have shot Sir Nathan's butler in the midst of his breaking into this house."

"And you will explain, Your Grace," responded Whitshire, "who is the gentleman behind you who has been spying upon Miss Patterson—Miss Paxton—ever since she came to London."

It was just then that Mr. Donnelly, aroused as had been the other servants by the pistol shots, stepped up to Whitshire to whisper that James, the first footman, was putting Mr. Tyrel to bed, that he, himself, would be pleased to valet his lordship this evening and then requested to know if his lordship's guests would be requiring tea.

"I should think so," declared Montegraham, having caught the word 'tea'. "Though brandy would be more the thing."

Lady Whitshire's urging and Ferdy's squawking between them convinced the gentlemen to move their discussion to the summer parlor where Whitshire poured cognac for them all and then lowered his long-legged form into a green wing chair. "Where is our spy in cloak and false nose?" he asked, glancing about for that gentleman.

"Gone to the kitchen, I expect. Conversing with your butler."

"With Donnelly? Why?"

"Because he is my butler, Whitshire," grinned the duke. "He would never think to sit in here with us. I thought I should die laughing when first I saw him this evening. No wonder Julia did not recognize him. He assured me she would not, but I did never think to see him done up like some actor upon the stage."

"Carpenter?" asked Lady Whitshire askance. "That was Carpenter? Oh, but perhaps you have a new man now."

"No, that was Carpenter, my dear. He is wearing a false nose and false eyebrows and I cannot think where he found that periwig."

Whitshire's gaze, bright with laughter, met Millard's across the room. "Andrew, we attacked a butler," he chuckled.

"You what?" asked the duke. "No, do not tell me. The footpads in the park that Carpenter wrote to me about— the two of you?"

"He was spying upon this establishment," grinned Millard, "and we had no idea why. Whit merely wished to discover his motives."

"Yes, but he escaped us," Whitshire chuckled. "And he gave as good as he got before he did, too. You have a most extraordinary butler, Your Grace."

Lady Whitshire, her blue eyes aglow as she studied the duke, who had chosen to sit beside her upon the sopha, smiled and patted his hand. "Had we known Julia was your niece we should have notified you at once that she was safe with us, William."

"No, we should not have done," declared a pouting Mr. Virtue adamantly. "At least, I should not have done. I do not give two hoots that you are a duke and her guardian. Only a blackguard would wager a wonderful girl like Julia in a card game! I have a mind to call you out for it! And she is not going back with you to be given over to that— what did she call him?—Knightsbridge! You may count upon that. Julia goes nowhere she does not wish to go!"

"And don't I know that," drawled the duke. "I vow, that child will be the death of me yet. You need not call me out, Mr. Virtue. I did not wager Julia in a card game. At least, it was not a true wager. I had broken my leg and my neighbor, Knightsbridge, came to keep me company for a time. Knightsbridge is a Methodist. It was extraordinarily kind of him to play cards at all. He would never actually have wagered on them. We simply made pretend wagers in order to keep things interesting."

"And Miss Paxton overheard?" inserted Mr. Millard.

"She must have," the duke smiled, "because she and Jasper disappeared that very night. I had word from Nathan's housekeeper four days later that Julia was with Nathan in London. I sent Carpenter to fetch her home, but Julia had fled Russell Square by then. And Nathan, bless him, was dead."

"What? Just days after your niece departed his establishment?" asked Whitshire.

"Indeed. A housebreaker they said in the papers. Thank goodness Julia had already fled or she might easily have been murdered as well! Carpenter expected that Julia would attend Nathan's funeral and so attended himself, intending to explain to her about the wager and bring her home. But when he approached her in the graveyard she was so very upset that she would not listen to a word. Ran off, and he could not chase after her without being confronted by someone for attempting to molest the girl. So I pondered upon it and then sent Carpenter word to simply locate Julia again and keep watch over her until I could come fetch her myself. It was his idea to wear a disguise so she would not run off again at first sight of him."

"It was not housebreakers killed Sir Nathan," muttered Justice.

"It was not?"

"No," Whitshire offered. "We suspect it was the gentleman you shot in my study. Mr. Curbridge is his name." And taking a sustaining sip of brandy, Whitshire began to explain about his theory and the trap they had laid and the fish who had taken the bait.

The evening grew quite late before all involved had had their curiosity satisfied and the Duke of Montegraham and Mr. Carpenter departed for Grillon's, Mr. Millard tripped off home, and the Runners came to collect Mr. Curbridge and carry him off to Bow Street, because the duke would not hear of Whitshire keeping him. It was nearing two o'clock by the time a weary Lord Whitshire made his way back to the kitchen and began to look about him for something interesting to eat. He had accumulated a slice of Vienna sausage, three slices of bread, four chocolate creams and a glass of ale, and was just sitting down to the table when the green baize door to the servants' staircase opened. He jumped up immediately and then grinned. "Hungry?" he asked, crossing to take Honor's candle from her and lead her to a chair. "Shall I make you tea?"

"I think I would prefer a glass of ale," murmured Honor.

"You drink ale?" The happiness in his eyes made Honor laugh.

"Yes, my lord, I have been known to drink ale upon occassion. It is one of my father's favorite beverages."

"Devil! A young lady who drinks ale!"

"Do cease teasing and fetch me some," Honor laughed, "or I will take myself back upstairs and put myself to bed. I should like a slice of that sausage, too, I think. And perhaps some bread. For some odd reason, I am becoming accustomed to a snack late in the evening. Did you ever imagine that Julia's uncle Monty would be the Duke of Montegraham? Is he the villain she thinks him to be?"

"No," called back Whitshire from the landing to the cellar where he was busy tapping the ale keg. "A misunderstanding is all. But Montegraham used to be a regular rakehell when he was young. There are countless stories told about him to this day," he added as he set the glass before her and turned to slice another piece of sausage. "No doubt the girl had reason to believe that he might wager her in a card game if she had heard any of those tales. He was the one," his lordship added, placing a slice of bread upon the plate and setting it before Honor.

"The one what? Who?"

"The duke who rolled up his sleeves and helped Mama with the tenants' cottages after my father died."

"Oh!" Honor smiled as Whitshire slipped into the chair directly across from her. "Then he is not only not a villain but actually kind. Now we must convince Julia of it, I think."

"That is not my main concern."

"You have a main concern, my lord? But surely, now that you have caught your murderer—"

"I did not catch him. Montegraham did. And he insisted that I turn the wretch over to Sir John and his Runners."

"Oh, Whit, I am so sorry."

The earl's eyes fairly blazed with goodwill. "You are? Truly?"

"Yes. I know how interested you are to speak with these villains and learn what you can of them. And Sir John will likely not let you, will he?"

"Well, he will give me an hour or so. But what can you learn in an hour or so? You truly do not think I am some—ghoul—for wishing to know more about why people commit murder?"

"Not at all. I begin to think it must be most interesting. Think what a sweet person Tyrel is and yet, he murdered a man."

"Tyrel is sweet," grinned Whitshire, "though he would not wish to hear you call him so. He killed his employer quite by accident, you know. Lord Harry had forced himself upon one of the parlor maids and was in the act of doing so again when Tyrel came upon them. Tyrel seized the nearest thing to hand and went after Lord Harry with it. Unfortunately it happened to be Lord Harry's short sword and though Tyrel meant only to wound the man and give both the girl and himself time to run, he did not know how to wield the thing correctly and—Well, I taught him how to wield one properly after he came to work for me, but he is still not adept at it."

"Perhaps not, but he was adept enough to stop himself in midthrust and keep from murdering us upon the stairs."

"Yes, well, he thought you to be our expected intruder."

"I realize. It was foolish of us to be there. But we all thought . . ."

"What?" asked Whitshire, munching on the sausage.

"That it was unfair for you gentlemen to be putting your lives in danger while we hid safely away behind locked doors. And it was too, but we ought to have been more aware of your plans before we came down those stairs."

"Yes, you ought to have asked," nodded Whitshire.

"Do you mean to say that you would have allowed us to help?"

"I should have welcomed it. I cannot speak for Millard and the Cub, but I should have been quite happy to have had you beside me—especially in that shirt and waistcoat and those breeches."

Honor's cheeks reddened considerably.

"I think Mama intended the same," he added, taking

a drink of the ale and laughing. "But your brother leaped upon poor little Spider before the lad could get Nev's clothes up to her. Speaking of which— Do have one of these creams, Honor. They are delicious."

"Speaking of which what?" Honor queried, taking one of the sweets from his plate.

"Speaking of which, Montegraham was sitting terribly close to my mama upon the sopha."

"Oh, Whit! You cannot possibly think—"

"Mama is a widow. Montegraham, it turns out, is a widower."

"Yes, and so is my papa, but I cannot think that your mama is the least bit interested in any gentleman but you. If she were considering marriage herself, she would not be so very worried about being sent to live in that house in Suffolk."

"That's true. I had not thought of that."

"Sometimes you do not think at all."

"Me?"

"Yes, you. Does it not occur to you that I have come down here in my nightrail and that we are sitting here alone once again, you and I, in the middle of the night?"

"Of course it does, but I thought it wiser not to make mention of it. Even such a slowtop as I, Honor," he grinned, "must finally grasp the idea that you have no wish to marry anyone simply because you are compromised. You are one of those ladies who will marry only for love, just like your sister and Miss Paxton and my mama."

It was early the following afternoon when Julia entered Whitshire's study upon Justice's arm. "I have come to tell you that I am sorry for fibbing about Jasper," she announced. "I did not realize then that you were in search of Uncle Nathan's murderer. I thought that perhaps you knew my papa, because of Jasper."

"Your papa? No. Never met the gentleman," Whitshire responded. "Will you not be seated, Miss Paxton?"

"No, but you may sit again. I shall not mind."

"Thank you," smiled Whitshire who had popped up out of his chair at her entrance. "Jasper is your papa's horse?"

"Papa is a cavalryman. Lieutenant Colonel James Paxton. He is the youngest of Uncle Monty's brothers and he remains upon the Continent until June. Uncle Nathan gave Jasper to Papa to ride into battle, but I quite fell in love with Jasper and so when Papa returned to his regiment last November, he would not take Jasper with him. Would it have helped for you to know that?"

"It would have saved me a number of hours searching for some nonexistent Captain Sharpe."

"And have made you less suspicious of Julia," added Justice.

"Me? You truly did suspect that I—?"

"It was merely that so many things seemed to point in your direction," Whitshire interrupted hurriedly. "Which reminds me!" He tugged open the first drawer of his desk and lifted out the ring and the hairbrush. "These, I think, belong to you, Miss Paxton."

"Oh! My hairbrush! My ring! Wherever did you find my ring?"

"In the bottom drawer of Sir Nathan's desk among the ledgers."

"Someone stole this ring." Miss Paxton frowned. She slipped the ring onto her finger and studied it thoughtfully. "I always thought it was Mrs. Curbridge took it. She said she would someday. She is the nastiest woman. Almost as nasty as Mr. Curbridge. Do you know that she sent Uncle Monty word that I was hiding at Uncle Nathan's when Uncle Nathan expressly told her not to do so? And she told me so right to my face. And then she laughed."

"Why is your eyebrow rising, Whit?" Justice asked. "Does that mean something?"

"It means that Sir Nathan did not rule his servants. Perhaps the Curbridges ruled him? Did Mrs. Curbridge know you would leave, Miss Paxton, if word was sent to Montegraham?"

"Well, of course. I went to Uncle Nathan's to hide from Uncle Monty. Anyone with half a brain would realize that—" Miss Paxton stopped in midsentence, and she gave the tiniest gasp.

"Just so," Whitshire frowned.

"What is just so?" Justice asked.

"Curbridge was planning to kill Sir Nathan even then, but he could not do so with Miss Paxton in residence, and so he got Mrs. Curbridge to drive Miss Paxton away."

"What a fool I was!" Julia exclaimed sadly.

"You did not know," murmured Justice.

"I was selfish. I knew that Mr. and Mrs. Curbridge were truly nasty people, but I did never once think that their nastiness was intended to hurt anyone but myself. Oh, poor Uncle Nathan! I will wager that they have been cruel to him in some way for a very long time, and he all alone with no one to help him fight them. Odds are they have been blackmailing him with something and draining the poor old gentleman dry."

Justice shook his head silently and Whitshire grinned. "It sounds remarkably like a plot from another Minerva novel, don't it?" Justice sighed. "She ought to be writing them, I think."

"I would purchase one if it had her name upon it," laughed Whitshire. "And read all three volumes straight through."

Honor could not help but smile as she passed by the summer parlor later that afternoon. The Duke of Montegraham, his hair gleaming silver and gold in the sunlight could be seen pacing into and out of view of the doorway, muttering under his breath, while Julia perched primly upon the green sopha. Farther down the corridor a most familiar pair of violet eyes laughed at her from the threshold of the drawing room and Whitshire waved her in his direction. "We are all in here waiting most impatiently," he grinned, escorting her into the chamber where Lady

Whitshire sat working upon her embroidery and Prudence lounged upon the fainting couch with her ankle delicately balanced upon a cushion and Mr. Millard delicately balanced upon a footstool beside her.

"But where is Justice?" Honor asked. "Has he gone off with his friends for the afternoon?"

"No, Miss Virtue," answered Mr. Millard. "Your brother is out upon the drawing room balcony pacing and tugging at his hair."

"What?" Honor strolled to the little set of French doors and peeked outside. Then she turned around and came back to sit upon the lyre-backed chair, her eyes alight with glee. "Why on earth is he in such a state? Did you see the duke and Julia?" she added, smiling up at Whitshire. "He is attempting to convince her, I think, that she has not been lost in a card game to Lord Knightsbridge and Julia is being most admirably aloof."

"No, that is not it at all," Whitshire smiled. "It is a deal more interesting than that."

"It is?"

"I should say so," delared Lady Whitshire, without looking up. "Justice has asked Julia to marry him, and Julia has just now announced to William that she will. And poor William has not a clue as to how to handle it."

"There is no way to handle it but for him to agree," Prudence announced, bestowing a most knowing smile upon Mr. Millard. "Fret and fume as he will, His Grace must give in at the last."

"He must?" asked Honor.

"Well, of course he must. If that young lady has decided to marry Justice, do you think anything that her uncle Monty can do or say will keep her from doing so?" Mr. Millard replied with what Honor thought to be unholy glee in his eyes. "And he will need to convince her papa to approve the match as well, because the two will have each other. Anyone with eyes can see that."

"I doubt her father would even think to deny her," added Whitshire. "It was he taught her to ride so well as to get the position at Astley's. If he could not deny to teach her acrobatics on horseback, he cannot deny her the husband of her choice. Must Andrew write to your father do you think, Honor?"

"Mr. Millard? Write to Papa? About Justice and Julia?"

"No, about himself and Prudence. You have been upstairs turning a hem, or whatever it is you ladies do when you say you are sewing, and have missed all the fun. Millard has asked your sister for her hand in marriage and she has accepted."

"You have? Oh, Prudence!" Honor was out of the chair and rushing to her sister without one thought but to give her a hug, and when she had finished that, she bestowed a most chaste kiss upon Mr. Millard's cheek as well. "Welcome to our family, Andrew," she said. "I have been hoping to have you for a brother."

"Yes, well, I am most happy for Prudence and for Justice," Lady Whitshire grumbled, staring defiantly at Whitshire and then Honor. "Most happy indeed."

"Of course you are, Mama. Oh! I almost forgot." Abruptly his lordship began to fish about in his pockets.

Lady Whitshire's eyes took on a new sparkle as she watched him do so, and Honor's heart began to pound in anticipation. Was he searching for a ring, perhaps? Was she, too, to have happy news to send home to Papa? And then the earl withdrew from his breeches pocket a much-folded piece of paper.

"What the deuce is that?" asked Millard, rising to join Whitshire as he spread the paper out upon a table.

"The map," announced his lordship with enthusiasm. "Longbourne's map. Now that his murderer is caught and gaoled, do you not think we ought to discover where it leads?"

Chapter 18

Mrs. Curbridge tweaked the edge of the curtain aside and peered out at the town coach and the four gentlemen who rode beside it as they paused before Longbourne House. One of the gentlemen took a piece of paper from his pocket, unfolded it and, moving closer to the street lamp which had been lighted early against the darkness of an approaching storm, stared down at it. Another of the gentlemen brought his horse up beside the first and studied the paper as well, the two pointing and talking as if there were some decision to be made. It was not until the second of the gentlemen removed his hat and ran his fingers through hair that glinted silver in the lamplight that Janie Curbridge had the first inkling of what was going forward.

"Montegraham," she muttered to herself. "The devil they said shot Desmond!" She squinted through the rapidly fading twilight with more concentration. "Whitshire," she mumbled finally, as the two gentlemen ceased to study the paper and urged their mounts up before the coach and four. "Nathan's map," she squeaked then as the realization snapped her into action. "They are following Nathan's map!'' She rushed to the little closet beneath the stairs, pulled her cloak about her, and in moments she was running through the house, out the back door and into the stables.

Janie Curbridge was not a city woman. She had been born and raised in the midlands and knew her way around a horse very well. Without alerting the one groom who yet remained to care for Sir Nathan's town hacks, she grabbed the tack from the wall and saddled one of the mares. With considerable deftness she tugged the back of the skirt of her black bombazine dress up between her legs and tucked it rapidly into the belt that held the household keys about her waist. Then she stepped up into the stirrup, swung a leg over the mare's back and urged the horse forward, ducking as they cleared the stable door. As she reached the street, she peered about her for a sign of the coach and riders. They were nowhere to be seen but she knew which direction they had taken. She guided the horse toward the first of the cross streets at the northwest corner of the square and was rewarded with a sight of the coach and riders turning into Spinnaker Street in the direction of Bloomsbury. Damn you, Nathan, she thought. How dare you put her initials upon that map. It is me you owe. Me. Not that snip of a child who did nothing but wreak havoc upon the household each time she came to town. Miss Julia Paxton was not the one comforted you in the night when that harridan of a wife of yours died, Nathan. Miss Julia Paxton was not the one warmed your empty bed. And Miss Julia Paxton will not be the one collects your fortune, Nathan, no matter that Bow Street has Desmond. With grim and angry determination, Janie Curbridge settled the mare into the rhythm of a slow trot and stayed as far behind the group as she was able without losing sight of them.

Whitshire paused beneath another streetlamp and peered down at the map again. ''North,'' he murmured as Millard rode up beside him. "We take the next street north until we come to a church. St. Michael's it is called."

"And then what?"

"And then we are within walking distance of our goal, I suspect. Look here, Andrew. Does it not appear that the X lies behind the church?"

"Why the devil would Longbourne bury his funds behind a church? How could he get to them when he required them quickly?"

"I suspect Sir Nathan patronized this church. It is close to his home, after all. He will have gone to it perhaps twice a week. And if the funds are not buried but somewhere above ground, it would be no different than patronizing one's own bank."

"I had not thought of them being above ground," mused Millard. "I have always thought of maps and *buried* treasure."

"Yes, you and Miss Paxton," grinned Whitshire. "My two favorite readers of novels."

"Enough," Millard chuckled. "The next street to the left, John," he called, spurring his horse back toward the coach. "As far as St. Michael's church and there we halt."

"We are almost there," whispered Prudence inside the coach. "Oh, is it not exciting?"

"Indeed," agreed Lady Whitshire. "What better way to entertain a duke than invite him to a hastily prepared dinner and then take him off into the midst of a pending storm to search for buried treasure. Garrett is a veritable genius when it comes to entertainment, I assure you."

Honor and Julia both laughed.

"Uncle Monty is enjoying every moment of it, my lady," offered Julia. "And what better way for him and Justice to come to know each other? Such an adventure shared must prove a bond between them, you know. And Uncle Monty will speak for him to Papa as he would speak for a compatriot. See, they are riding side by side now," she added, her gaze falling fondly upon her intended through the coach window.

"A born romantic, my Garrett. Devoted to providing happy endings," Lady Whitshire mumbled.

"He is, Lady Whitshire," declared Honor. "It was he told Prudence how much Mr. Millard loved her, was it not, Prudence?"

"Yes, and urged me to give Andrew a chance to win my heart."

"And it is Garrett," pronounced Lady Whitshire in dire accents, "who alone among the gentlemen remains unattached."

"Uncle Monty is unattached," offered Julia blithely.

"Pooh! William was married to Margaret for twenty years."

"Yes, but he is not married now."

"No, and neither is Papa," Prudence added, "though perhaps he does not count because he does not accompany us."

Honor took one look at Lady Whitshire's regally raised eyebrow and giggled. It was not truly humorous, she knew, but the other girls' comments were so very far from the point which Lady Whitshire was attempting to make that she could not help herself.

Truly, she had been almost as disappointed this afternoon as Lady Whitshire when Whit had produced a map instead of a ring.

"We are here," announced Justice, looking in at the window as the coach pulled to a stop.

"And where is here?" Lady Whitshire queried.

"At the church of St. Michael's. What we seek, Whit thinks, is around to the rear of the building."

"Not inside?" asked Julia.

"Not according to the map. We shall leave the horses and the coach here in John Coachman's charge and walk the rest of the way. You ladies do wish to join us? It is not raining as yet."

"This is Garrett's expedition," Lady Whitshire sighed. "It will not rain until we are out in some field without the least hope of staying dry. I am certain of that."

* * *

Janie Curbridge halted the mare at the entrance to St. Michael's Lane and watched from the shadow of an oak as the gentlemen dismounted and helped four ladies from the coach. "Damnation, they are making a veritable picnic of stealing my riches," she hissed. And with a fierce growl, she dismounted, tied her horse to the limb of a small elm, and moved on foot toward the church. Above her thunder echoed ominously, but Janie Curbridge paid it not the least heed. They would regret their interference in her affairs! The whole lot of them!

It surprised her that not one of them entered the church itself because she thought it would have been most appropriate for Nathan to have hidden his cache behind the statue of Michael the Archangel which stood in the far corner of the sanctuary. He had presented that statue to the church and she would not have put it past him to have had a niche somehow incorporated into the marble figure to hold his wealth. But the party of ladies and gentlemen ignored the church entirely and wandered along the side of it into the tiny graveyard at the rear.

"How delightful," mused Lady Whitshire aloud. "A graveyard."

Whitshire, who was strolling between his mama and Honor and swinging one of the coach lamps, laughed uproariously at that.

"It is not *that* humorous, dear heart," his mama advised him.

"No, I am sorry, Mama. It is not *that* humorous. What think you, Montegraham? There?"

The duke, who strolled upon the other side of Whitshire's mama, brought the entire group to a halt as he crossed to stare down at the map in Whitshire's hand. "I should think so, Whitshire. We have merely five more paces to take to comply with the map's instructions. What a grim place to hide one's monies, eh? I can see I ought to have taken more time to argue with Nathan about banks."

"It is a tomb, Andrew," whispered Prudence, leaning upon Mr. Millard's arm as she hobbled forward a few more steps.

"Give us the light up here, Whit," urged Millard. "Let us read whose tomb it is."

Whitshire passed the coach lamp forward.

Lightning crackled and thunder shuddered above the group in the graveyard as Mr. Millard swung open the gate to the low iron fence that surrounded the moss-covered brick building. "Elizabeth Anne, Lady Longbourne and Sir Nathan Longbourne," he read quietly.

"I remember now," nodded Julia. "This is the church from which Uncle Nathan was buried and this the tomb where they laid him."

"But where did Nathan lay the funds?" asked her uncle Monty.

"Perhaps there is a niche behind the plaque?" Justice mused, stepping up to the bronze marker and attempting to move it. "No," he sighed, "not a bit of wiggle to the thing."

"Perhaps there is a loose brick or a special place cut in the side of the tomb," Honor offered.

"We shall take a look, shall we?" smiled the earl as he took her hand into his own and raised the lantern high. By its flickering light they made a circuit of the small building. "Nothing at all noticeable," Whitshire announced as they returned to the group. "I expect we ought to have come in daylight."

"But it would not have been nearly as much fun," observed his mama drily. And then a slow rain began to fall. Lady Whitshire gazed up at the sky and chuckled.

"I knew you were enjoying this, Melinda," accused the duke.

"All it needed was rain," laughed Lady Whitshire girlishly. "Garrett's flair for adventure is unrivaled among men. Even the rain cannot deny him. Are we going to look inside or not?'' she asked then. "I cannot imagine simply walking away now.''

"It takes a key,'' announced Justice, taking the coach lamp into his hand to study the door. "Did a key come with the map?''

Lightning flashed again and the earl turned to peer over his shoulder. Thunder rolled and the rain increased.

"Yes,'' replied Whitshire at last and loudly. "There was a key.'' And he began to reach inside his waistcoat pocket.

"What is it?'' Honor whispered when he seemed to freeze with his fingers in his pocket. When he did not answer she stood upon her toes to whisper in his ear. "Garrett Forester, speak to me!''

Whitshire grinned. "That tickles, when you hiss in my ear. Devil it!'' he exclaimed then at practically a roar. "It is beginning to rain harder and the wind is picking up.''

Which was true, but Honor could not think why he should state the obvious so loudly. "Honor, come, let us return to the coach before you catch your death,'' he commanded.

She was about to proclaim that she was not afraid of a bit more rain when she was already wet. And besides, all he need do was use the key to open the tomb and give them all immediate shelter. But then she saw his lordship flash a most speaking look at Mr. Millard and then at Justice and then at the duke. "I shall return as soon as I have got her safely in the coach,'' Whitshire announced, and grabbing her hand, the earl steered her back toward the church.

"We have left the lamp behind,'' Honor protested. "I can barely see my feet. We shall fall over a marker and break our necks.''

"Hush, sweet girl,'' he replied in a murmur. "We are going only as far as that willow to our left and as we come within reach of its branches, I am going to duck into them and you are going to turn about and hurry back to the others.''

"Why?'' Honor whispered back. "What is going on, Whit?''

"Mrs. Curbridge. I was hoping she might turn up and she has. She is behind the willow. I glimpsed her in the lightning."

"Well, then you are not going in there alone. What if she has a knife or a pistol?"

"I doubt she has a pistol, dearest. And it will be me she attacks because now she believes me to have the key."

"And you do not have the key."

"No. It must still be at Longbourne's establishment. Now!" he shouted, giving Honor a quick and gentle push. "Run!" And he was ducking under the branches of the willow.

Honor stumbled back, caught herself, and dove quickly among the willow branches after him. In the deepest of the shadows she could barely make out two figures. They were struggling and so close to each other that at first glance they seemed but one.

"Give it me!" panted a woman's voice. "Give it me or I will slip this blade up between your ribs and do the same with that pretty filly of yours, too."

"Devil you will!" cried Honor, leaping toward them and grabbing a fistful of hair as the two spun about.

And then Whitshire raised one of the woman's arms into the air and, in a flash of lightning, steel glittered at the end of their fingertips. Honor, infuriated that anyone should raise a weapon against Whit, let go the woman's hair and landed a good solid kick against the back of her leg.

Janie Curbridge cried out as the kick landed and the knife was wrestled from her hand at one and the same time. In a blaze of anger, she hissed and spit and spun away from them both and attempted to dash toward the church. But as the lightning flashed yet again and the thunder boomed, she saw a tall figure waiting for her at the very corner of the building. She spun to her left and a figure waited there as well. And on her right another. And then the man who had taken the knife out of her hand was plunging out of the willow after her. Janie bolted in the only direction unguarded by the men. She dashed madly toward the tomb where the coach lamp flickered and three women huddled in the pouring rain.

The ladies! She was not intimidated by the ladies! She would run straight into them, snatch up the lamp and be gone around the back of the tomb, through the graveyard and around the hill to the street. The ladies would do nothing and the men, hampered by a late start in the race and a dismal lack of light, would never catch her before she reached her horse. And then she would ride back here, because they would not expect her to do so. She would urge the mare straight at that arrogant wretch with the key in his pocket. She would ride him into the ground, filch the key and be off. Time enough to open the tomb when they carried his broken body away through the night, the ladies wailing at his heels.

"Do you see?" Prudence whispered. "She is coming straight for us just as Andrew said she might."

"Yes, and we must hope she does not veer off," Julia replied. "Though Justice is to one side and Mr. Millard to the other."

"Your uncle Monty has started after her now," hissed Prudence.

"Where in the name of heaven are Garrett and Honor?" Lady Whitshire asked, squinting beyond Janie Curbridge to the willow tree. "Garrett ought to be upon her heels."

And he would have been upon her heels if he had not stopped to plant a hearty kiss upon Honor's astounded lips. "You do not take orders well, but I love you anyway so I will learn to deal with it," he said as he released her from his arms, grabbed her hand and tugged her after Mrs. Curbridge and the duke.

In what seemed like forever and no time at all combined, Janie Curbridge was at the tomb and reaching for the coach lamp. A good four yards behind her, the duke's boots were pounding across the sodden ground and behind him, Honor and Whitshire were closing the gap.

From both sides, Millard and Justice were advancing. But Janie saw no one except the cowering ladies and a victorious smile lit her face as she snatched the coach lamp up.

And then something pounded against her head, and her smile disappeared as she sank to her knees.

"Oh, I say!" exclaimed Julia, retrieving the coach lamp from Mrs. Curbridge's slowly opening fingers as that woman crumpled to the ground at the ladies' feet.

"Melinda!" roared Montegraham.

"Mama!" shouted Whitshire.

"Well, of all things!" exclaimed Lady Whitshire, placing her hands upon her hips and turning to stare at those two gentlemen. "As if I should allow this game of hare and hounds to go on the entire night when I am standing here wet to the core."

Honor was holding onto his lordship's hand and running and laughing at one and the same time. "G-game of h-hare and h-hounds," she laughed. "G-Garrett, your mama is s-so funny!"

They came to a stop behind a quickly stooping duke, Whitshire twirling Honor into his arms. "Mama, you ought not have done that," he protested. "We were coming."

"Yes, I can see I ought not," declared Lady Whitshire. "My reticule is ruined and everything is spilled all over the ground. No, do not bother, William. Garrett, open this door at once so that we may get in out of the rain. William, I shall collect my things in daylight. Garrett will drive me back. Do get off your knees."

"I cannot open the door, Mama. I have not actually got a key."

"No, but I have got a hairpin, dear heart. Do not look so very innocent, Garrett. I have been aware of what you can do with a hairpin since you were ten."

"Yes, but this lock is much too large, Mama."

"Too large for this?" asked Montegraham, holding up an enormous brass key.

"No wonder you felled her, Mama," Whitshire laughed, taking the key. "Thank God I took you with me to Longbourne's. This is the reticule you carried with you to Russell Square, is it not?"

"Yes, but whatever—"

"Just so," the earl interrupted with a significant glance at Honor, and stepping forward he placed the key into the lock. He turned it once, lifted the latch, and the door swung inward.

In a matter of moments the ladies had been hustled inside, Jane Curbridge carried in, and the coach lamp lifted to illuminate two coffins, each on its own marble stand.

"Nothing," sighed Justice and Julia together.

"Ha!" exclaimed the duke. "Just like children to be disappointed before they have given anything a decent try. Shine it this way, Whitshire. Nathan will not have left his valuables lying about in the open for any eyes to see."

"There," Mr. Millard said, his arm firmly about Prudence's waist. "In that odd nook at the back corner, Whit. Can you see it?"

Whitshire nodded, strolled with the lantern to the nook and came back with both lantern and a metal box. "Now I can use a hairpin, Mama," he murmured, handing the lantern to Montegraham and setting the box upon the top of one of the coffins.

Janie Curbridge moaned, but no one noticed as all eyes fixed upon Lord Whitshire. Truly, he has the most elegant hands, Honor thought as she watched his long, lean, ungloved fingers fit the hairpin into the lock and turn it slowly one way, jiggle it, turn it slowly the other. And then the lock snickered and rasped and in a moment the box was standing open.

"Well, I'll be deviled," murmured Montegraham, lifting a thick stack of bank notes from the top of the pile and revealing a veritable rainbow of jewels sparkling beneath.

Janie Curbridge groaned again and put a hand to her aching head. She stumbled uncertainly to her feet and the glint of the jewels darted across her vision. "They are mine," she mumbled, tottering unsteadily toward them.

"I was not his mistress all these years for a bit of a pension an' a pat on the back, I was not!"

Justice was beside her in a flash and Millard with him, each taking one of the woman's arms, but she did not appear to notice either of them. "Mine. All mine," she mumbled again.

"You were Nathan's mistress?" asked Montegraham with a cock of an eyebrow. "Nathan's mistress and his butler's wife? What a busy lady you have been, my dear."

"Desmond is my brother," stated Janie in a most disoriented fashion. "Desmond is my brother."

"Well, you shall like to get to the very bottom of this, shall you not, Garrett?" asked Lady Whitshire with an unholy gleam in her eye. "Perhaps Sir John will loan you the Curbridges for a year."

"No, I do not think so, Mama."

"You do not wish to study the Curbridges, dear heart?"

"Ah, not at the moment, Mama."

Honor watched with considerable curiosity as the earl backed away from the metal box and began fishing about in his pockets. Above them a great clap of thunder shook the tomb to its very foundations, but no one appeared to truly notice.

"What the deuce are you looking for, Whit?" muttered Millard. "You have not got another map somewhere, have you?"

"No, no, not a map. Ah, Miss Virtue," he said, clasping something in his hand and turning toward Honor. "We are not alone together in the summer parlor? Say no," he prompted.

"N-no," stuttered Honor, uncomprehendingly.

"We are not alone together in the attic or the kitchen?"

"No, my lord. We are standing dismally wet in a dank old tomb in the presence of family, friends and quite possibly a murderess."

"Yes, well, I did intend for us to step outside into moonlight and stars at this point, but we cannot possibly. So, I will just say my piece here. Miss Virtue, your eyes are like a glass of ale in candlelight, always sparkling, always changing, always seductive. And your hair is—well, it is falling down and miserably wet at the moment because you have lost your bonnet—but it is generally very attractive. You are the most beautiful woman, Miss Virtue, that my eyes have ever seen."

"Yes," whispered Lady Whitshire. "You are doing admirably, dear heart."

"Just so, Mama," nodded Whitshire, a grin tickling at his lips. "You are honorable, courageous and as curious as I about some things, Miss Virtue, and you are not adverse to a bit of excitement now and then. Are you?"

"I should think you would know," giggled Honor.

"Just so. You are not adverse to a bit of excitement now and then. And we are most admirably suited, you and I, despite the fact that Lord Sandsquire told Justice that our fathers were enemies and fought a duel over Mama. Obviously your father has relented. He did let you come to London with Mama. And my papa will not say a word."

"That is not at all to the point. That was jealousy on Loyal's part and nothing more," Lady Whitshire mumbled.

"And you wish, Honor, as do I to set my mama's mind to rest and to put an end to her fears of Cousin Freddy and the wretched house in Suffolk because then she will not—well, we know what she will not—never again."

"What?" asked Lady Whitshire. "What is he babbling about?"

"Indeed," Honor chortled. "I do wish to set your mama's mind to rest, especially about Cousin Freddy and the house in Suffolk."

"Just so. And in that vein, I know that you would make me a most desirable helpmate in *all* of my undertakings."

Honor's chortle grew into bubbling laughter. She knew very well what kind of undertakings. He wished her to help him put back all the things his mama had stolen for one and to help him catch more murderers for another.

"Do cease laughing for just a moment, Miss Virtue, because I have not finished quite."

"I sh-shall t-try, my lord."

"Good. Because I wish to say, Honor, that I love you with all my heart and that is the true reason I wish to marry you, not because you are compromised or anything else. Will you have me?"

"Yes," grinned Honor.

"Good. I will kiss you, sweet thing, in a moment," he said with a wide smile, "but first this." He took her hand and slipped onto her finger a most exquisite topaz ring edged in diamonds. "That is just to let the world know that you are taken." And then he swept her into his arms and kissed her tenderly and then passionately and then teasingly and tenderly and passionately and teasingly again until they fell apart laughing and gulping for air.

"He could not do this in the summer parlor this afternoon?" queried Lady Whitshire of no one in particular. "He must wait until he has run the poor girl ragged?"

"The ring had not come then," offered Millard.

"Andrew, you knew he meant to propose?" asked Prudence.

"Yes, and I know where they will go on their bridal trip—to visit any number of friends and relations," Millard chuckled. "Some of them mine, my precious Prudence. And we are going with them."

"Julia and I are going as well," declared Justice from around a still groggy Janie Curbridge. "We shall all be ambassadors scattering cheer as we go."

"And scattering other things as well, Prudence," Julia hinted at the mystified young woman. "Things people will be happy to discover are not lost."

"Oh!" gasped Prudence abruptly. "Oh! Scattering *things*. Of course! We will all of us take our bridal trips together and—and—scatter *things!*"

"They are all as mad as hatters," stated Lady Whitshire, taking Montegraham's arm. "Mad as hatters. But I do not care. I thought I should never marry the boy off and I am so relieved that Honor will have him that they may all scatter whatever wherever and I will not mind a bit."